KILL
SHOW

KILL SHOW

A True Crime Novel

DANIEL SWEREN-BECKER

HARPER

An Imprint of HarperCollins*Publishers*

HarperCollins books may be purchased for educational, business, or sales promotional use. For information, please email the Special Markets Department at SPsales@harpercollins.com.

FIRST EDITION

Library of Congress Cataloging-in-Publication Data

Names: Sweren-Becker, Daniel, author.
Title: Kill show : a true crime novel / Daniel Sweren-Becker.
Description: First edition. | New York, NY : Harper, [2023]
Identifiers: LCCN 2023013177 | ISBN 9780063321403 (hardcover) | ISBN
    9780063321427 (ebook)
Subjects: LCSH: Abduction--Maryland--Frederick. |
    Murder--Maryland--Frederick.
Classification: LCC HV6574.U6 S84 2023 | DDC
    364.15/40975287—dc23/eng/20230513
LC record available at https://lccn.loc.gov/2023013177

23 24 25 26 27 LBC 5 4 3 2 1

A tip of the hat to
RS
who knows where all the bodies are buried.

CONTENTS

It's been ten years since sixteen-year-old Sara Parcell disappeared without an explanation on a crisp April morning in Frederick, Maryland. The ensuing events captivated, shocked, and divided the American public. But what really happened? The case was examined and litigated from every angle, yet the full story has never been told. Until now. The principal participants have finally agreed to speak.

This is the testimony of twenty-six people who played a role in the events surrounding Sara's disappearance. They answered questions about the ensuing search, the media frenzy, the tragic and scandalous conclusion, and the reckoning that followed.

In the words of the people who lived through it, here is what actually happened . . .

When quoted, each individual is identified by their name at the time of Sara Parcell's disappearance, and either their relationship to Sara or their professional title at the time.

Dave Parcell*: father
Jeannette Parcell (now Jeannette Geary): mother
Jack Parcell: brother
Beverly Geary: grandmother

Felix Calderon: detective, Frederick Police Department
Dmitri Russo: patrolman, Frederick Police Department
Christine Bell: district attorney, Frederick County

Olivia Weston: friend
Nellie Spencer: friend
Brandon Grassley: neighbor and classmate
Veronica Yang: principal, Frederick High School
Miriam Rosen: music teacher, Frederick High School
Travis Haynes: bus driver, Frederick Unified School District

Tommy O'Brien: sales associate, Geary Home & Garden

Evelyn Crawford: wife of Manny Crawford (deceased, mechanic at Frederick Shell station)

Olaf Leclerq: ice cream shop owner, Sara's boss

Mike Snyder: news reporter, *ABC-7 Frederick*

Casey Hawthorne: producer, *TNN*

Marcus Maxwell: network president, *TNN*

Anthony Pena: video editor

Zane Kelly: camera operator

Alexis Lee: associate producer

Becca Santangelo: admin, *SareBears* Facebook group

Bruce Allen Foley: chief reality officer, *Unfounded*

Ezra Phillips: pop culture critic, *Slate*

Molly Lowe: professor of sociology, University of California, Berkeley

The following people were contacted for interviews but declined to participate:

Herb Geary: grandfather; owner, Geary Home & Garden

Frank Grassley: neighbor; bank officer, Frederick Savings & Trust

Tim Walker: assistant volleyball coach, Frederick High School

*All interviews with Dave Parcell were conducted over the telephone per the visitation restrictions at Cumberland State Prison.

KILL
SHOW

CHAPTER 1

"Our Last Good Morning"

Jeannette Parcell (*mother*): It was a normal day. I hassled the kids out of bed, fixed breakfast. Jack was filming himself trying to eat Froot Loops off his nose—he was always posting silly videos like that back then. Sara was fixing the strings on her violin. We had bought her new strings that weekend. Thirty dollars, for the good ones. Dave was reading the sports section, complaining about the Orioles' bullpen, I bet. Everyone in their own world. I'm sure the four of us barely talked, but still—it was our last good morning.

Dave Parcell (*father*): I had a pit in my stomach, for sure. When the kids left for the bus, I tried not to make a big deal of it. But I gave Sara an extra squeeze on the shoulder. I remember what I said: "Have a good day, Sare-Bear." She didn't even blink.

I stood in the doorway, staring after them as they walked to the bus stop. Jeannette saw me. I don't know if she thought anything of it.

Jack Parcell (*brother*): We didn't take the same school bus—Sara's went to the high school—but we waited at the same corner with some other kids from the neighborhood. When my bus came, she probably said, "Later, dude," and flicked my ear or something like that. I don't remember.

We got along, even if I annoyed the hell out of her sometimes. She would kick me out of her room when her friends came over, that's for sure. I get it, who wants to hang around with their little brother? Sara was five years older, but she was still nice to me, always looked out for me. Especially when our parents fought.

Jeannette Parcell (*mother*): Dave and I, our marriage was . . . good. It was fine. We just never had enough money, that was pretty much the problem. We laughed a lot, but when you don't have enough money, there's also a lot to fight about. I know that was hard for Dave. Maybe I could have eased up on him a bit. But our water heater needed to be replaced, Jack needed braces, Sara had outgrown her track shoes. I couldn't pretend these things weren't real.

Dave Parcell (*father*): It had been a rough few years. I was bone-tired and out of ideas. We owed a lot. The bank was coming after our house. I had started doing this crazy thing, I would leave work on my lunch break, drive home, check the mailbox for any new bills, and leave the rest of the mail for Jeannette to grab later. I didn't want her or the kids to see how bad it was.

I thought if we could just get a little breathing room to get back to even, we'd be fine. But when you've got a music prodigy in the house, there's a sense of urgency, a timeline you don't get to control. One missed opportunity could change everything.

Jeannette Parcell (*mother*): We'll never know how far it could have taken her, but she really was quite talented. It was always such a kick to me—where did this come from? Dave and I wouldn't have recognized Mozart if he was our uncle.

Dave Parcell (*father*): She got her musical genes from me. I followed Aerosmith around one summer, played a lot of guitar in the arena parking lots. A guitar's not that different from a violin, you know. And Jeannette? She couldn't carry a tune if she had a bucket with a lid on it.

Jeannette Parcell (*mother*): My God, Sara could take your breath away, just practicing up in her room. I'd be doing the dishes at night and hear her start to play. I'd creep up the stairs and stand in the hallway, put my hand lightly on the door. Close my eyes and just listen. I'd picture her onstage. She was so small when she started, she looked like a baby horse trying to wrestle that bow, all arms and legs. She was so young, so innocent. But she played with such power. It lit me up.

Jack Parcell (*brother*): I never learned an instrument. My dad tried to teach me guitar one weekend when I was eight or nine years old. My fingers were hurting so bad, and he was getting frustrated and yelling at me . . . I threw it on the ground and ran off crying.

Dave Parcell (*father*): Sara wanted to do the teen summer program at Juilliard that year. It was expensive, but she deserved it, she had worked so hard. It's the best program, the best music school in the world.

So, yeah. That's how this whole mess got started. When Sara left the house that morning, I thought it was her first step to Juilliard.

Brandon Grassley (*neighbor*): I don't really remember anything unusual from our bus stop that morning. We did the same thing every day, stood around and waited. Just a regular old suburban street corner. It wasn't very exciting.

Nellie Spencer (*friend*): Sara got on the bus and walked down the aisle to me and Olivia. We normally sat in the back, showed each other stuff on our phones, maybe put on a little makeup. Sometimes I copied Sara's homework.

Olivia Weston (*friend*): Nellie was freaking out about something. Sara and I were trying to calm her down.

There had been a field party that weekend, it had kinda got out of control. Giant bonfire, a couple of kegs, kids from other schools.

Nellie had snuck off early in the night and we couldn't find her, she wasn't answering her phone. But Sara and I stayed. We stuck together because I remember there were definitely some sketch balls hanging around.

Two days later, on the bus, Nellie told us where she disappeared to, and it became a whole thing.

Nellie Spencer (*friend*): I needed their help responding to a text message. It had been a crazy weekend, and now this guy was blowing up my phone and I didn't know what to say. I remember being really stressed, but maybe I was being dramatic. I was definitely a tad dramatic back then. I know Sara didn't approve of the whole thing, but she was still trying to help me. You know, with the . . . situation I found myself in.

Olivia Weston (*friend*): Nellie was fucking our volleyball coach.

Nellie Spencer (*friend*): I was involved with an older guy who worked at the school. *Assistant* volleyball coach. I mean, he was like twenty-three, it wasn't some Woody Allen thing. And we hadn't even slept together yet. I left the field party early that Saturday night and went to his place.

That's when his roommate, or housemate, whatever, found out about us. And the roommate was applying to law school and all of the sudden got scared about being an accessory or witness to some crime. Like God forbid he was in the next room while we hooked up. It was ridiculous. Maybe try actually going to law school before you start worrying about imaginary crimes?

Anyway, it was turning into a huge mess. Coach Walker—yes, that's what I called him—he was trying to get our stories straight. I'm positive that's what we were talking about on the bus that morning.

Brandon Grassley (*neighbor*): Those girls never shut up. I never knew exactly what the drama was, but it was always something. Usually,

I'd put my headphones on and try to tune them out, but I caught bits and pieces. It sounded like there had been a big party that weekend. I wasn't there. But I think that's what they were worked up about.

Olivia Weston (*friend*): We all got off the bus together, walked toward school. Before we got inside, that's when Sara realized she had left her backpack on the bus. Me and Nellie kept going to our lockers, and she ran back to get it.

Nellie Spencer (*friend*): The three of us were at our lockers when Sara realized she only had her gym bag, not her backpack. She told us not to wait for her, then ran back to try and catch the bus.

Travis Haynes (*bus driver*): I did exactly what I was trained to do, followed the protocols to a T. Finished my route on time, drove back to the depot, did recon up and down the aisle, cleaned up all the stupid shit these kids throw on the floor, soda cans, gum wrappers, you know, and then I saw the backpack. Nothing crazy, so I brought it to the depot office where the lost and found was. The door was locked, that's someone else's fault, not mine, but that's what screwed me. Meanwhile, the bus is all the way across the lot, the office is locked, my car is right there, I'm heading home, so what else am I supposed to do with it? I took the backpack with me.

And no, I know what her little friends told the police, but she never came back after everyone got out at the school. Once Sara Parcell got off my school bus, I never saw her again.

Dave Parcell (*father*): I spent the morning checking my watch, checking my phone, every five minutes. Just a normal bullshit day at Geary Home & Garden.

Jeannette Parcell (*mother*): Dave worked for my father, at the home supply store he owned. It had been a few years at that point since Dave's roofing business went under. He was always a hard worker, but he didn't have the head to run a whole business. I convinced him to finally give up, then asked my dad for a favor. The situation at the store wasn't ideal, I knew that, but we needed the steady paycheck.

Dave Parcell (*father*): Seriously? How do you think I felt about it? It was a reminder every single day that you're a failure who can't take care of your own family. And as a bonus, you get to carry around fifty-pound bags of fertilizer. What's not to love?

Tommy O'Brien (*employee, Geary Home & Garden*): I always liked Dave. He bought me beer on Fridays sometimes, after I lost my fake ID. Yeah, he would grumble about his father-in-law, but it wasn't so bad working there. Mr. Geary was a nice boss. There was no convincing Dave, though, he was just pissed off to be there, pretty much pissed off at the world. I remember something he said once: "Sometimes you're the hammer, sometimes you're the nail . . . and I'm tired of always being the goddamn nail."

When he first heard something happened with his daughter, we were out on a job together. Putting in an automated sprinkler system in an office park.

Dave Parcell (*father*): We left the store around noon, me and the kid, what was his name . . . Tommy. We were supposed to go plant maple trees in somebody's backyard. Took the work truck, trees tied down on the flatbed. Stopped at the fill station to get gas. Manny was there. We looked over at each other for a second or two. Nothing more than that.

Evelyn Crawford (*wife of Manny Crawford, mechanic at Frederick Shell*): I had never met Dave Parcell, still haven't to this day. Had never heard his name, to be honest, before everything happened.

Manny was friends with a lot of people who frequented the station.

Self-proclaimed mayor of Route 15. You could ask anyone from here to the Potomac, you wouldn't hear a cross word about my husband. The only problems that man ever had were with yours truly, when he wouldn't charge people to fix their cars. Yeah, that was his business strategy—lots of loyal customers and no one ever pays.

I'm sorry, give me a second. Manny was . . . a very good man. Generous, thoughtful, had a laugh like a foghorn, and smoked a rack of ribs that danced off the bone. It seems crazy now that I would yell at him for fixing our friends' cars for free. I'm sorry I ever did that.

So, yeah, we weren't rich. We were always a little behind. But even that doesn't explain it. I have no earthly idea what made him get involved in such a stupid idea.

Tommy O'Brien (*employee, Geary Home & Garden*): We left the gas station, made it to the office park, started working, and about an hour later Dave answered his phone. I could tell it was about his kids, something to do with their school. He seemed surprised at first, then upset. I wasn't paying too much attention, but I remember after he hung up, he rushed back to our truck and took off.

Miriam Rosen (*music teacher, Frederick High School*): I was surprised that Sara was absent from our rehearsal. The spring concert was in two days, and she had a big solo. She was our star performer, the only real attraction, to be perfectly honest. At that point I wasn't even teaching her that much, technically speaking. I was just trying to fortify her with the energy and discipline she needed to keep up with her talent. It can be scary at that age—to be so good.

Some sixteen-year-old girls don't want the attention, and I mean literally: They don't want people staring at their bodies. Or they can't manage the expectations of being so good. Sara was handling it, but I could tell it was weighing on her.

It wasn't notable for a student to be absent, but when I was in the office later, I did ask if Sara was in school that day. It was so unlike her to skip rehearsal. Of course, at that point, I was only worried about her missing the concert . . .

Veronica Yang (*principal, Frederick High School*): Our school's policy is to notify the parents if a student has an unexcused absence in their first three periods. I didn't make the phone call myself, but someone in our office got in touch with her father, I believe.

Jeannette Parcell (*mother*): I worked at a catering hall, doing their bookkeeping. I was in a meeting, so I missed the call from the school that Sara was absent.

Dave Parcell (*father*): Yeah, I got a call on my cell. The attendance office at the school, they said Sara hadn't shown up. I immediately called Jeannette.

Jeannette Parcell (*mother*): When Dave finally reached me, I was worried instantly. We had seen her head out to the bus that morning. And Sara would never ditch school. I told my boss I had an emergency, left work, and met Dave back at our house.

Dave Parcell (*father*): We kept trying Sara's cell phone. I mean, this was the whole reason why kids get these stupid phones, right? Or so I had been told. But there was no answer. I left Tommy to finish the trees and drove straight home.

Jeannette Parcell (*mother*): I tried to reassure myself that Sara was literally the most responsible person I knew. She cleaned her room. Finished her homework. Had a job. I knew she wasn't caught up in anything dangerous. So when she wasn't responding, deep down, I knew it was bad.

Dave Parcell (*father*): Jeannette was freaking out pretty quickly. I tried to calm her down.

Jeannette Parcell (*mother*): I could feel my body go into panic mode. My stomach, my skin, my heart rate, the taste in my mouth . . . everything just went haywire.

Dave Parcell (*father*): Jack came home from school around three o'clock. We kind of told him a white lie about needing to talk to Sara, and asked if he knew where she was, but he didn't know anything. Last he'd seen, she was still waiting for the high school bus. There was nothing more he could tell us, so Jeannette had one of her friends pick him up and get him out of the house for the afternoon.

Jeannette Parcell (*mother*): School had let out and we still hadn't heard anything. I started contacting all of her friends.

Olivia Weston (*friend*): Sara's mom called me, and that's when I started to get scared. I told her I last saw Sara going back to the school bus for her bag. And that's all I could really say. I had been wondering where she was all day, too. She wasn't answering any texts, I knew something shady was going on.

Nellie Spencer (*friend*): Her mom was sobbing on the phone, begging me to tell her anything, promising we wouldn't be in trouble. Yeah, I was not in a great headspace for that. The first thing I thought of was that maybe something happened at the party after I dipped out early on Saturday. Maybe Sara was dealing with that. But I wasn't about to start speculating out loud. It didn't seem like that big of a deal at first.

Dave Parcell (*father*): It got to the point where the choice was obvious: We had to call the police.

Jeannette Parcell (*mother*): I don't remember what happened. Dave did it.

Dave Parcell (*father*): I could barely bring myself to make the call. I knew once we did that, this whole thing would become real. Sara would officially be a "missing person." But I forced myself to do it. I made the call, made the report.

After I hung up, I immediately had this awful feeling in the pit of my stomach. Was literally shaking as I put the phone down.

I couldn't have predicted what came next, but I just knew that I had ruined all of our lives.

CHAPTER 2

"Then We Better Find Her Real Soon"

Felix Calderon (*detective, Frederick Police Department*): I had already clocked out for the night when my captain called me. It's not like Frederick has a lot of experienced detectives. Or detectives in general. He wanted me to handle this case. It was a combination of best man for the job and only man for the job.

I left my house and arrived at the Parcell residence at 8:47 p.m. on the Monday Sara Parcell disappeared. I had received a preliminary report from the dispatcher based on the parents' phone call. Our department had issued an APB already. My objective during the initial visit was to gather any information that would help us find Sara—if, in fact, she had gone missing due to criminal activity.

Dave Parcell (*father*): The first time I called the police station, they weren't too alarmed. I don't remember who I spoke to, but they took down some general info about Sara. They suggested we wait till later in the night to file a formal missing person report.

Jeannette Parcell (*mother*): I didn't appreciate that. I knew my daughter. Something bad had happened. We waited maybe an hour and called back. I made the call this time. Mama-grizzly mode. I told them my daughter was missing and they needed to get their ass in gear.

An hour later, Detective Calderon showed up at our house. He didn't seem too thrilled to be there, if I'm being honest.

Felix Calderon (*detective*): I had fifteen years of experience at that point, mostly in Houston. I had been in Frederick for two years. Small city of about seventy thousand, and it was as quiet as I expected when I applied for the transfer. My instincts told me this was not an abduction case.

Jeannette Parcell (*mother*): He asked a lot of uncomfortable questions. If Sara had boyfriends, if she did drugs, if we ever hit her, for chrissakes. He asked about her social life, parties, what her curfew was, if she ever broke it. That was the one thing that made me think. I knew she had gone to a party that weekend. And I knew she had gotten home late. But Sara didn't even have an official curfew. Like I said, she was too responsible.

Felix Calderon (*detective*): I made a note about the late night out two days prior. Frankly, it was the only thing that was slightly suspicious.

Jeannette Parcell (*mother*): He claimed he would start the search process immediately but expected Sara to be home within a few hours. He thought he was so smart, Detective Calderon, but what did he know, really? Nothing, as it turned out.

Dave Parcell (*father*): He was doing his job. I didn't have a problem with him.

Felix Calderon (*detective*): A teenager missing one day of school and ignoring phone calls is not a serious red flag. Kids go on joyrides, benders, have secret relationships, lose track of time. Honestly, the most likely explanation in these cases is that they bring some beer into the woods, and it gets too dark for them to find their car. Then the parents overreact and imagine there's a serial killer running around.

Probably because they watch too much TV. But from the way the Parcells described Sara, I understood their alarm. I took it seriously, even as I expected her to walk in any minute.

After we were done, Dave walked me out to my car. It was clear he wanted to have some kind of straightforward man-to-man exchange. I told him I really didn't think he had reason to worry, that ninety-nine times out of a hundred, this ends with a kid getting grounded.

He wanted to know about that one other time, the unthinkable outlier. I told him not to go there, it wasn't healthy or helpful. But he kept staring at me, waiting for an answer. So I was straight with him. If it's that one other time, I told him, then we better find her real soon.

He just nodded. What an asshole.

Dave Parcell (*father*): I remember that conversation. Does he want an apology or something? Gimme a break. In the grand scheme of things I wish I could take back, that little talk in the driveway is nowhere near the top of the list.

Jeannette Parcell (*mother*): Heaven help me, that first night was bad. It wasn't near the worst, as it turned out, but it was still brutal. I thought she'd come home, so of course I didn't sleep. Paced around the house. Made Jack sleep at our friends' so he didn't have to see us. I kept walking into Sara's room for no reason. Every headlight that went by, I jumped for the window. Dave was very sweet. Each time, when it wasn't Sara, he came over and held me tight.

Felix Calderon (*detective*): I was up early the next morning. I checked in with Dave and Jeannette, there was no word from Sara. I was starting to share their concern. We were deep into the red zone, that first forty-eight hours that usually makes or breaks these cases. Halfway through already, with no leads. I didn't even go to the station, I drove straight to the high school and got started on my interviews.

Olivia Weston (*friend*): The cops took over a classroom and questioned all of Sara's friends. It was stressful. I hadn't done anything wrong, but I kinda felt like a criminal.

Nellie Spencer (*friend*): The main detective asked if he could look through my phone. I told him no. I mean, I wanted to help Sara and all, but I knew whatever was going on had nothing to do with me. I'd throw my phone off a cliff before I let a cop look through it.

Felix Calderon (*detective*): At first glance, it appeared that Sara wasn't in the middle of any kind of crisis. My impression from her peers was that she was happy and well liked. But it was clear her friends were nervous about something. I wasn't ruling anything out. Kids hide things. Then their friends protect them out of misguided loyalty. I really wish they had just told me what was going on.

Olivia Weston (*friend*): I remember he was hung up on the field party. I recapped the night for him: I met Sara at nine when her shift at the ice cream shop ended. We walked around town for a bit. Got food at Burger King. Then we got a ride with some friends out to the field. I didn't have an exact address or anything, but I mean, who cares, she wasn't kidnapped there, right? We dropped her off at home at the end of the night. I tried to tell him who was at the party, but it was literally like hundreds of people.

Nellie Spencer (*friend*): I didn't say anything about Coach Walker. Dude freaking owes me.

Brandon Grassley (*neighbor*): I remember trying to be as helpful as possible. I told the detective what Sara was wearing on the morning she went missing: black jeans, checkered Vans, purple zip-up hoodie. I lived across the street, so I was trying to think of anything weird I'd seen recently, you know, like a creepy van or a suspicious person. I really wanted to be the one who solved the case, obviously. But there wasn't much to say.

Veronica Yang (*principal*): It was quite traumatizing for our students to go through that questioning. Some of them are afraid of the police, for valid reasons. And all the while, their peer is missing. We tried to make it as comfortable as possible, but they were all terrified. We had contingency plans for everything—fire, tornado, active shooter—but not for this. It was uncharted territory.

It always came as a surprise to me, how sensitive their antennae are—the students could be so reckless in myriad ways, posturing as adults, but the minute they sensed true, genuine danger, they become scared children again. They all knew Sara; they knew she didn't run away and join the circus. They knew it was bad. So that was the energy that permeated our school: genuine fear.

Felix Calderon (*detective*): After all the questioning, we got one legit lead—Sara's friends told me she had gone back to the school bus to get her backpack.

I went straight to the bus depot. Got the name of the driver on Sara's route. They had a storage closet for lost-and-found items—I checked that, no sign of Sara's bag. So I went to find Travis Haynes.

Travis Haynes (*bus driver*): This asshole rolls up on me in the parking lot of my apartment complex just as I'm getting in my car to head back to work for the afternoon route.

He starts questioning me. Yeah, I'm Travis. Yeah, I drive the East Meadow route in the morning. License, work ID, the whole nine. And then he asks if I've seen a green backpack with a troll key chain attached.

This can't be real, I'm thinking. I know at this exact moment—I'm about to be railroaded! Of course I can't help but look in my car, and the bag is sitting right there, riding shotgun, the dumb-ass troll staring us in the face.

I was in handcuffs three seconds later.

Felix Calderon (*detective*): It was a bittersweet moment. You're excited because you think you're about to find the victim, but on the other hand, it's a sickening confirmation that some piece-of-shit degenerate is involved. At that point you're prepared for the worst, really just hoping that she's still alive.

I did a preliminary search of Haynes's car and apartment. It was messy, disorganized, lots of beer cans and motorcycle posters, but I didn't find anything. So I drove him back to the station for questioning.

Travis Haynes (*bus driver*): I sat in their stupid interrogation room for a while, they kept yelling at me, and I just told them the same thing over and over: I found the bag, brought it to the office, but it was locked, so I threw it in my car. I didn't know who it belonged to. Didn't open it.

Didn't even know anyone was missing.

Felix Calderon (*detective*): The room at the bus depot with the lost-and-found bin didn't have a lock. I had been there earlier that day. Travis's story didn't hold up.

Travis Haynes (*bus driver*): Eventually, I told him either shit or get off the pot, you know? And they let me go. I know there's like a weird prejudice against school bus drivers, like we are all mentally ill weirdos, but that's not me.

Felix Calderon (*detective*): Travis Haynes was an idiot and a criminal. He should not have been driving a school bus full of children.

Travis Haynes (*bus driver*): I had my buddy pick me up, and it was obvious right away they put a tail on me. Probably thought I was some kind of idiot.

Mike Snyder (*news correspondent, ABC-7 Frederick*): I received my tip on the afternoon after the young lady went missing. She'd been gone twenty-fours at that point, people were worried, but the police had a suspect. I made my first report outside the police station. I didn't use the suspect's name, but I did identify the girl as Sara Parcell. If I remember correctly, the family gave us permission.

Dave Parcell (*father*): I don't know who would have authorized that. It certainly wasn't me.

Felix Calderon (*detective*): I tipped off my contact at the local news station—this useful haircut named Mike Snyder. I wanted Sara's photo on TV. I wanted to put pressure on the bus driver. By letting him go so quickly, I was hoping he would panic and lead us to her now that we had eyes on him.

Pushing those buttons—releasing Sara's name and letting Travis Haynes walk—there are consequences to that. It's not great for the family, I get it. It scares the community. But it is helpful from an investigation standpoint. The Parcells wanted their daughter back, so I stand by that decision.

Jeannette Parcell (*mother*): By sundown that night, there were four satellite vans in our front yard, just in time for the local news. It felt like an invasion. They had already staked out Jack's school and filmed him leaving that day.

Jack Parcell (*brother*): I didn't go to school that day. I stayed home, looking out the windows as all the news vans set up. From Sara's bedroom . . . that's where I was hanging out.

Mike Snyder (*local news*): The reason we go to the house is to give our viewers the visceral sense that this is happening in our community. We'd also love to get a word with the family, but they have every right to decline. I get it. We're not trying to harass anyone, but a missing girl is newsworthy. And we go where the news is, so to speak.

Dave Parcell (*father*): I was ready for this. I didn't know it would happen so quickly, but I knew the news crews would descend, and I had thought about how to handle it.

Jeannette Parcell (*mother*): I had no prior knowledge of what Dave was going to do.

Mike Snyder (*local news*): That moment on their doorstep was TV magic, I'll never forget it. They came outside, the mother and father, and gestured for the cameras to come over. The sun was setting, it was that perfect light, magic hour. I can still tell you what Dave said, word for word: "Sara, we love you and we miss you . . ."

Dave Parcell (*father*): "Sara, if you can hear this, we love you and we miss you. We are doing everything we can to bring you home. All your friends and family are praying for you, praying that you're safe. Keep us in your heart, and stay strong, Sare-Bear."

Mike Snyder (*local news*): Then he pulled those papers from his back pocket. His actual bank statement! Held it up for the cameras. "We have seventeen hundred and sixty-two dollars to our name . . . it's everything we've got, and we're offering it as a reward to whoever helps us find our daughter. No questions asked, we just want her back." It was incredible! Ten minutes later, it led every news broadcast in our area.

Felix Calderon (*detective*): I didn't have a problem with it. I wanted the community aware and mobilized. I thought it was admirable.

Evelyn Crawford (*Manny's wife*): When we ate dinner, Manny liked having the news on. I liked *Jeopardy!* Well, I bet you already know, I didn't see a lick of *Jeopardy!* that night. He damn near stared a hole through that television set.

Miriam Rosen (*teacher*): My heart broke for that family when I watched. So many of us wanted to help. I was ready to do whatever I could.

Tommy O'Brien (*employee, Geary Home & Garden*): I got in my truck and started driving around in circles, looking for her, hitting all the bridges, drainage ditches, you name it. Not for the reward or anything like that. Just seeing Dave so broken down, I had to do something. Had the floodlights on my truck, the scanner going and everything.

Evelyn Crawford (*Manny's wife*): The news broadcast painted a very sympathetic picture of the family and what they were going through. The man accomplished his goal. Shame on him.

Jeannette Parcell (*mother*): I was shocked when Dave did that. It's so awful to say, but I was worried about the money. Not actually, of course, but that was my first reaction: We can't give away any money! But within a second, I was so grateful he did it, I fully supported it. We would have given anything to get Sara back.

We stepped back inside our house, and I felt like I finally took a breath. I had tried to put on a brave face outside, but I was suddenly overwhelmed by everything—that Sara was really gone and that we were in the middle of this frenzy. The awful reality had set in, and I totally broke down. I collapsed into Dave, you know, hysterical, sobbing. He held me up, stared into my eyes, and I remember exactly what he said: "Sara is strong, she's brilliant, she's tough. She'll find a way. We're gonna get her back home. She'll be playing her violin upstairs again in no time, I promise."

Dave Parcell (*father*): That was one of the toughest moments. Trying to pull my wife back from the edge of darkness. She was being tortured. I did the best I could at the time.

Jeannette Parcell (*mother*): "We're gonna get her back home." He promised me. He said it with such conviction. And in that moment, I believed him. Clearly, I did, because I know I embraced him and smiled back through my tears. And we just stood there forever, holding on to each other.

Of course, neither of us had any idea we were being filmed.

Jack Parcell (*brother*): Yeah, my parents had no idea I was filming them after they came inside. It was almost an accident. I had been upstairs, filming the craziness outside from the window. You've got to understand, think about how boring Frederick is—this was definitely the wildest thing that had ever happened to me. I don't even mean Sara being gone, but just everyone in front of our house, yelling, pushing, the lights, the cameras.

So when I heard my parents come in, I had my phone out. I was at the top of the stairs, looking down. They were having this intense moment, whispering to each other. I kinda froze, just, you know, scared and confused about what I was seeing. When you're a little kid, there's nothing more terrifying or uncomfortable than seeing your parents vulnerable like that. I didn't want to interrupt or let them know that I had seen anything. But I still filmed it. I really don't know why.

Jeannette Parcell (*mother*): Jack was being sweet, in his own way. I don't blame him for anything that happened after. All of us can look back on specific moments when we did something to cause the dominoes to keep falling. So many little crossroads—if we had done one thing differently, Sara would still be alive.

Jack's decision was innocent. Not everyone else can say the same.

Jack Parcell (*brother*): Later that night, I snuck my phone into my room when I was going to sleep. I wasn't supposed to have it, but I guess there were bigger things going on. I lay in bed and kept watching that moment between my parents over and over. I couldn't stop. Like I said, it made me uncomfortable, but it also made me feel safe. Hopeful, even. I think I put it up on YouTube because I thought it might somehow help us find Sara.

Sara died because I posted that video. I have these scars on my wrists because of that video. It ruined my life. It ruined all of our lives.

Dave Parcell (*father*): Jack's video changed everything, obviously. It was a godsend at first. I mean, I couldn't have set things up better if I'd tried.

But then, yeah . . . the next thing we knew, we were in way over our heads—the Hollywood circus came to town.

CHAPTER 3

"Hollywood Loves a Viral Video"

Casey Hawthorne (*producer, TNN*): You have to remember what I was doing with my life back then. I was producing *Arm Candy*!

Do you know the story line for the episode we were shooting that week? Okay, get your popcorn ready: Amber's boyfriend bought everyone a round of shots. He ordered tequila. Amber hates tequila, and he knows it. But her roommate, Lindsey, loves tequila. Boom, that's our episode, Tequila-gate. So yeah, it's fair to say I was looking for a change.

I had been in LA for like ten years at this point. Came out to attend AFI, did the whole broke-filmmaker thing afterward, waitressed, made little shorts with my friends on weekends, some played at a few tiny festivals—it was fun for a minute, then awful. I had to pay bills, I had student loans. Then a random PA job on a reality show turned into a shitty producing job, which turned into a real producing job, and suddenly, I was making too much money to say no.

Without planning it, I had a career: I was a reality TV producer. At first I was embarrassed to say that out loud. But look at me now . . . it worked out.

Marcus Maxwell (*president and programming executive, TNN*): I knew Casey secretly hated her job back then. She was an artist at heart, and *Arm Candy* offended her precious film school sensibilities. But not every artist gets to have a career in this town. We have a lot of very talented waiters. And God forbid one of them finds out you're a TV exec . . . you start getting Shakespeare monologues with your specials, it's a nightmare, you might as well stay home.

Anyway, Casey was good at her job but a pain in the ass even then, before she got famous. Always thought she was the smartest person in the room. Probably was, but she still had to let you know it.

Casey Hawthorne (*producer*): Yeah, I was an artist, but I wasn't an idiot. I understood what the network wanted. They wanted money. Money comes from ads. Ad prices are set by the number of viewers. And viewers are attracted to . . . what, exactly? They would never admit it, but we had it pretty well figured out by then—the audience is attracted to hot people in bathing suits throwing drinks at each other. You can only produce so many episodes of that before you go crazy. We were on Season Five.

Anthony Pena (*video editor, TNN*): Casey would get pretty loopy during our late-night editing sessions. We'd be jacked up on gummy worms and coffee, and she'd ask me to cut together some gonzo sequence that revealed how stupid the whole thing was. You know, like a moment when you could hear Casey off-camera feed someone a line to escalate a fight. Or when she'd have a character repeat something a few times so she could get the right coverage. I guess we would make these goofy outtakes to remind ourselves that we were above the material in some way, that we were in on the joke. Obviously, we would never leave them in the final cut, but it was clear Casey was at the end of her rope.

Casey Hawthorne (*producer*): I've never touched a gummy worm in my life. But yes, I was slowly losing my sanity. I had moved to LA to tell stories. My North Star had always been that I wanted the audience crying when the credits rolled and they saw my name. I wanted to move them. Not sell them car insurance.

Anthony Pena (*editor*): After the first few seasons, Casey would always talk about wanting to do something different. I would ask what she meant, and she'd just say, "I'll know it when I see it." I think she had given up on making serious feature films, but the ambition behind that was still burning inside her.

Casey Hawthorne (*producer*): I saw Jack's YouTube video while I was driving. I was stuck at the light where Wilshire hits Santa Monica, prime location for scrolling through your phone, and I clicked on the link.

It was so raw, so tender, but I didn't fully understand what I was watching. Someone honked at me, so I kept driving. At the next light, I saw the news story about Sara, and then I saw Dave and Jeannette making that little speech in their driveway. I shouldn't say "little"— making that powerful speech in their driveway.

By the time I made a U-turn on Santa Monica, I had the whole show figured out.

Marcus Maxwell (*executive*): Casey marched into my office and shoved her phone in my face. She made me watch two videos, first the parents outside with the bank statement, then the one inside the house with them embracing. She had only seen these herself ten minutes earlier, but she made a full pitch on the spot.

Casey Hawthorne (*producer*): I knew this was what I was looking for. Frankly, this is what the country was looking for. The family was straight out of central casting. The flannel shirts, the bad haircuts, the pickup truck, the messy house. And they were dealing with everyone's worst nightmare. But they were standing strong, standing together, being vulnerable, looking for help, literally and figuratively asking you to join their ordeal. And then that stolen moment, husband and wife, embracing and holding each other up through their tears—who wouldn't fall in love with them?

And finally—you can believe me or not, I don't care—I truly thought I could help them find their daughter.

Marcus Maxwell (*executive*): I looked up from the videos and stared at her. Casey was just nodding. Nodding very confidently. There was no discussion. I gave in . . . I told her to get on a plane to Maryland. What can I say? Hollywood loves a viral video—it's existing IP!

Casey Hawthorne (*producer*): I ran home, packed a bag, and left for the airport. I remember taking off over the Pacific, then curving around to fly east. I was stuck in a middle seat, but I craned my neck to look down at the coastline, that beautiful blond sliver of sand that runs forever. We were supposed to be shooting in Malibu. Hell, my crew was probably still shooting without me. Amber, Lindsey, the whole gang, right below the plane. But if you had made me go to the set of *Arm Candy* that day, I would have driven off a cliff right into the sea. Fuck California—Frederick, Maryland, was my new paradise. Because there was something meaningful worth doing there. A story that would move people. From that first moment stuck at the traffic light on Wilshire, I was consumed with making this show.

Marcus Maxwell (*executive*): Of course we never should have made it. But Casey convinced me we were doing a public service. And I was excited to be a pioneer. It was 2013, everyone was already doing true crime by that point. But we were going to be the first show that did true crime in real time, without the safety net of looking backward.

In hindsight, there's a reason it's not done like that. Or not done by this network anymore—Casey still does it, obviously. It's too hard to stay removed from the story. And it's too unpredictable. When the stakes are high, which is what you want, there's always the risk of something unspeakable happening. And then you're compelled to air it. Everyone in this business, we're all showmen, none of us have the willpower to sit on amazing footage, no matter how unseemly.

But I gotta be honest—after what happened in Frederick, I lost the stomach for it.

Casey Hawthorne (*producer*): Look, Marcus was a sweetheart, still is, and he is pretty smart and not an asshole and never grabbed my ass at a holiday party. Solid foundation right there, give that man a medal! But he was always kind of a pussy. I'm sorry, it's just true. That's why he's still banging around at TNN and I'm not.

Marcus Maxwell (*executive*): It's funny, after we did *Searching for Sara*, I had this flashback to when my daughter was five or six years old. She would come downstairs when my wife and I were watching TV, and sometimes we'd quickly turn it off or change the channel. She'd ask why, and we'd say it wasn't appropriate for kids to watch. But my daughter came up with her own name for it, you know, for shows that were too violent for her. She'd ask, "Is it a kill show?" That's what she'd call it. "When will I be old enough to watch a kill show?" We think we shield our kids from this stuff, but they know what's out there.

I thought about that after the finale of *Searching for Sara*. We never set out to make a kill show. But we were being naive.

Ezra Phillips (*pop culture critic,* Slate): *Searching for Sara* as an artifact and Casey Hawthorne as the human embodiment represent the nadir of the true-crime industrial complex.

They did not invent the form, of course. They owe plenty of credit to Dumas, Dostoyevsky, Conan Doyle, Capote, et cetera.

And Hollywood has depended on and then mythologized true-crime stories since its inception—from *Public Enemy* to *Bonnie and Clyde* to *Goodfellas* to, one could even argue, more modern examples of corporate malfeasance like *The Social Network* and *The Big Short*.

But only recently have we seen this frenzied, symbiotic relationship between contemporaneous criminal events and the various products—books, movies, TV series, podcasts—that repackage them for our entertainment.

I say "frenzied" because the minute an attractive young woman gets murdered, journalists and producers fight for the story rights. And I say "symbiotic" because often these entertainment products are necessary vehicles to bring attention to miscarriages of justice. Good luck getting your conviction overturned without a hit podcast in your corner.

But Casey took this grotesque relationship one step further: a reality show that follows the search for a missing girl in real time, all from the perspective of the victim's family. Remember, Casey didn't know beforehand how it would end! Something like that had never been done. And for good reason. The moral hazard should have been abundantly clear.

Molly Lowe (*professor of sociology, University of California, Berkeley*): True-crime obsession is nothing new, and relatively easy to explain from a sociological perspective. We know violence is titillating. Adding the veneer of truth makes it even more so. Every true-crime story carries an implication that makes it scarier than fiction: Look! This could have happened to you! But it didn't, because you're either luckier or smarter or more deserving. Congratulations.

But there's another dopamine hit embedded in the best true crime. What people crave even more than a thrill is being involved, feeling a sense of belonging and purpose. Whether it's a family, fraternity, political party, any number of things—we all register significant boosts in happiness when we are part of a group. Even better, a group with a clear objective that reinforces this heady bond. And if the objective is perceived as noble? Watch out. Individuals will give away their whole lives to pursue that goal.

Now what's more noble than saving the life of an innocent girl? It is literally the archetypal epic story. A girl out there somewhere who needs our help. A damsel in distress. That's what Casey Hawthorne tapped into with *Searching for Sara*. This was her genius—she got her viewers to believe they were joining the rescue party. That's why millions of them became obsessed with it. That's why I wrote my dissertation about it.

Casey Hawthorne (*producer*): Before any show could exist, I had to win over the family. So I spent my entire plane ride catching up on the story and thinking about how to pitch them.

I felt like I already knew who these people were. I had grown up in the same kind of town—"all-American," "the heartland," people would say. I had gone to the same football games and Christmas pageants and harvest festivals. I personally found it all boring, flat, suffocating, homogenous, and don't even get me started on the food. But that type of town was still in my blood.

I knew the people in these towns didn't want anything I had to offer. If I could smell the casseroles a mile away, they could smell my condescension. They had a feeling of contempt for those of us who had left and succeeded and were proud of it. Fair enough, even if that contempt was rooted in jealousy, fear, frustration, self-loathing. But come on, no one there understood this; it's not like a single one of them had been in therapy.

So I knew the Parcells weren't going to welcome me with open arms. They only wanted their daughter back. I had to figure out how to make them see me as a vessel for that.

Marcus Maxwell (*executive*): Casey is a wolf in wolf's clothing. She comes straight at you, no buttering you up with false charm. That doesn't work for a man trying to win anyone over; people are rightfully turned off by the naked aggression. But when they see a woman with that unabashed swagger, there's an implication that she had to walk through some serious shit to reach that point . . . and if she's offering you a spot on her team, if she's going to take that same attitude and wield it on your behalf, then you're excited to trust her. I had every confidence she would close the Parcells.

Casey Hawthorne (*producer*): I rented a car at the Baltimore airport, pointed it west, and almost immediately got a speeding ticket. But hey, that's what production budgets are for.

I got in to Frederick kind of late that first night and found a Hampton Inn. There's a cute little downtown there—quaint, but with some cheesy tourist stuff, lights on trees, a gazebo, stuff like that. It's a big Civil War town, I guess that whole area was a real hot spot for battles.

I did a lap on Main Street and found a restaurant where they were still serving food at the bar. Ordered a martini and a burger. There was one other person sitting there.

Oops.

Felix Calderon (*detective*): Of course I regret sleeping with Casey. Absolutely unprofessional, and it's impacting my career even ten years later. But you have to remember, she conveniently didn't tell me who she was that first night. She said she worked in "medical sales." I bought her a drink after she made it abundantly clear I should approach her, and we had a nice conversation.

I don't want to get into it any further.

Casey Hawthorne (*producer*): I was sitting alone, staring at my phone like a normal human being. He kicked out the barstool next to me and practically said, "Do you come here often?" I was bored and lonely, so I didn't bite his head off.

Look, being single in your early thirties, working your tail off, successful in LA . . . it's complicated emotionally. You feel like you're kicking ass, but there's a part of you that wonders about popping out a few kids, joining a country club with a tall husband, and baking vegan cookies until you drop dead in your kitchen. I'm making it sound gross, but I'm not going to lie, some version of that appealed to me. And at that age, it was still possible, so every minute you're not going down that path, it feels like this weighty, intentional decision. Which leads to coping mechanisms to deal with the stress. One of mine was convincing myself how fun my life was, being footloose and fancy-free. So when a hot stranger approached me at a bar, it was on.

Felix Calderon (*detective*): It's the lying I have a problem with. Part of me wants to defend Casey when people nowadays call her a con artist. I know it's more complicated than that. I want to believe her heart is in the right place. But then I remember our first encounter. She was lying from the start.

Casey Hawthorne (*producer*): Yes, I misled him about why I was in town that first night, that's true. But he knew the truth eventually, and that didn't put a stop to anything!

I don't know why he has to act like such a Puritan about our little tryst. The only two decent-looking adults in a fifty-mile radius met at a bar, of course we went home together.

Felix Calderon (*detective*): Do I think she was using me for the sake of her show? Yes.

Casey Hawthorne (*producer*): All I knew that first night was that he was a local cop. Maybe I had a sense that he was a detective, I can't remember, but I didn't know he was the *main person* on Sara's case. Or I didn't know that for sure. I guess I might have assumed it was possible.

He sat down next to me, and we ordered fresh martinis. I like mine with a lemon twist, but he does his dirty. I confessed that I hated olives, and he got very cutely offended. He told me that some of his family were olive farmers in Spain. He had gone there for the summers, to Andalusia, as a kid. So we sat at the bar, and he spent the next thirty minutes mansplaining olives to me. Like he was the Forrest Gump of olives. That sounds so boring, hearing myself say it out loud, but it wasn't. It was sexy. The way he described the mist in the groves, the rays of sun kissing the delicate skins, the breeze that tiptoed in at dusk to cool things down . . . I had goose bumps.

I promise you, I didn't sleep with Felix as some kind of strategic play. Come on, I tried that for about a month after grad school in LA—not for me. No . . . he fully charmed me, and I was into him.

Afterward, when it became clear over the next few days that we were antagonists, so to speak, it didn't bother me that much. Yeah, it was messy, but I love messy, I thrive on messy. We all run toward things we're good at, right?

And to anyone who judges me for continuing on with him once I knew he was the detective, I'd put it like this: I know for a fact that we never would have found Sara if Felix and I hadn't been sleeping together.

Felix Calderon (*detective*): It was a giant mistake. And a disservice to the family. God knows what I could've discovered earlier if I wasn't caught up in her web. Remember, at the end there, a few hours could have made all the difference.

Anthony Pena (*editor*): I hate that dude. Our production would have gone so much smoother if he wasn't constantly mooning over Casey.

Marcus Maxwell (*executive*): No, I did not know she was sleeping with the lead detective. I only found out when the scandal broke. And then learned way too much about it during the lawsuit. It obviously was not a good look for TNN, and we took steps to ensure something like that didn't happen again.

Ezra Phillips (*pop culture critic*): I think it came out after the show was already popular, after Casey had some notoriety . . . not only is this woman impeding and impacting a police investigation, but she's also sleeping with the detective! Unbelievable! We all understand why he lost his job. But Casey? What recourse is there for her? Hmm, how about an ethics censure from the reality producers' guild? Come on, do you hear how ridiculous that sounds? No, there was nothing. Quite the opposite, in fact—she gets picked up for more seasons and doesn't skip a beat.

To take this matter seriously for a second, it begs an important question: For the creators of this content—the producers, podcasters, executives—who do they answer to? They're not law enforcement.

They're not journalists. There are no voters or public officials or professional regulations to hold them accountable.

I guess the sick answer is that they are beholden to stockholders and board members . . . stockholders and board members in giant multinational entertainment conglomerates that want to earn money. So why does an exploited underclass have their bleak lives sucked dry by the entertainment industry? It's actually pretty simple: capitalism.

Casey Hawthorne (*producer*): I had a job to do. So the next morning, right as the sun came up, I kicked Felix out of my hotel room. I told him I had a big sales pitch—not a lie! You would have thought he had stuff to do, too, right? I mean, we had sex again, don't get me wrong, but I had to start my day. No lying around afterward staring at the ceiling, please.

I grabbed coffee in town, read the local newspaper, went over my notes. Then it was time. I drove to the Parcells' house.

Dave Parcell (*father*): That morning was a lot of waiting around. We kept Jack home from school, and Jeannette and I were trying to have a talk with him about his video. It had exploded like wildfire the day before and was a bit overwhelming for all of us. I mean, the main landing spot for this story was now our eleven-year-old's YouTube page.

Jeannette Parcell (*mother*): Everyone we knew had reached out, they'd all watched it, everyone *they* knew had watched it. The views on YouTube just kept going up, and Jack was freaked out about what he'd started. When I first saw it, I thought it was sweet of him to capture that moment.

We weren't angry with him, we knew how scared he was, but we tried to let him know that some things weren't appropriate to share on his phone. He understood.

And then there was a knock on the door.

Felix Calderon (*detective*): She should never have been let through. The department had been instructed to keep a strict perimeter around the house. Four of our patrolmen were on the scene.

Casey Hawthorne (*producer*): The street was crammed with news vans. I parked a couple blocks away. It was a cookie-cutter neighborhood, modest homes, small lawns.

A few uniformed cops were milling around in front of the Parcells' driveway. I'm not even kidding, I think they were huddled around a box of doughnuts. So I ducked under the police tape and walked past everyone, straight to the door.

Dmitri Russo (*patrolman, Frederick Police Department*): We were not sitting around shoveling doughnuts in our faces, give me a break. That woman is in showbiz. She says whatever she thinks her audience wants to hear.

Casey Hawthorne (*producer*): Someone shouted at me as I crossed the lawn. I didn't turn around, I acted like I belonged there. I got to the door and knocked quickly, three times.

Jeannette Parcell (*mother*): I opened the door and saw this glamorous stranger standing there. I don't know how she was let through. The cops were already running up from the curb.

Casey Hawthorne (*producer*): I heard them yelling at me. I knew I only had twenty seconds, tops. Jeannette opened the door and Dave joined her. I had three points to make, had practiced them all morning, and delivered them as clearly as I could:

"I want to make a reality show that follows your family as you search for your daughter . . .

"This is the best hope you have of finding her . . .

"And yes, you'll get paid . . ."

As I finished my last sentence, I handed them my business card. Jeannette took it, almost robotically. And then the cops caught up to me, dragged me away, and threw me into a police cruiser. I turned to look back at Dave and Jeannette as they stood in the doorway.

I could see it on their faces. Wheels were turning, they were pro-
cessing what I had just said. When they'd answered the door, they had
seemed so forlorn. Now I saw something else: surprise . . . curiosity . . .
maybe even a glimmer of hope.

I knew I had a chance.

Dave Parcell (*father*): Honestly? What was I really thinking? I remember it exactly: I looked down at that business card and thought, This is
a miracle, it's a golden ticket . . . *my little girl is going to Juilliard.*

Jeannette Parcell (*mother*): I can't remember what I thought. I just
know what happened next. We sold our soul to the devil. It was the
worst decision of our lives.

CHAPTER 4

"This Show Could Be That Miracle"

Dave Parcell (*father*): I was ready to say yes right away. But I knew I had to seem like I was reluctant. If this thing was going to work—the new version, I mean, the one that had fallen into our laps—I needed Jeannette to be driving it.

Jeannette Parcell (*mother*): I remember watching Casey walk back across our lawn. She had talked so fast, I wasn't sure what had happened. I began to process what she had just said.

There is no other word for it . . . it was crazy.

I turned to Dave. He seemed to be in shock, too. But after a few moments, he got his head around it sooner than I did. My first instinct was to throw the business card away. Dave agreed with me at first, he said something like "Yeah, of course, it's insane." I actually did it, I tossed that thing in the trash. But then Dave started pacing around. I asked him what he was thinking about. He was reluctant to say anything. I had to pull it out of him. He finally looked at me and said, "What if she has a point? What if this could actually help us find Sara?"

Dave Parcell (*father*): Jeannette had put the business card down on our kitchen table. I picked it up again, to take a second look. Then, very cautiously, I said maybe we should find out exactly what this producer had in mind. That it couldn't hurt to ask a few questions without committing to anything. That maybe there was another way she could help without us doing a whole ridiculous TV show.

Jeannette was still horrified by the idea, but I saw that she had softened just the slightest bit as I talked. I reminded her that it had been fifty-four hours since anyone had seen Sara.

Fifty-four hours, I said again. I'd be happy to throw the card away, but it was up to her. Jeannette thought about it for another minute; I could tell it was killing her. Then she told me to make the call.

Casey Hawthorne (*producer*): I was stuck in the back of the cruiser for a little while. But I wasn't panicking, I knew wheels were turning without me. Finally, one of the cops let me out, and I talked my way out of a trespassing charge. I walked down to my rental car, then drove back to the hotel to wait for their call. I stared at the phone for about ten minutes, and then it rang. I manifested that shit.

Dave wanted to meet. He and Jeannette had questions before they committed to anything. Totally understandable, I said. He suggested a roadside diner twenty minutes out of town. I said that was perfect.

Dave Parcell (*father*): I drove out to McGraw's, outside of town. I didn't want anyone to see us if I could help it.

Casey Hawthorne (*producer*): It was one of those old boxcar places. I loved it. There were serious *New-York-Times*-reporters-come-here-to-interview-voters-type vibes.

I got there early, and then Dave arrived and slid into the tattered booth, across from me. You know the famous diner scene from *Heat*? That's what it felt like. Pacino and De Niro. Intense. Charged. Cat and mouse. Then we ordered some blueberry pie, and he asked me to explain what I had in mind.

Dave Parcell (*father*): She had made some pretty bold claims on our doorstep. I didn't know if she was a serious person or some lunatic. I googled her before I left the house. *Arm Candy*? We didn't watch that junk.

Casey Hawthorne (*producer*): I told him this was going to be different. I gave him my longer pitch, but I didn't even have to lay it on too thick, because it was all true: "It seems like you have five idiot cops working this case . . . I can turn that into a hundred. You've got friends and family driving around, looking out for any sign of your daughter . . . I can turn that into millions of eyeballs, literally. If the people who have Sara think this will all blow over, they'll know that's not possible anymore."

I tried to be respectful, but I put it pretty plainly: "Look, I get it, there's a lot to be said about small-town values, but no one wants a small-town investigation for their missing kid. You want big-city spotlight. Resources, experts, awareness. Most people can't snap their fingers and demand that kind of attention. *You* can—because of what you said on your doorstep and because of Jack's video, the world is ready to help you. But they're also ready to forget you in about five minutes. If you want the world to help find your daughter, you'll do this show."

He sat there thinking for a long time. Really made a meal out of it, now that I think about it.

Dave Parcell (*father*): Hardest two minutes of my life. Well, to that point, at least. I wanted to jump across the table and hug this woman. But I had to sit there, playing with my pie, literally biting my tongue.

I finally looked right back at her. I told her we'd have to think about it, me and Jeannette. But just in case we came around to it, how would it work?

I can't remember all the details she threw out that night. Production schedules, turnaround times, broadcast windows, all that stuff. But I know I heard this: fifty-thousand-dollar-episode fee for our family. Ten-episode guarantee, or at least until Sara was found.

I thanked Casey for her time, got up, and left. Floated out to the parking lot. For the first time in my life, I was about to be rich.

Felix Calderon (*detective*): I spent that night driving around Frederick, digging into Travis Haynes. We had let him go, put a tail on him, and I still thought he was the odds-on favorite.

I talked to his boss at the bus company. Talked to his landlord. Not exactly glowing reports but no smoking guns. I drove across town to the dive bar where he hung out most nights, pulled up a stool. It took me all of fifteen minutes sipping a Natty Bo to learn that Travis was running a very unsophisticated prescription-pill scheme. He would drag himself into the VA every month, tell them he was still having headaches from his tour in Afghanistan. They'd prescribe Vicodin, Percs, Oxy, whatever else, then Travis would sell loosies at the bar for ten bucks a pop.

I decided not to arrest him right away. We had just taken our run at him, anyway. But it was good to know we had leverage to hold over his head whenever we wanted.

Travis Haynes (*bus driver*): He said that? He's airing out my private medical records from the VA? This is a total HIPAA violation! I can't believe it's ten years later and this asshole is still running his mouth about me. I'm living rent-free in his head, I guess.

I was using those pills for myself. For valid medical reasons. I didn't see Detective Calderon over in Afghanistan, so he can kiss my ass. And yeah, maybe when a buddy was in really rough shape, I'd be a good friend and hook him up with a pill or two. That's called kindness. But hell no, I wasn't operating a drug ring. I should sue him for saying that. I would, too, if it weren't for, you know, the statue of limitations and all that.

Felix Calderon (*detective*): For the record, Travis was a quartermaster in the army. I checked. He worked on a base unloading food supplies.

Beverly Geary (*grandmother*): I had no idea what Dave and my daughter were contemplating that night. I just knew there was a candlelight vigil in the town square. They had decided not to attend, it was too overwhelming for them, but I went with my husband. It was really beautiful, so many people came out. By then everyone had seen the little video Jack made. They were all holding candles, leaving gifts for Sara at the base of this giant photo collage her friends had made.

Olivia Weston (*friend*): We didn't know what else to do. We were all just hugging, and crying, and praying. I left a pack of sour Skittles there, Sara's favorite. Someone was passing out yellow ribbons to pin on our coats.

Nellie Spencer (*friend*): I was kind of weirded out by the whole thing. It felt like she was already dead. But she wasn't. Like, if Sara is missing, I don't see how all of us standing around crying is going to help anything, you know?

Olivia Weston (*friend*): It was truly terrifying. Of all people, I knew for sure that Sara hadn't just run off and done something crazy. She was the mom-friend in our group—she made us text her when we got home. She always had that extra tampon for you. She made us drink a glass of water in between every beer at parties.

Nellie Spencer (*friend*): Oh my God, her freaking one-for-one rule! So much water, so much peeing. Yeah, we spent a lot of time in bathrooms, the three of us. But those are kinda the best moments of your life, aren't they? Crammed into a random bathroom, laughing with your friends, ignoring the knocks on the door . . . I'd go back in a second.

Olivia Weston (*friend*): Sara wasn't reckless or unhappy or impulsive . . . someone had to have kidnapped her. The vigil really made that hit home. I was physically sick for days afterward, just thinking about what might be happening to her.

Miriam Rosen (*teacher*): This town is a special place. Neighbors really care about each other here. The whole town was at that vigil. They all would have stood there waiting, rain or shine, for however long it took, if that would have been any help.

Mike Snyder (*local news*): I did a stand-up report there, we got some really terrific footage. Led our news hour with it that night, obviously. As you might imagine, it was our top story for quite a long time.

Evelyn Crawford (*Manny's wife*): No, Manny and I did not attend the so-called vigil. I do remember mentioning it to him that afternoon. He wasn't interested.

Dmitri Russo (*patrolman*): I attended the vigil and did several walk-throughs applying the profiling techniques I had learned at the academy. You'd be surprised how often the perpetrators of a crime attend these types of things. I think they get off on it—these are disturbed individuals. So I was on high alert. But I didn't see anything suspicious.

Beverly Geary (*grandmother*): The only thing that put a damper on the evening was when we ran into that man from the bank. Grassley. Frank Grassley. He had a lot of nerve showing up to a vigil for Sara. He's lucky that Dave and Jeannette weren't there.

It was enough for me just to give him the stink eye, but not my husband. He marched right over to Frank and started giving him a piece of his mind. That's why Herb wouldn't do this book, by the way—he said talking about this stuff would just set him off. He does have quite a temper.

Anyway, when he was confronting Frank Grassley . . . I can't say I didn't approve. This man lived across the street from our daughter and her family. And what he did with all that loan business between him and Dave . . . well, it wasn't neighborly, I know that much. That's why Dave lost his roofing business, you know. The bank, the Grassley fella, they were totally out to get him. It was shameful.

Brandon Grassley (*neighbor*): Yeah, I didn't really know what that confrontation was all about. I knew Sara's dad didn't really like my dad. That was kind of obvious. Some awkward moments in the driveway, stuff like that. But it wasn't like, as a kid, I knew about every loan my dad approved at the bank. Or why her grandfather was so upset at him. I can't imagine he did anything wrong. But I guess her whole family got it into their heads that my dad was some kind of villain.

Dave Parcell (*father*): By the time I was driving back from the diner, the vigil was over. But I could see what they had done in the town square. It was . . . yeah, it was really touching to see how much people cared. I knew they would, of course. I mean, you'd have to be made of stone not to care.

I got back home and sat down in the kitchen with Jeannette. I recapped Casey's pitch. Tried to keep a poker face. Then I told her the numbers Casey had offered. I saw her react.

Jeannette Parcell (*mother*): The money had nothing to do with it. I'd be the first one to admit if it did. If anyone understood how desperate we were financially, what just a single fifty-thousand-dollar windfall could do for us, it was me. I don't even remember the money coming up that night, to be honest. The fact that we would get paid at all was a surprise to me. I didn't know how show business worked, I thought all the people on these reality series were volunteers!

Forget the money, it still felt wrong to me. Taking this horror we were going through and turning it into entertainment? I mean, who would want to watch that? And why would we want anyone to see our family like this?

But I kept thinking about what Casey had told Dave: "A million eyeballs looking for Sara." When it was put like that, I started to understand.

Jack Parcell (*brother*): I came downstairs, but my parents wouldn't let me stay in the kitchen. Of course, I waited around the corner and tried to listen. Had the good sense not to film, at least. I didn't understand exactly what they were discussing. But it seemed like my dad was doing most of the talking.

Dave Parcell (*father*): I leaned into how guilty we would feel if we didn't do it. What if something awful happened to Sara and we hadn't done everything we could to save her? What would our excuse have been? That it was too inconvenient having cameramen in the house? That it was embarrassing? That we'd be ridiculed by some pencil-neck snobs in their ivory tower? Who cares! We wanted to get our girl back.

Ezra Phillips (*pop culture critic*): I think about that moment all the time, when the parents actually sat down and agreed to do this. To this day, I cannot wrap my head around it. I've heard all the justifications, all the rationalizations, and still . . . no. They literally agreed to make a reality show about the search for their missing daughter. How could they ever imagine that was a good idea? The mom, specifically. Jeannette. What could have possibly convinced her?

Dave Parcell (*father*): Once I saw that Jeannette was almost there, I grabbed her: "We have to do this. Now. What do we have to lose?"

Jeannette Parcell (*mother*): He was holding me tight, staring at me, almost shaking me. He repeated something that he said Casey had just told him: "Sara needs a miracle . . . this show could be that miracle."

That stuck with me. I had always believed in miracles.

Casey Hawthorne (*producer*): The show could be the miracle? No, I definitely never said that. I'm not the religious type. It's a good line, though! Must have been Dave's. I would remember if it was mine.

Jeannette Parcell (*mother*): I would have done literally anything to get my little girl back. Walked through the fires of hell if that's what it took. So how bad could it be to have a few cameras follow us around? If there was any chance it might help, I couldn't say no.

Dave Parcell (*father*): Jeannette finally nodded. She was in. I let go of her and went to call Casey.

Casey Hawthorne (*producer*): Of course I remember where I was when I got that call. Or voicemail, I should say. Shockingly enough, I didn't pick up. I was . . . busy.

Felix Calderon (*detective*): Ironic? That she was at my house when Dave called her? No, I wouldn't say ironic. Ridiculous. Annoying. Embarrassing. Shameless. Intentional, for all I know. Not ironic.

Casey Hawthorne (*producer*): Felix had asked me out again. He hadn't been at the Parcells' earlier, so he hadn't seen me there, didn't know what I was doing in town or that I'd already had a brush with the law.

He texted me, said he was working late, but he'd love to cook me dinner at his place when he was done. If I was still in town and free. He told me he had some special Portuguese fish recipe. How could I say no?

Felix Calderon (*detective*): Bacalhau. It's a traditional stew with salted cod. Grandmother's recipe, even though it's technically Portuguese, not Spanish. It's very good, and I don't make it for just anyone.

I shouldn't have made it for Casey.

Casey Hawthorne (*producer*): He had a nice little house that I could walk to. I put on a cute top and stopped off to pick up a bottle of wine. I asked the shop owner if she sold any natural wines, and she looked at me like I had three heads. But I found something decent.

I got to Felix's and was pleasantly surprised. There was jazz playing when I walked in. He had a fire going, there was art on the walls. Sure, it was mostly that generic black-and-white photography, you know, stuff for people who think they're arty, but at least it wasn't posters! I kicked my shoes off, curled up on his couch with a blanket, and we opened the wine. The stew he was making bubbled away in the kitchen, that garlic-and-white-wine scent wafting over us. If I wasn't me, I would have been halfway in love already.

Felix Calderon (*detective*): I had been in Frederick for two years and hadn't met a lot of people like Casey. I was married once before, briefly, and divorced at twenty-nine. It was hard for me to get excited by someone new. But the way Casey walked into my house . . .

I mean, in hindsight, you never know with her—what's a performance? is she just manipulating you?—but I had no reason to doubt her back then. She tossed me the wine bottle she was carrying, literally threw it to me. Walked through the kitchen, dipped a finger into the pot on the stove, licked it, and said in a condescending tone of surprise, "Hmm, tastes good." And then she kicked her feet up on my couch and asked what was taking me so long to open the wine.

Casey Hawthorne (*producer*): The stew was good. He looked great in an apron, of course. Apron, suit, uniform, briefs . . . he looked great in anything. We got a little drunk. We stared into each other's eyes. We *talked*. I had to hear a little more about olives and his summers in Spain. I told him about my family's summer road trips to the national parks. My parents were both teachers, so we went hard in that station wagon once school let out. I could fall asleep instantly on any straight highway.

We went deeper. He confided in me about what caused him to leave Houston. Heartbreaking, I felt awful for him. I told him about the films I had wanted to make in LA, the graveyard of my artistic dreams. We dropped the facade and didn't pretend that we were perfect or happy.

I think we could both feel that something cool was happening. We had different lives, but our chemistry made sense. He spent all his time being serious—he was desperate for someone to make him laugh. And I spent my days doing the most frivolous job imaginable—I was desperate for someone with substance. That's why I had come to Frederick, to do a different kind of show, something that mattered. And then I met this guy straight away who dedicated his life to stuff that mattered. Of course I was attracted to that. We were tearing each other's clothes off while the dessert burned in the oven.

Felix Calderon (*detective*): It was a nice evening, I will concede that much. But you have to remember, I still thought Casey was a traveling salesperson. Yeah, she kind of lost track of her cover story when she told me she had wanted to make movies. And when I asked about the specifics of what she was doing now, she brushed it off. But I didn't push too hard. She made it sound unimportant. And I really didn't think I'd see her again.

Casey Hawthorne (*producer*): Later, in bed, we were in the middle of one of those heavy silences—not the bad kind but one of those moments with the invisible buildup of energy and both people are fully attuned that whatever comes out next is important. And he just blurted it out, it was so sweet. Something like "It's a shame you're just passing through, I could really see myself falling for you." He was totally smitten, the poor guy! I almost started to make fun of him for being such a softie, but I didn't. To be fair, I had developed a little crush, too. It was nice to hear him say that.

Felix Calderon (*detective*): Casey is notorious for hearing what she wants to hear, whether it actually happens or not.

Casey Hawthorne (*producer*): I got out of bed at one point and found my phone in the other room. Maybe the longest I had gone in years without checking it. I saw Dave had left a message. He and Jeannette were in! The show was on! I silently screamed and did a little dance in my birthday suit. My heart was racing, I was ecstatic. It had all worked out, I was really going to produce this show that had never been done before. The show that I had conceived of days earlier. The show that I truly believed would change my career, change my life, even. I took a couple deep breaths, then put the phone away and went back into the bedroom.

I laid back down next to Felix, got nice and tangled with him, and then the other reality hit: He would find out who I was the next day, why I'd come to Frederick. I thought he would hate me, and I was right. So there was no way I was going to say anything that night. I didn't want to burst the bubble. I was relishing the realness. I wanted one more pure, honest night together. He was half asleep, but of course I woke him back up.

Felix Calderon (*detective*): One more *honest* night? That's really what she said? Unbelievable.

But I shouldn't be surprised. That's Casey for you.

Casey Hawthorne (*producer*): Afterward, I slept so soundly. It had been an exhilarating night. Forget the soft hum of highway miles in the back seat of your parents' car . . . for a grown-ass woman, there's nothing like an orgasm and a greenlit show to help you drift off to sleep.

CHAPTER 5

"Turn the Cameras On"

Marcus Maxwell (*executive*): Casey called me and said she got the family. Needless to say, I wasn't surprised. She told me she wanted to start filming the next day. I told her to do whatever she needed. From that moment on, her show was the network's number one priority. My only question: Did she have a name for it?

Casey Hawthorne (*producer*): *Searching for Sara*. You always want people to be able to know what the show is about just from the name or the poster. *Survivor, The Bachelor, Arm Candy* . . . it's not rocket science.

Marcus Maxwell (*executive*): I had our business affairs team rush out some contracts for the family. I approved flights for a production crew. It was a hectic day, so I never really had that moment of: Are we really doing this? I obviously never thought they'd be writing books about our show a decade later. I simply had faith in Casey. She was a terrific producer, and she had a battery up her ass for this idea. That's the secret sauce right there: Empower talented people to do what they're passionate about. My job is to sign the checks and get out of the way.

Zane Kelly (*camera operator*, Searching for Sara): I was at my climbing gym when I got the call. Boss told me to pack a bag and get to the airport in four hours. Barely had time to drop my dog off at a friend's house, then walked onto the plane with my fingers still chalked. Didn't know much about the project. We were told Casey would fill us in when we landed.

Alexis Lee (*associate producer*, Searching for Sara): I hadn't worked with Casey before. Her normal crew was in the middle of *Arm Candy* production. But I knew her reputation: smart, demanding, a little condescending, but not a bitch. I was excited. Until we actually got to Frederick. All of our other shows were in Hollywood, Malibu, Orange County. This was flyover country, you know? Except instead of flying over, we actually landed.

Anthony Pena (*editor*): Casey had called me and begged me to come. She explained that this was going to be different than anything we had done. "An editor's dream," she said. Of course, when they say that, that usually means an editor's nightmare.

Casey wanted to rip and run, film all day, start cutting at night, turn around episodes every few days, get them on air in almost real time. Marcus Maxwell was giving her whatever time slots she wanted. Two or three nights a week if we could move fast enough. I had to admit, it sounded exciting. So I shipped a bunch of equipment to the hotel, flew out there, and set up an editing bay in one of the suites. I basically didn't step foot outside for a month.

Alexis Lee (*associate producer*): The most stressful part was trying to find a decent meal. Forget about finding a ripe avocado. Everything you ordered had some weird gravy on it. The place next to the hotel — Shoney's, with the buffet? Sturdy chairs in that place, for good reason.

Zane Kelly (*camera operator*): I loved Shoney's! Walk around with a Steadicam rig all day, you're not turning your nose up at a buffet.

Anthony Pena (*editor*): The local cuisine wasn't great. Casey is usually a rah-rah type when we are in production, she tries to keep up the morale, but even she was complaining about it. Before I flew in, she made me stop at the health food store near her house in LA, Moon Juice or whatever. I had to travel with fifty strawberry-rose-geranium bars, loaded down like a pack mule. Casey was living on those while we edited. I tried one, they're disgusting. I stuck to my gummy worms.

Alexis Lee (*associate producer*): We had a production meeting the next morning. Casey explained her vision for the first time. I was definitely a little apprehensive. I mean, forget the production challenges, it just felt like the stakes were really high. This girl was actually missing. Yellow ribbons tied around all the trees, everyone in town on edge. It's hard to remember now, but at the time we thought there was a predator on the loose. So yeah, I was a little freaked out.

Casey made it sound like we had come to the rescue. She had a real sense of purpose to make something meaningful. It was inspiring but also unnerving to see her so determined. I didn't feel like we—you know, just this basic reality TV crew—were qualified for the self-appointed humanitarian mission she had on her vision board.

Casey Hawthorne (*producer*): Marcus and TNN were great. They gave me everything I asked for, and we had boots on the ground the next day. It was mostly a new crew for me, but I had no problem with the people they sent—not yet, of course—and we were ready to roll right away. I briefed them, laid out my plan and expectations for them, and then we were off to the Parcells'.

Zane Kelly (*camera operator*): When we rolled up to the house, there was a bunch of cop cars and news vans out front. We just parked in their driveway. Started unpacking the van and doing our load-in. You could feel everyone staring at us.

Alexis Lee (*associate producer*): It felt like we were driving into battle. There's always some jitters on the first day of shooting, but usually, there's some levity and excitement, too. Not here. It was clear as we approached the house: This was ground zero for where a child had been kidnapped. It made you want to whisper.

And I guess no one else knew we were coming, you know, besides the parents. After we parked, one of the local cops runs over, starts yelling at us. I tried to explain what we were doing, that we had permission to be there, but he didn't believe me.

Dmitri Russo (*patrolman*): This big Sprinter van shows up, and people scurry out and start unloading gear. One of them said they were filming a TV show at the house. It didn't make any sense. I was just trying to protect Dave and Jeannette, you know, spare them from answering the door with more cameras in their face. But I guess they saw me arguing with these people in the driveway. Dave came outside.

Alexis Lee (*associate producer*): He told the cop we were good. And that was that.

Dmitri Russo (*patrolman*): Dave said they'd be coming in and out every day and not to stop them. It definitely struck me as odd. And you could tell he was almost a little embarrassed.

Zane Kelly (*camera operator*): We spent the first couple hours setting up inside, not shooting yet. There's a lot more to these shows than just turning a camera on. We had to rig a bunch of lighting setups, wire up the whole family with lav mics, install remote cameras. Even when our crew wasn't there, our cameras would have access to the house.

And honestly, the most important thing to do is establish a rapport with the people you're shooting. So I was making a point to say hello, chat a little bit, ask about something on their shelves. It obviously wasn't a very jovial mood, but you still try. Just being extra thankful for a glass of water can go a long way. I'm about to stand three feet away from these people for God knows how long. We end up seeing them at their most unguarded moments—tired, angry, crying, we're right next to them. We're there for every fart, burp, and booger, there's no hiding. So it helps if you build up a little camaraderie.

Jack Parcell (*brother*): I had never seen such cool camera equipment. The lead camera guy, Zane, was super nice. He let me carry some of the cases. Even let me try out the Steadicam rig, it was like putting on a jet pack. My mom saw me running around in it and made me take it off.

Zane Kelly (*camera operator*): Yeah, Jack was a little eleven-year-old tech geek. So I let him be my assistant or whatever. It's always fun to show off the fancy gear to kids who appreciate it. And besides . . . I knew he was in a tough situation emotionally or what have you. He asked me that first morning if we were going to help find his sister. I could tell he was desperate for good news. I told him I hoped so. We ended up getting pretty close, me and him, you know, with inside jokes, stupid games. I . . . fuck . . . this is bringing up some shit I didn't expect, I'm sorry. I found out a few years ago he was in bad shape. I didn't reach out, but I was really sorry to hear that. You can't help but wonder, you know, if it wasn't for us going out there for the show . . .

Casey Hawthorne (*producer*): Our load-in was almost done. The only problem was that it felt like half the neighborhood had wandered over to the house. Usually, when we shoot, we're in a much more controlled environment. Or if we're out in public, we've got an army of PAs to secure the area. This was a leaner operation, more vérité, if you will.

Ezra Phillips (*pop culture critic*): Vérité? Um, no, I won't. D. A. Pennebaker is vérité. Frederick Wiseman is vérité. Casey Hawthorne is not.

Brandon Grassley (*neighbor*): I was playing video games and saw what was going on from my house and walked outside. My dad, too. There was, like, a production crew going into the Parcells' house. I didn't know why. My dad said something like "These people don't know what they're doing." And then we went back inside.

Mike Snyder (*local news*): I certainly didn't approve, I can tell you that much. We hadn't gotten any updates from the family since that first night. And now they're letting these Hollywood carpetbaggers stroll right through the door? While I'm getting yelled at for stepping too far up on the sidewalk? It didn't sit right with me. We, ABC-7 Frederick, had been there from the start. It was our broadcast that put this story on the map. Dave and Jeannette were happy to use us for their little bank-statement stunt, then suddenly, they were big-timing us.

Casey Hawthorne (*producer*): While the crew did some tech setup, I sat down at the kitchen table with Dave and Jeannette to look over the contract. Pages and pages of boilerplate stuff, but they were trying to read every word of it, like they knew what any of it meant.

Dave Parcell (*father*): We had a question about who owned all this footage afterward, like forever. I was a little nervous about that. It felt like we were signing our life away.

Jeannette Parcell (*mother*): I didn't care about any of that. The point was to find Sara. I would have signed anything.

Casey Hawthorne (*producer*): I was brutally honest with them. I shuffled the papers away and said: "Look, you're probably right to assume you're getting screwed ten different ways in this contract. That's the business. If you want to get an entertainment lawyer to review this and start negotiating, you can probably get some numbers changed. Foreign merchandise rights, second-run airline residuals, all that irrelevant stuff will get bumped up ten percent, sure. But it's gonna take weeks to sort out. The whole point of this show is getting the word out as fast as possible. For Sara's sake, right? The contract in front of you today is fine. And it means we can start shooting right now. And of course your check for Episode One is already cut. Do you really want to bog this thing down?"

Dave Parcell (*father*): She had some good points. And she had the check ready to go. We signed the contract. And then Casey told her crew, "Turn the cameras on." Just like that, we were part of the Hollywood machine.

Jeannette Parcell (*mother*): It was awkward at the beginning. They were just hovering around us, filming. I didn't know how to act or where to look. And it's not like we were doing anything. I mean, we were mostly waiting around—waiting for the phone to ring, for an update from the police, from some of the local volunteers who were out searching in the woods. I didn't understand how Casey would ever make a show out of it. We just sat there for a while, not talking, really. And then Hurricane Beverly swooped in. I guess that was a little bit of drama, at least.

Beverly Geary (*grandmother*): I was about two steps in the door when one of these new people told me what was going on. I found my daughter and asked if it was really true. They had just signed the contract, apparently. Now someone was shoving a clipboard in my face and asking me to sign a waiver. They were literally filming the conversation we were having!

Casey Hawthorne (*producer*): Jeannette asked me to stop filming when her mom came in yelling. I didn't want to, obviously. It was good content. But that wasn't a battle worth having on the first day.

Zane Kelly (*camera operator*): Casey gestured for me to cut the camera. But there are different levels of going dark. Our usual trick was to point the cameras at the floor and act like we aren't recording anymore. People tend to let their guard down when they see that.

Casey Hawthorne (*producer*): We knew we'd still have audio. Sometimes playing out a meaningful conversation over a black screen can be far more dramatic.

Alexis Lee (*associate producer*): I'm sure Casey would call it a gray area. It's not. It's just wrong.

Beverly Geary (*grandmother*): I told Jeannette the truth. It was shameful what they were doing. Our poor Sara is missing, and they're getting paid and making TV programs? I wasn't going to stand for it. There was nothing I could do, but I wouldn't stand for it.

Dave Parcell (*father*): I think that was the diciest moment, as far as Jeannette being on board. Between the contract stress, all these people stomping through our house, and now her mother screaming at her . . . she wanted to pull the plug.

I took her aside. I reminded her that we had prepared for this. It was going to be ugly and hard and confusing, but if it helped find Sara, it was worth it. I reminded her how strong Sara was. How we had to be strong for her and endure all the criticism, no matter who it came from. I talked Jeannette off the ledge.

Jeannette Parcell (*mother*): Of course I remember that conversation. Think about what that man did right there. Think about the state I'm in—my daughter is *gone*. God knows what she's enduring, if she's even alive. It made me physically ill to think about for one second. And now all this other stuff is blowing up in our face, my mother is yelling at me, and what does Dave do? He gives me a pep talk. A locker room speech. *Knowing what he knew at the time.* He can rot in hell for that.

Beverly Geary (*grandmother*): She chose Dave over me. You always know your children will grow up and find a partner, and that's who will come first. It's natural, but still an awful shock when it happens. I remember the first time I sided with Herb against my mother, may she rest in peace. I told her we were going to live together before we were married. She cried and cried and didn't talk to me for a month. So I wasn't surprised that Jeannette went along with Dave.

What could I say afterward? "I told you so"? Trust me, I said it.

Casey Hawthorne (*producer*): Dave talked to Jeannette. He calmed her down, and we were back on track. For about ten minutes.

Dmitri Russo (*patrolman*): I had called Detective Calderon when the TV crew was let into the house. He didn't sound too pleased about it.

Casey Hawthorne (*producer*): We'd just started getting our rhythm again when suddenly Felix barges in, basically kicks down the door. I was upstairs, but even from there, I can hear he's ready to explode. And this is before he even knows I'm there! I'm sorry to laugh. I know there's nothing funny about what happened, broadly speaking. But seeing Felix flustered always got me.

Felix Calderon (*detective*): One of my guys called me at the station. Gave me a heads-up. I rushed over. I guess by that point it was clear what was going on, there was no attempt to hide it: The Parcells had agreed to do a reality show. Over my dead body, I thought.

I walked in and tried to shut the whole thing down. I saw Dave and Jeannette first. And some camera guy following them around. My message to them was simple: "Have you two lost your minds? None of this is going to help find Sara. If anything, if this actually gets broadcast, it might provoke whoever took her." They needed to trust me and my department to do our jobs. Doing this show would only end up hurting Sara.

I didn't know how, exactly, in that moment. But I was right in the end.

Jeannette Parcell (*mother*): I lit into Detective Calderon. Just absolutely unloaded. I obviously wasn't the biggest defender of the show, but getting criticized by him, specifically, really triggered me. How dare he tell us how to behave when all we wanted was to find our daughter? We didn't care who did it or how it was done. And what had he accomplished, anyway? Three days had gone by, and they had nothing! Nothing! The idiot bus driver had run circles around him. For all we knew, he had left Sara in a ditch, and Mr. Brilliant Detective over here hadn't figured it out. He was the same guy who told us Sara would be home after curfew the first night.

On some level, looking back, it just felt good to scream at someone. I had all this anger but no one to blame. And I probably would have kept going, but then Casey came into the room.

Felix Calderon (*detective*): What did I think when I saw Casey? Well, for about half a second, I was excited. And I thought, Well, this is a weird and awkward place to bump into *you*, the traveling medical salesperson I slept with as she passed through town. And then it hit me. I put it all together and thought, You have got to be fucking kidding me. I felt like the biggest asshole in the world.

What else was there to think?

Casey Hawthorne (*producer*): I said hi. Asked if we could speak outside for a second. He just stared back at me with such contempt. And shame, too. I didn't like seeing that. I never wanted to hurt or embarrass him. After what seemed like forever, all he could say was "How could you do this?"

Dave Parcell (*father*): It was a weird question. The way he said that to Casey . . . that's when I started to get suspicious.

Casey Hawthorne (*producer*): How could I do this? I didn't know how he wanted me to answer. Professionally or personally. I thought it was better for all of us to keep it professional.

I explained what we were trying to do with the show. How it dovetailed with his goals. That my production team intended to stay out of his way.

He didn't answer me. Maybe he had wanted the other answer, about how could I do this to *him*. He stared at me and didn't say a word in response. I saw something break inside him. And I saw him try to hide it and start to move on from me. Then he turned back to Jeannette and Dave.

Felix Calderon (*detective*): I asked them with total sincerity if they really wanted to do this. They nodded. There was nothing else I could do. I told them I was totally against it but I was still going to try and find their daughter. Then I walked out.

Casey Hawthorne (*producer*): I caught up with him outside. I wanted to apologize. He didn't deserve to be blindsided like that, and it had hurt him worse than I expected. And selfishly, I wanted to salvage it, to keep this good thing going. The type of thing that we had . . . that was rare for me. But Felix didn't want to hear it.

Felix Calderon (*detective*): What could she possibly say? Once you're a liar on that scale, I can never trust you again. All that staring into each other's eyes, baring our souls bullshit? She was playing me the whole time.

Casey Hawthorne (*producer*): I was never playing him. Once all the cards were out on the table, I wanted him to know that I cared about finding Sara. That we were on the same team and there was a world where we might even be able to help each other. That we owed that much to the Parcells.

And I didn't want this to end things for us. I tried to bring back that feeling from the night before. I smiled at him and said, "Hey, it's not all bad news, your wish came true, it turns out I'm not just passing through town . . . you can fall for me now."

He stared back at me, seething.

Felix Calderon (*detective*): I told her to stay the fuck away from me.

Casey Hawthorne (*producer*): I mean, I didn't *love* hearing that. But I also didn't believe him. And I couldn't afford to dwell on it. My work always came before my flings. I compartmentalized, tamped down my feelings. I had a show to produce.

Zane Kelly (*camera operator*): Casey came back inside. It was kinda awkward. She didn't address anything then. She just told me to get my ass upstairs, she wanted B-roll of Sara's room.

Alexis Lee (*associate producer*): Sara's bedroom was exactly as she had left it. I think the cops had poked around a bit, but other than that, just a normal sixteen-year-old's room. Casey wanted some footage to show the viewers who Sara was.

Zane Kelly (*camera operator*): We went into the room. Casey stood behind me and was telling me what to shoot. Actually, Casey *and* Jack. He followed us in there. I was getting her track trophies. Her music stand. Photos of her and her friends. A collection of spray-painted trucker hats. Jack was guiding us through what Sara cared about. It was clear Casey wanted more.

Jack Parcell (*brother*): She asked me if Sara had any stuffed animals. I didn't really know. I mean, I remember she used to, every kid did at some point, right? But it's not like Sara kept them out anymore. I told Casey there might be some in the closet. I knew there was a box of junk in there.

Casey went in and found an old teddy bear. She asked me if Sara had loved that one. I said sure. I didn't know what she was getting at.

Alexis Lee (*associate producer*): Casey took the teddy bear and brought it over to Sara's bed. She placed it on top, resting on the pillows. She thought for a second, then pushed the bear over. Instead of sitting perfectly atop the bed, now it looked like it had fallen. She stepped back and told Zane to shoot it.

Zane Kelly (*camera operator*): I did a slow pan on the overturned teddy bear. Casey asked me to get shots from a few different angles. I spent a couple minutes on it. That's why they pay me the big bucks.

Jack Parcell (*brother*): I said something at the time. I tried to, at least. I told them Sara would hate this. She would think it was so cheesy, she didn't keep stuffed animals on her bed. My sister was sixteen. But Casey just brushed me off. She said, "Don't worry, we won't show it on TV."

Alexis Lee (*associate producer*): The whole thing gave me goose bumps. And not in the way that Casey wanted. This was her crossing the line, I realize now. Everything that came after . . . I should have known from the moment she brought out that teddy bear.

Casey wasn't there to tell the truth. She was there to tell a story.

CHAPTER 6

"Frederick's Most Wanted"

Brandon Grassley (*neighbor*): Obviously, the first episode of *Searching for Sara* changed my life instantly. It was a total surprise. None of us knew what Casey was going to do.

Casey Hawthorne (*producer*): I wanted to get our premiere out as soon as possible. I told the crew forty-eight hours . . . I wanted a killer episode ready for air forty-eight hours after we started filming. We had a lot of work to do.

Alexis Lee (*associate producer*): We hit the town hard. My job was to line up interviews with basically anyone close to Sara. Some people were apprehensive, but most were excited about potentially being on TV. And everyone was still buying into the idea that the show was going to help find Sara.

Casey Hawthorne (*producer*): I wanted viewers to feel like they knew Sara. But more importantly, I wanted them to fall in love with Jeannette and Dave. With Sara gone, they were our protagonists. That had worked out great when they weren't trying. But once the show became a reality, I started to sense them getting in their own heads. I needed them to loosen up a bit, to let us in.

I had them sit down for standard talking-head interview sessions.

Asked them about Sara, their family, their marriage. It didn't work at all. They were so stiff. And in their defense, it was awkward to be engaging in so much artifice with their daughter missing. That wasn't the show I set out to make, and their discomfort helped me remember that.

Dave Parcell (*father*): I can laugh at it now, but for my first sit-down interview, I put on a nice shirt and combed my hair. I don't know what I was thinking. After about ten minutes, Casey scrapped the whole thing.

Casey Hawthorne (*producer*): I called an audible and decided that all of our Dave and Jeannette engagement would be organic. I would still corner them for questions but only while they were going about their day—driving to work, making dinner, that type of thing. It worked so much better.

Jeannette Parcell (*mother*): All of it was weird for me—you know, talking with the camera hovering around you. I really didn't have much to say. Casey wanted anecdotes that involved Sara. I told the story of her first loose tooth: This thing was hanging by a thread for days, and she was so nervous about it. Dave finally convinced her of a fun way to yank it out—they made this whole obstacle course throughout the house, Sara ducking and diving and walking on top of the furniture, and at the end of the line, there was a long piece of dental floss tied to a doorknob. Sara had to loop the floss around her loose tooth and slam the door to finish the obstacle course. Her tooth went flying, and she loved it! No fear, no pain, she was laughing and panting and giddy from racing through the house.

That was a nice memory. It's hard to remember now, but we had a lot of those times.

So it was stuff like that. Casey kept emphasizing to us: The more sympathetic we came across, the better. The more exciting, the better.

"Exciting," can you believe that? She really said it. I gave her a look,

I didn't even mean to, but it must have been one hell of a look. She got flustered and apologized.

Zane Kelly (*camera operator*): We were running around like crazy those couple of days, zigzagging all over town, filming anyone Sara had known. Casey would do all the interviews, standing right behind me as I filmed. She always ended with the same question.

Casey Hawthorne (*producer*): I don't remember. I'm not sure he's right about that.

Zane Kelly (*camera operator*): "What would you say to Sara if she could hear you right now?"

Casey Hawthorne (*producer*): Oh. Right. It's so morbid to think about now. Sadly, no one ever got that chance.

Alexis Lee (*associate producer*): As we drove around town, something occurred to me in the van that morning. I asked Casey: "What happens if Sara turns up today? Like what if this is all some boring misunderstanding . . . what happens to the show?"

Casey was speechless for once. Like it had never occurred to her that this was possible.

It made me wonder, just on a human level, what she was rooting for.

Anthony Pena (*editor*): At the end of our first day of shooting, Casey and I were back in the editing suite. I had caught up with the rest of the crew earlier, and they were all gossiping about when the detective had shown up at the Parcells' house. You know, about the vibe between him and Casey.

So I asked Casey about it. We were tight like that. Enough late nights and weekends will do that. She kinda smiled and shrugged and gave me a "yeah, shit happens" expression. We all knew that people can get freaky on these out-of-town productions. So I just shook my head and laughed. But then I asked if this was something we'd be navigating for the rest of the shoot. She said, "I don't know, maybe."

I knew Casey pretty well. I had seen all her other relationships, if you could even call them that. "I don't know, maybe" meant that she was practically in love.

Marcus Maxwell (*executive*): Casey sent me some raw footage from the first day. To be honest, it didn't seem very promising. In fact, it was downright bleak. The Parcells doing chores. People in town crying. What the fuck happened to the groundbreaking docuseries I was pitched? So I challenged Casey: "Is this going to be anything other than sad people being sad?"

I know this will make me sound like a dinosaur, but in a previous century, we used to talk about the watercooler test, you know, like what are people going to talk about when they congregate at the watercooler in the office the next day. Well, by the time we made *Searching for Sara,* we were already deep into the "holy shit"–text era. What was going to make our viewers text "holy shit" to their friends? I prodded Casey on that, because it was hard to imagine getting that moment from the footage she'd sent. She told me not to worry, she'd find something.

And she did.

Casey Hawthorne (*producer*): We did a lot of interviews. Some of the early ones were duds . . .

Veronica Yang (*principal*): I told Casey and her team what a wonderful student Sara was and how talented she was on the violin. I gave her a tour of the school and facilitated some introductions to Sara's peers.

I really deliberated over that decision. Clearly, we had no policy in place to guide us on students participating in a reality series about the disappearance of their peer. Ultimately, I decided I didn't want to close off a potential avenue for the kids to process the trauma. I'm a modern educator, I take the world as it is.

Olaf Leclerq (*ice cream shop owner*): Sara had worked at Big Olaf's for three years at that point. She was one of my best girls. Favorite flavor: black raspberry! Very smart and totally trustworthy. I was planning on making her the weekend key holder that summer. It was devastating when she disappeared—I immediately gave a thousand dollars to the local reward fund that got set up.

Casey Hawthorne (*producer*): Some of the interviews didn't have much use at the time . . .

Brandon Grassley (*neighbor*): We did the interview in my house, can you believe that? My dad thought it was stupid, but I wanted to. Casey and her crew set up in my bedroom. I remember trying to clean it up a little, but it looked ridiculous, you know, my posters, my gaming console, I had some old-school turntables I was messing around on, trying to learn how to DJ.

I walked them through the morning Sara had gone missing, starting at our bus stop. I basically just repeated what I had already told the police, it wasn't that interesting. Casey was pressing me for anything else going on with Sara at school. But I really didn't know anything. I knew everyone else had been at a party that weekend. I told Casey to ask Sara's friends about it.

Casey Hawthorne (*producer*): And some interviews I really had to work for, but they proved totally worth it . . .

Nellie Spencer (*friend*): Yeah, I wanted to be on TV, but I wasn't dumb. I had seen enough reality shows to know that once they filmed you, they could portray you however they wanted. Like they can make it seem like you're stupid or an asshole even when you're not. It's called selective editing, look it up. So when Casey asked originally, I said no.

Olivia Weston (*friend*): I was happy to do the interview. I knew that's what Sara would have wanted. Casey suggested that Nellie and I do it together, to give it more of a casual vibe. But Nellie wasn't down at first. I guess she thought all her stuff with Coach Walker was gonna come out. Like she was going to blurt it out accidentally, I don't know.

Nellie Spencer (*friend*): The same day I said no to the interview, Casey followed me on Instagram. She started messaging me, and she saw that I followed this one clothing brand in Los Angeles. She told me she was friends with the owner or something. The next thing I knew, Casey was back in our school the next day. Not sure why she was even allowed there, but she was.

She called me over and handed me her phone. The owner of the clothing company was on FaceTime. We chatted for a minute, it was kind of awkward but cool. She said she was always needing to send out new samples for feedback. She asked for my address.

Me and Olivia sat with Casey for the interview that afternoon.

Olivia Weston (*friend*): We started off just talking about Sara and how fun she was. The crazy birthday cards she'd slip in our lockers that were really just glitter bombs. The summer she made us get super into fedoras. The way she cured hiccups by drinking water, doing a hand-stand, and practically choking to death. We talked about what our plans were, you know, for college, and after. Sara wanted to live in New York, of course.

Casey asked what a typical night looked like for us when we all hung out together. She asked about the field party. That kind of caught us off guard, I don't know how she knew about it. We mumbled some vague answer. Then Casey asked about any secrets we all shared.

You know, I actually went back to watch this scene before we talked today, I found the clip online. You can see Nellie and me look at each other, like "Should we really do this?" I was nervous. But to this day, even with all the chaos it caused, I think it was the right thing to reveal that secret.

Nellie Spencer (*friend*): I knew Olivia would never do it, so I finally just blurted it out: "Sara has a stalker." I remember Casey's face, she was so fucking stoked.

Olivia Weston (*friend*): Nellie made me say the rest, and I told Casey everything. Showed her the texts, too, just to prove it was real.

They were from Sara, almost every weekend from the previous few months. She always worked at Big Olaf's on Saturday afternoons. And she would text us from work, stuff like: "The creeper is here again . . . OMG, caught him checking out my ass . . . if you don't hear from me later, I might be dead in the deep freezer lol."

I mean, we were all just laughing about it. It was normal joking around, or half joking around. Every sixteen-year-old girl deals with skeezy men eyeballing us, it's a sad fact of life. We have to laugh about it or we'll go crazy. It really didn't seem like a big deal until Sara went missing.

Felix Calderon (*detective*): To be honest, I was getting pretty frustrated. We didn't have any obvious suspects besides Travis. First instinct in these cases is always a boyfriend or family member. But that didn't make any sense here, we ruled it out pretty quickly. Next on the list are people the victim works with, so I started digging deeper on Sara's boss at the ice cream shop and another guy who worked there. Moved on to a few teachers at her school. Then the usual pro forma check-ins with sex offenders in the area. There was a recent parolee who had abducted a teenage girl thirty years earlier. I paid him a visit, but he was in a wheelchair attached to an oxygen tank.

None of this was paying off. We had a tip line set up, but nothing worthwhile was coming in. The only intel I was picking up was about Casey going around town talking to everyone. Some people I would get to, they'd be frustrated to have to repeat what they'd just told

Casey. One of them, her English teacher, was pretty aggravated. He suggested I ask Casey for her footage so he wouldn't have to waste his time answering the same questions again. His whole attitude definitely put him on my radar.

So, yeah, that was the state of the investigation before Casey's premiere aired.

Anthony Pena (*editor*): We pulled an all-nighter getting the episode ready, fueled by candy and Moon Juice bars. Locked it in Thursday morning for a prime-time premiere on Thursday. Biggest night of the week in TV. An old-timer explained it to me once: Everyone used to do their shopping on the weekends, so companies paid the most to advertise on Thursdays. Plant those jingles in your head before you hit the stores on Saturday. Not sure that makes sense anymore, but it was cool that we got that time slot. I knew the first episode was gonna land like a nuclear fucking bomb.

Alexis Lee (*associate producer*): I didn't get to see the cut. I wasn't inner-circle like that. But if I had, I wouldn't have been comfortable airing it. It was a straight-up character assassination.

Marcus Maxwell (*executive*): I had wanted a "holy shit" moment. Ask and ye shall receive.

Zane Kelly (*camera operator*): I don't ever watch the shows I work on. But this one, yeah, I was curious. Even though it was my night off, I flipped it on in the hotel room.

Casey Hawthorne (*producer*): I wasn't nervous for the premiere. From the minute I saw Jack's viral video of his parents in their foyer, I knew this thing would be a hit.

Dave Parcell (*father*): We watched in our living room when it came on, just like everyone else did.

Jack Parcell (*brother*): I was excited. I was going to be on TV.

Jeannette Parcell (*mother*): I had an absolute pit in my stomach. I guess part of me thought that the show would air and then our phone would ring and someone would've found Sara. That was the idea, anyway.

Beverly Geary (*grandmother*): I refused to watch, I was so disgusted with their decision. But Herb put it on in the den, and I sat there with him. I was doing my crossword, but I saw bits and pieces on accident.

Nellie Spencer (*friend*): I don't want to say "party," but a bunch of us got together to watch in my basement. You know, popcorn, pajamas, that type of thing.

Miriam Rosen (*teacher*): It was all anyone could talk about, of course we watched. I'm sure you could have walked stark naked down Main Street at that hour and no one would have seen you.

Tommy O'Brien (*employee, Geary Home & Garden*): It really got to me, seeing Dave and his family hurting like that. The show did a good job of taking you behind the scenes. Like I had always seen Dave as this tough, macho guy with all the answers. But sitting there with his son, peering out the windows with his wife . . . suddenly, you saw how helpless he was.

And then that moment with the sad teddy bear on Sara's bed . . . Jesus. Yeah, I can admit it got a little dusty where I was watching.

Becca Santangelo (*founder of the SareBears Facebook group*): I know exactly where I was when I first met Sara Parcell. LOL, I shouldn't say "met"—when I first *heard* about Sara Parcell.

Sophomore dorm, my suitemates and I were just hanging out, normal night, watching reality shows. And *Searching for Sara* came on. I hadn't really heard about the case till then. But they showed the backstory, you know, the dad with his bank statement, then hugging his wife inside. And the little brother filming it, oh my God, it broke my heart. I just became obsessed with finding Sara. *Obsessed.*

I started the SareBears group as soon as the episode ended. We took the name from what her dad called her. By the next morning, we had six thousand members. And it just grew from there.

Back then, before all the drama, it was really simple. Being a Sare-Bear meant one thing: Mama bears will do anything to protect their young . . . that was our attitude toward finding Sara.

Ezra Phillips (*pop culture critic*): It's hard to pinpoint the exact moment *Searching for Sara* entered the zeitgeist. Was it the minute it premiered? Halfway through, when people started to truly understand what they were watching? At the end, when they revealed the new suspect?

I would argue the exact moment was actually five minutes after the premiere ended.

Everyone watching had a moment to think about what we had just seen. And I'm sure it occurred to all of us almost simultaneously: My God, that dude is so fucked.

Marcus Maxwell (*executive*): Casey delivered. She had cozied up to Sara's friends and gotten them to spill it: Sara had a stalker. Someone she was worried about, who was freaking her out at work, who she told her friends about. Someone from town. Someone who lived on her block.

Olivia Weston (*friend*): Frank Grassley. That's who was harassing Sara.

We told Casey, and that's how she ended the first episode. Me and Nellie saying the name Frank Grassley.

Marcus Maxwell (*executive*): Every story needs a villain. Now we had one. The quiet banker from across the street. It was perfect.

Nellie Spencer (*friend*): It was heavy. When we talked with Casey the day before, I didn't realize what was going to happen.

Dave Parcell (*father*): I went nuts. I almost ran outside to go break down his door. Jeannette stopped me; she thought I might kill him. We called the detective.

Felix Calderon (*detective*): I was seeing this in real time along with everyone else. I literally had no idea who Frank Grassley was. But the way Sara's friends talked about him was definitely alarming. I quickly determined I needed to find him. It felt ridiculous—taking marching orders from Casey's show. Those girls should have given the information to me, not Casey. I was still waiting on the phone company to send me all of Sara's info. There were procedures I had to follow, it was going to be days—weeks, even—before I saw any of those text messages.

And Casey . . . Casey wasn't a scared teenager, she should have told me the instant she found out. I did the math—she kept it to herself for twenty-nine hours, saving it for her big premiere. Imagine if Frank Grassley had killed Sara sometime in those twenty-nine hours? We would have charged Casey as an accessory.

Travis Haynes (*bus driver*): Best thing that ever happened to me, I'll tell you that much. I fucking loved it. Frank Grassley, Frederick's most wanted. It was an honor to be replaced.

Olaf Leclerq (*ice cream shop owner*): I was devastated. To think that this harassment took place in my store . . . shame on that man.

Becca Santangelo (*SareBears*): Frank Grassley. That's all we messaged about that night. The SareBear den was activated.

Beverly Geary (*grandmother*): I wasn't surprised, to be honest. He was a vile man.

Felix Calderon (*detective*): The Parcells kept calling me. They wanted Frank Grassley arrested immediately, questioned, his property searched. It was complicated. I had never requested a warrant based on info from a reality show. But they were right to feel a sense of urgency. If Sara's friends had nailed it, God knows what he was doing now that he had been accused on national TV. Even if all the official warrant business would take a few hours, I drove over to his house right away.

Brandon Grassley (*neighbor*): Yeah, we were watching. Everyone was. It caught me totally by surprise. I looked over at my dad. He was just as surprised as I was. He said something like "I have no idea what those girls are talking about . . . I don't even like ice cream."

It was surreal. Did I think my dad had kidnapped Sara Parcell? Well, no. But that's what they were saying on TV. And there was already a lot of weird stuff going on with our family. I mean, my mom had moved out two years earlier. She was living in Florida with my sister. My dad was going out at night, and I didn't really know where. Things were . . . complicated.

But what they were accusing him of . . . it was ridiculous! And so easy to disprove. So after a minute or two, we kind of laughed about it. But we were being naive. Idiotic, really. We didn't understand the power of the Internet. We didn't realize what was happening outside our house. Forces were gathering. My dad was now the main suspect in what had just become the most well-known case in the country. He had been accused, tried, and convicted during a commercial break. We couldn't imagine what that would make people do.

We found out, though. Within minutes, our life became a living hell.

CHAPTER 7

"These Are Sick People"

Christine Bell (*district attorney, Frederick County*): The case was an absolute mess. The investigation was taking place on TV, and now everyone expected to watch the indictment, the trial, and the conviction on TV, too. No way, honey, that is not how I operate. Anyone could have asked around and found out real quick that I'm not to be trifled with. Third in my class at William & Mary . . . second woman ever to edit the *Law Review* at UVA . . . took down a good ol' boy incumbent here in Frederick after ten years of private practice. I don't like having a mess in my house, in my car, or in my district. So after the first episode of the show aired, it became abundantly clear that I would have to exert some control over things.

Felix Calderon (*detective*): I was summoned the next morning to meet with our local DA. She kept the door to her office open, yelled at me for twenty minutes so her staff could hear, then sent me on my way. I believe she had invited some press to hang around and listen as well. The next morning she had the headline she wanted in the local paper—"DA Bell Cracks Whip to Crack the Case" or something like that.

Christine Bell (*district attorney*): This is a law-and-order community. When a crime happens, citizens here expect us to find the culprit and prosecute them to the fullest extent of the law. That's what I always promised, and that's what they were entitled to.

The whole thing with Frank Grassley being announced as a suspect on a TV show upset the natural order of things. I told Detective Calderon that he better find this girl and find the person responsible faster than green grass through a goose.

Felix Calderon (*detective*): My entire focus at that point was determining whether Frank Grassley had abducted Sara Parcell. I was inclined to believe her friends, who claimed that Grassley had been harassing Sara. We brought him in for questioning the morning after Casey's show aired, and I took a run at him.

He didn't bother with a lawyer or anything, which didn't make sense to me. He calmly denied being involved and denied any interactions with Sara at the ice cream shop where she worked or in the neighborhood they shared. And he had an airtight alibi for the hours when Sara disappeared. He was at the bank all day, confirmed by colleagues, employee security devices, and surveillance footage. Didn't even leave for lunch.

I was disappointed but ultimately confident: It was impossible for Frank Grassley to have abducted her.

Dave Parcell (*father*): Detective Calderon calls us and tells us that he's sure it isn't Frank. Alibi this, surveillance footage that, there was no chance he took Sara. Look, I obviously knew all along that Frank didn't do it, but he was still an asshole. I would have appreciated if he had to sit in the slammer a little longer.

Felix Calderon (*detective*): We let Frank Grassley go home. He was cleared, as far as we were concerned. But the rest of the world still thought he did it.

Brandon Grassley (*neighbor*): My dad spent the whole day at the police station. I didn't go to school . . . how could I? I knew everyone there had watched the show. So I was by myself at our house all day. The phone started ringing in the morning. A few calls here and there. I don't know how they got our number. As the day went on, it wouldn't stop. Death threats. I'd pick up, and crazy people would start screaming about how they were gonna cut my balls off and shove 'em down my throat, and on and on. I was sixteen years old, I didn't know what to do . . . call the phone company and have them change our number? Eventually, I unplugged it, I couldn't take it anymore.

My dad finally came home. He assured me that everything had been cleared up with the police. They knew he didn't do it. He was exhausted but relieved. Again, we were naive, we thought the worst was over. So we sat down and tried to have a normal dinner. And that was the first time we were SWATed.

Dmitri Russo (*patrolman*): SWATing was something that had been around for a while but we hadn't ever dealt with here in Frederick. It's when someone calls in a fake hostage scenario or bomb threat or that type of thing and gives a specific address. But it's just a prank. Or harassment, I should say. The caller wants a SWAT team to go break down the door of someone's house. Hilarious, right?

After Frank Grassley had been released, our department got a call, a male voice was on the line saying he was hiding from his father, who was threatening to kill both of them, and that his father was heavily armed. He gave his address as the Grassley residence, said his name was Brandon. We had no choice but to take it seriously.

Brandon Grassley (*neighbor*): We were eating pizza in front of the TV when we heard the vehicles race up onto our lawn. Lots of lights, no warning, then our door was smashed in. A bunch of storm troopers rush in, guns pointed at us, flashlights in our eyes, all of them are screaming, we can't understand a word.

Our dog, Roscoe, goes nuts trying to jump all over them. They start shooting at the poor guy, these assholes. Rubber bullets, it turns out, but still. My dad and I are thrown on the ground. I've got a knee in my back. Roscoe's whimpering. The rest of them are racing through the house, crashing into everything, looking everywhere. "Living room, clear! Kitchen, clear! Garage, clear!" Yeah, no shit, it's just the two of us eating dinner.

They finally sit us up after realizing nothing's going on. They explain there was some kind of prank call, apparently. A half-assed apology, and ten minutes later, they're gone. The same damn episode of *Survivor* is still on the TV. Our dinner's on the floor, but the same episode of *Survivor* is still playing.

My dad and I just look at each other. Our new reality was fully sinking in. We have to move, we realize. We have to live like fugitives, even though we did nothing wrong. I saw how scared he was. Not of the cops but of all the crazy people who had seen the show. Who now thought he was a serial killer or something. And seeing that look on his face . . . it made me fucking terrified.

Jeannette Parcell (*mother*): We heard all the commotion—the trucks, the sirens—and went out on the street to look. Everyone else on the block, too. Our poor neighbors . . . our quiet little street had turned into a war zone.

Dave Parcell (*father*): I guess it was some prank or something. Look, we can all agree it's messed up to jerk around the police like that. They have more important things to do. But as far as getting his life inconvenienced a little bit? Frank had done much worse to other families. Foreclosures, evictions, you name it. I didn't make the SWAT call, but no, I didn't shed a tear when that happened.

Beverly Geary (*grandmother*): Frank Grassley deserved everything that came his way. As far as I'm concerned, you can draw a straight line from him coming after my son-in-law's business to what happened to Sara. He set all these wheels in motion by being an asshole, and you can't tell me any different.

Becca Santangelo (*SareBears*): Yes, we spent time digging into Frank Grassley. People in our group found his address and phone number. Someone might have even posted it on our page, and I took it right down. But a true SareBear would never SWAT anyone. We were fans. A support network. We weren't trying to attack anyone.

I know those other groups existed, though. Much crazier. They would literally try to show up and get involved in the case. When I heard about what happened to the Grassleys, I wasn't surprised that someone would do something like that.

Molly Lowe (*professor of sociology*): Online vigilante mobs are a problem with no easy solution. They are essentially a perfectly evolved version of what we can call the ur-mob. This original prototype mob provided anonymity, camaraderie, and strength in order to accomplish goals that would be impossible or too shameful to attempt on one's own. Of course, for a mob to form in the traditional sense, it requires a critical mass of people in one location, efficient communication, homogeneity of thought, and an absence of sufficient deterrence.

All of these barriers to entry are lower online. Anonymity is the de facto setting, physical location is irrelevant, cognitive dissonance to absolve one's responsibility is much easier to achieve, and, as we've learned over and over again, social media companies refuse to police the mobs that form on their platforms.

The result is a perfect primordial stew for arm's-length vigilantism. And the costs can be harrowing. Remember the Boston Marathon bombing? A group on Reddit was convinced that their online sleuthing had identified the culprit. The online mob turned into a real mob and marched to that person's house. He was totally innocent, it turned out. The mob was wrong. It was a miracle that no one was killed.

Sara Parcell's disappearance triggered this type of reaction, unsurprisingly. The mob formed and went after Frank Grassley. But more interesting to me, there's another online archetype drawn to events like this, and their behavior is even less comprehensible. This group isn't trying to impact the events . . . no, these conspiracy-addled contrarians deny that the events even happened.

Bruce Allen Foley (*chief reality officer, Unfounded*): Where to even begin? I mean, it's kind of hard to talk about a crime that never actually transpired.

Dave Parcell (*father*): Tell me you are not interviewing Bruce Allen Foley for this book . . .

Casey Hawthorne (*producer*): Please tell me that man is not walking around freely. Is he really out of prison already? Where is he? I'm being serious, tell me, I have a right to know.

Bruce Allen Foley (*Unfounded*): Let's start with the basics: Sara Parcell was never kidnapped. That much we can all agree on, I hope! Now, did she ever even exist? I would say the jury is still out on that, in some respects.

Was the dead body of a sixteen-year-old girl found? Sure. Probably. It's not difficult to produce the body of a teenage girl and say, "Hey, look over here, this is so-and-so, you have to believe us." But was that body—and please note that my fingers are making air quotes here—"Sara Parcell"? Well, no, I don't believe so.

Felix Calderon (*detective*): Of all the lowlifes and examples of abhorrent behavior associated with this case, I rank him the lowest. Below the liars, scam artists, opportunists, confessed murderers, silent accomplices . . . fathoms below that, that's where you'll find Bruce Allen Foley.

Bruce Allen Foley (*Unfounded*): Our group, Unfounded, which I created and continue to serve as chief reality officer, is devoted to exposing the lie that there is an epidemic of child kidnappings in this country. We have demonstrated that over ninety-nine percent of so-called child abductions are either wholly fictional or grossly exaggerated. The claims are *unfounded*, and there are no children to be *found* . . . get it?

The lie is in service to an authoritarian power grab. We believe and can prove that this fabricated epidemic of missing children is perpetuated in tandem by the media and tyrannical elements in our government determined to increase surveillance on everyday citizens and limit our freedoms. The more fake crimes, the more they can invade our privacy.

And I forgot Hollywood. That's a big part, too. They take the lies and turn them into entertainment, all part of the plan to brainwash people into believing kids are getting snatched off the street left and right.

As soon as the Sara Parcell case started getting media attention, our members identified it as a classic "Hiroshima event"—a fake event designed purely to instill fear. This is the label we give to whichever major kidnapping the government springs on us every twenty years or so to remind the sheeple how dangerous the world is. The Sara Parcell story fit all the criteria. We mobilized right away, and I was on the road with several of my devoted brothers and sisters to go shine a light on the lies in Frederick, Maryland.

And before you even ask, I know what you're about to say, and I'll beat you to it. The answer is simple: well-paid, well-trained crisis actors.

Molly Lowe (*professor of sociology*): These are sick people, clinically speaking. They reject the objective facts of real tragedies and then traumatize the victims even further with denials and accusations. But they didn't start out this way, they went on a journey to eventually align with groups like Unfounded. It's a radicalization process that is relatively easy to chart and understand.

The starting place is always a sense of dissatisfaction. Maybe it's financial, sexual, or social, but they're frustrated with their lives. Like all of us, they crave meaning and a sense of belonging. When this is offered in the form of conspiracy theories, they are vulnerable targets easily magnetized to new beliefs that absolve them of responsibility for their failures and blame larger power structures instead. Unhappiness plus shame is unbearable. But unhappiness plus blame is galvanizing.

And then you have the truly insidious part: The deeper these people go, the crazier the theories get, the harder it becomes to shake them back to reality. Because once they've invested so much time and emotional energy, to renounce these beliefs would assassinate their identity. In plain English, it would make them look like fools. So once they're in, it's very hard to bring them back.

Bruce Allen Foley (*Unfounded*): One of our operatives is a real computer whiz. While some of us were driving to Frederick, he was back home working out how to hack into everyone's phones, computers, social media, all that. You wouldn't believe how dumb people are with their passwords.

So we knew they were all pretending. The mother, the father, probably even the brother, although sometimes I try to give these very young collaborators the benefit of the doubt. And now they had set up a classic patsy, Frank Grassley, the neighbor down the street who was going to take the fall for the whole charade. We assumed he was a crisis actor as well.

All of us know the script by now: frantic investigation, hero cops, big show trial, conviction, then suddenly, a whole new round of laws and restrictions get passed in the name of stopping these fake abductions.

And who do these laws target? Well, you can't throw a dart at a newspaper without reading the lie that middle-aged white men are the most likely to commit these "crimes"—please note the air quotes again. So that's the demographic they come after, no surprise. Totally ridiculous. A white guy can't walk down the street without drawing suspicion. It's dystopian!

Anyway, sorry for the rant. Back to my computer guy. He successfully gets into Frank Grassley's cell phone, and we're thinking this will prove Grassley is performing a role in this whole charade, you know, maybe we can find instructions from his handler or his real identity. So we go through the phone . . . and whoa, boy, did that lead to some interesting revelations.

And yes, I am all for privacy for regular citizens, but not for the government contractors participating in these schemes.

Brandon Grassley (*neighbor*): Someone hacked into my dad's phone. It turned out to be the psychos from Unfounded. They were parked in front of Sara's house, waving signs and yelling most of the day. I guess they thought we were all part of some conspiracy faking Sara's disappearance. So they leaked all my dad's info on their Twitter feed. Doxed him. Photos, private messages, videos, everything.

So, yeah . . . my dad was gay. Or bisexual, I guess, I don't know, we didn't really ever talk about it afterward. But he was using a gay dating app. And now everything he had ever said on that app was on the Internet.

I stopped going to school. My dad stopped going to work. My mom, in Florida, wanted me to come live with her. But to be honest, I was worried about my dad, I didn't want to leave him. We both just kinda stayed in the house, alone in our rooms, for a long time after that happened.

It was a rough time.

Olivia Weston (*friend*): There was a weird vibe right after the first episode. At first everyone was calling us heroes, saying we had solved the case and we'd find Sara now. I was proud, excited, hopeful. But I guess within a couple days, the cops found out that Frank Grassley was actually innocent. And then his life was ruined. It kinda felt like Nellie and I had caused that.

I wanted to apologize to Brandon, but I never saw him again.

Nellie Spencer (*friend*): I don't know what to say. Sara sent us those texts about Brandon's dad, they were real, we didn't make anything up. Casey practically begged us to talk about them on TV. One minute we were getting yelled at for keeping it a secret, then a day later we were getting yelled at for spreading lies. We just did what we were supposed to do. It's all the assholes on the Internet who went after that family, not us.

Becca Santangelo (*SareBears*): Nellie and Olivia didn't do anything wrong. They are the original SareBears.

Zane Kelly (*camera operator*): I think the first episode was a wake-up call for a lot of people. I noticed a big difference in everyone we filmed before and after it aired. They realized they weren't just talking to our crew but essentially to the whole world. I had seen this happen plenty of times over the years but never this quickly—our show was turning people from anonymous to Internet-famous in forty-eight hours.

Jeannette Parcell (*mother*): That first trip to the grocery store after the premiere was rough. People wouldn't stop coming up to me. Most of them were supportive, but a few said something nasty. A parent from Sara's school told me that Dave and I should lose custody if Sara was ever found. I left my cart in the middle of the freezer aisle and walked out. I couldn't take it.

I went home and started sobbing with Dave. But he convinced me it was a good thing—it proved everyone had watched the show . . . everyone would be looking out for Sara. A million eyeballs.

Casey Hawthorne (*producer*): The pressure really ratcheted up after the premiere. People were spooked to talk to me. There was all that drama with Frank Grassley. The girls felt bad. Jeannette was freaking out. We had just started, and already everyone was tense.

Marcus called with the overnight ratings. They were through the roof, just like I suspected. He asked me when I would have a new episode ready. I didn't know, and he got on my ass about it.

I realized I had a decision to make: Should the next episode be about the ongoing search for Sara? Or about the fallout from the premiere?

Alexis Lee (*associate producer*): Casey was doing Reality TV 101. Create conflict with the airing of your show and then film the new conflict that ensues as the participants deal with the fallout. Rinse and repeat. I get that it's useful, and we've all done it, but it's a cheap trick, and it made me queasy to be doing it while Sara was still missing. That's not how Casey had pitched the series.

That's when I should have quit.

Casey Hawthorne (*producer*): The answer about what to do for the next episode was forced on me. Because, in all honesty, the search for Sara had kind of stalled out.

Felix Calderon (*detective*): I got another call from District Attorney Bell. More pressure to solve the case.

Christine Bell (*district attorney*): We had gone from the bus driver, then to the neighbor discovered by Nancy Drew, and then to zero suspects. It was a disaster. The girl had been missing four days now. I was ready to turn the case over to federal investigators.

Felix Calderon (*detective*): I had no leads. I went digging through the tip line again. My third or fourth time. Something finally stuck out. It was kind of confusing, but a woman had called in to report that her brother had seen her car near Sara's school on the morning of the disappearance. Not that interesting, obviously, except for the fact that her car had been left in the repair shop that week.

At the Frederick Shell station.

Evelyn Crawford (*Manny's wife*): Yup, my husband was questioned by the police. Along with everyone else at the shop. He brushed it off as nothing when he told me about it.

Felix Calderon (*detective*): Those were early days, when I talked to Manny Crawford. I can't believe how close we were. But everything checked out with him, and I moved on.

Dave Parcell (*father*): I was over at the Shell a few days after that. Just gassing up, no agenda. Went inside to buy a soda. When I came back to my truck, I noticed I had four flat tires. Someone had let the air out of all of them.

The air hose was around the back of the garage. So I pulled my truck back there. No one around. Except Manny, kind of concealing himself in a doorway.

He told me the cops were up his ass. Something about a car spotted near Sara's school. I assured him they didn't have anything real or he wouldn't be standing there. Tried to pretend I was just filling up my tires. He gave me a look . . . he wasn't happy. But it wasn't the place or time to get spotted together. I told him not to panic, and a minute later, I was gone.

Felix Calderon (*detective*): I couldn't see it then, what was actually going on. I was back to having nothing. It was extremely frustrating, the feeling that Sara had vanished into thin air. So I swallowed my pride and did what was right for the case.

Casey Hawthorne (*producer*): Felix reached out to me, clearly with his blood still boiling. He gruffly asked for a meeting. We decided on the lobby bar at the hotel.

Felix Calderon (*detective*): I asked Casey what else she had heard. Obviously, people were talking to her. She had a knack for getting people to open up, I conceded that. If there was any information being kept from me, I needed her to share it. The stakes were too high, I couldn't just wait for her next episode to air. I knew if anything else came out on her show before I knew it, Bell would take the case away.

Casey Hawthorne (*producer*): He attacked me, basically. Accused me of hiding details that could help find Sara. Of only caring about my show. Playing games with people's lives. It was incredibly insulting.

I told him I wasn't hiding anything. And that if he was serious about doing what was best for the case, he should participate in the show. Give viewers a POV from inside the police investigation.

Felix Calderon (*detective*): She wanted to team up and run around like two kids in a comic book. It was ridiculous. I blew my stack. I'm sure I said some things I shouldn't have. I was under a lot of pressure.

Casey Hawthorne (*producer*): If he wanted to make it personal, I can go there. I told him the truth: All this anger coming out of him, it wasn't about the investigation . . . no, he was hurt that I lied to him, that I had ruined his little love-at-first-sight fantasy. I told him to grow up.

Felix Calderon (*detective*): It became clear that we couldn't continue like this . . . and by "this," I meant her show and my investigation. They couldn't coexist. I stood up, walked to my car, and drove to the Parcells' house.

Dave Parcell (*father*): Detective Calderon charged up to the house with his hair on fire and took us by surprise. I was working by myself in the garage.

Jeannette Parcell (*mother*): He came in and gave us an ultimatum. We had to pull the plug on the show. He made a big speech about how it couldn't work to give Casey more access than the police. Of course, Casey drove up two minutes after him, and we let her have her say, too. It was a regular old debate.

Casey Hawthorne (*producer*): I was right behind him at the Parcells'. Of course I knew where he was going. To tell on me with Mommy and Daddy or whatever he thought he was accomplishing.

I told Dave and Jeannette that the plan was working. I shared the ratings Marcus had given me. Five million people were looking for Sara. They were desperate for the next episode. And what had Felix accomplished? Nothing. I said it to his face, right in front of them: "You want access? Information about Sara's life? Do your job. Go talk to people. Investigate! I'm not stopping you."

Jeannette Parcell (*mother*): She had a point. But I didn't know what to do. I looked at Dave. He made the call.

Dave Parcell (*father*): We told Calderon that if we had to choose, we were sticking with Casey. If he didn't want to help us, he could put someone else on the case. And that was that.

Casey Hawthorne (*producer*): I walked down to the curb with Felix. He wasn't talking. I couldn't help myself. I told him he was hot when he was angry. Then I slipped the key card to my hotel room into his pocket. Told him he could blow off steam any time. Patted the card and walked away.

Felix Calderon (*detective*): I didn't have time for Casey's head games. I saw that the garage door was still open. That's where Dave had been working when I arrived. Then he had met us inside the house. But now, as we were leaving, I peered into the garage. Dave was coming back out again, I guess to finish whatever he had been doing. He didn't see me watching, but I saw him rush to grab something off the workbench and slip it into his pocket. It looked like a cheap flip phone. At least that's what I thought. One of those burners you can buy at any convenience store. The urgency with which he grabbed it and hid it away . . . it just struck me as odd.

I got in my car and sat there without leaving for a minute. Just thinking about everything that had happened so far. Finally opening my mind to any and all possibilities. And now, after seeing that little panic he had grabbing the phone, it sealed a new idea for me.

For the first time, I knew it had to be true: This guy, this newly minted local hero, this sympathetic dad of the year . . . he was definitely hiding something.

And even though it wouldn't be popular, that meant I needed to go after him.

Dave Parcell (*father*): After they left, my mind was racing. Jeannette and I were now all in with Casey. She and her cameras would be poking around for weeks. That changed everything.

It meant I needed to make another long hike into the woods.

CHAPTER 8

"Dave, the Monster"

Felix Calderon (*detective*): Something didn't seem right about Dave in those early days. He was almost . . . smug. I never saw him truly panicked about the situation. Sure, he cried for the news cameras, and ranted and raved in front of me, and comforted his family. But it all seemed controlled . . . like a performance. I should have noticed it sooner.

Christine Bell (*district attorney*): We needed a suspect. Someone, pardon my French, whom we could tar, feather, and hang. My election was coming up in six months. The local machine was running some blowhard who was trying to outflank me on law and order. Bless his heart, that wasn't going to happen.

But I couldn't sit around and do nothing. This was the biggest case ever in our county, a prosecutor's dream. Some of us wait an entire career for a chance to lead a trial like this. I knew my reelection hung in the balance, so I was prepared to do whatever it took, even if I had to request federal assistance. Generally speaking, we don't like big government agencies coming around these parts, but I like unsolved abduction cases even less. Calderon must have sniffed out that I was about to go begging for help. He called me and told me he was onto something promising, convinced me that we could wrap this up with our local manpower.

That was appealing to me, until I heard what he had in mind.

Felix Calderon (*detective*): I wanted to bring in Dave and formally question him. Bell told me absolutely not. You've got to remember, he was still the main sympathetic figure at the time. The dad with the bank statement. "Bad optics," she said. She didn't want to risk the impression that law enforcement was harassing the brave parents.

Bell told me I'd be taken off the case if I went after Dave. I tried to argue with her, but all I had was a hunch, no evidence. She wanted a new suspect and gave me until the end of the week to bring her something real. I was determined to use that time to bring her around on arresting Dave.

It was a tough spot. I was now racing the clock to pin something on this guy but forbidden to go directly at him. I needed to find a way that kept my fingerprints out of the situation. Eventually, I hit upon a pretty good idea.

Christine Bell (*district attorney*): The Dave angle made no sense, but I gave Calderon one more chance to dig up something else. While I waited on him, I figured why not, might as well accept the invitation I had received from that producer girl. Everyone else was getting their share of the limelight. I thought it couldn't hurt to have my face out there, start building a more national profile.

Casey Hawthorne (*producer*): Christine Bell reached out to us. Several times. We never thought to interview her. When we finally did, at her insistence, we didn't even use any of the footage. She tried to turn it into a campaign ad.

Felix Calderon (*detective*): I got a call from my buddy at the courthouse. Casey and her crew had just arrived, and they were setting up to interview Bell in her office. My reservoir of anger was pretty depleted by that point, but this chapped my ass. It just confirmed what I already knew: Some public servants are there to serve the public, some are there to serve themselves.

I wasn't going to cause a giant scene, but I walked over to the courthouse. If Casey and Bell were going to mess up this case even more, to further blur the line between the show and the investigation, then I was going to make them do it in front of me. This was back when I thought every person could feel at least some measure of shame.

Casey Hawthorne (*producer*): Felix was loitering around the courthouse after the interview. He asked how it went, you know, just being a jerk about it. I told him the truth, that Christine Bell was a charlatan and a moron. He laughed. I could tell he didn't want to, but he laughed.

I asked if he had held on to the hotel key I slipped him.

Felix Calderon (*detective*): I hadn't tossed the key card. But I never used it. Well, I guess technically, I used it once, but that was different.

I told Casey, "If you're expecting me to sneak up to your room, don't hold your breath."

Casey Hawthorne (*producer*): I told him holding my breath could be fun sometimes, he already knew that. He blushed. Then I told him I had to run, I was doing a ride-along with Dave, he was going to be out driving around, looking for Sara.

Felix Calderon (*detective*): Something about the idea of her riding around alone with Dave caught me. I grabbed her as she was walking away. Leaned in and told her I had to tell her something. She looked back at me, sensing I was serious. Her whole crew was waiting. I told her it had to be in private. We looked around. Not a lot of private spaces in a crowded courthouse lobby. But the elevators were right there. I pushed the button, the doors opened, and I pulled Casey inside. Once the doors closed, it was just us. I hit the disable button so we couldn't move and couldn't be disturbed. Then I looked right at her.

Casey Hawthorne (*producer*): We had seen each other a few times since that moment in the Parcells' living room when he discovered who I was. Never alone, though, and each time, he had been so angry. But suddenly, in that elevator, he spoke to me like a person again. He was honest and open and warm. He admitted to being hurt by my deception. And even if a part of him wanted to see me again, he had resolved not to.

But he said he couldn't forgive himself if something happened to me. So he told me what he suspected about Dave. He knew I was about to go off alone with him. He warned me: "Be careful about trusting that guy . . . he might not be who you think he is . . . make sure you protect yourself."

And then he kissed me. Softly, slowly. A goodbye kiss, it felt like. I leaned in to him for more, but he was already pulling back and pushing the button for the elevator doors. They opened up and he walked away.

Felix Calderon (*detective*): I had to. I had to tell her about Dave.

Casey Hawthorne (*producer*): That kiss was . . . confusing. It was a lot of things.

I composed myself, walked through the lobby, felt everyone staring, and made it outside to our van. I'll admit it, Felix had me totally thrown. I couldn't tell if he loved me or hated me. If I should chase after him or try to forget him.

But beyond that confusion, I had a whole different set of wheels turning. I wasn't just thinking about Felix, I was thinking about Dave. "He's not who you think he is," what the fuck did that mean? And in an instant, walking down those courthouse steps, it all clicked for me. I shoved my boy drama aside and transformed back into a producer—I finally knew what to do for Episode Two.

For two days, I had been struggling to figure out how to shape the next episode. All the stuff we had started to put together—Nellie and Olivia dealing with their new fame, reactions to the Frank Grassley drama, Olaf showing us every inch of his ice cream shop like it was a crime scene—that shit was boring. And worse, it was tacky. I'm actually pissed that no one on my team had the balls to call me out.

People wanted a look inside this family. At the time, I didn't have any new ideas about what to show them beyond the Parcells being scared and sympathetic. But then Felix cracked it for me. I could psychoanalyze that kiss later . . . the real headline from the elevator was that he had given me an incredible gift for my show.

What if Dave was actually the villain? A sociopath who killed his daughter and then cultivated all this attention? Now, *that* was a story line.

Alexis Lee (*associate producer*): We got back in the van, and Casey was in a fog. She wouldn't tell us what happened in the elevator. But then, out of the blue, she ordered us to cancel the rest of our shoots for the day. We were scrapping the episode outline and starting from scratch.

Casey told me to make sure we found time to film Dave back at the house. The new episode was going to be all about him.

Basically, I came to realize, she wanted us to frame him.

Casey Hawthorne (*producer*): I never said "frame" him. I said, "Let's take a look at him without the benefit of the doubt. Forget the conflict of interest in him being a partner in the series — let's portray him just like we would any other suspect in the case." Which, in fact, he was. I shouldn't have needed Felix's comment to remind me of that.

Of course Alexis didn't like it — she didn't like any idea if it came from me.

Alexis Lee (*associate producer*): It made no sense. The entire premise of the show, as Casey said a million times, was that this family, these parents, were straight out of central casting, sympathetic avatars of decency and courage. And suddenly, we were going to do a hit piece on the dad?

Casey Hawthorne (*producer*): Look, my North Star never wavered. The show was a vehicle to help find Sara. That missing girl deserved our best and broadest efforts. If the lead detective thought her dad was suspicious, I had a professional duty to convey that to our audience, and a moral duty to Sara to expose him for who he was.

Marcus Maxwell (*executive*): I loved the new angle. That's why Casey is Casey. She is fearless.

Anthony Pena (*editor*): It was a bitch to cut the new episode together in time. We worked through the night, Casey right over my shoulder, nitpicking every frame and munching like a rabbit on her special snack bars, getting the crumbs all over me.

In our business, we call this episode "the turn"—it's when we show a character in an entirely new light and coax the audience into reversing their sympathies. There's an art to this type of editing, and not to brag or anything, but I've been called the Picasso of the turn. Yes, by other people!

So much of this technique is timing. Viewers are accustomed to shows moving with a certain rhythm. When you mess with that rhythm but only with one character, it's very impactful. Just holding on his face a beat longer. Or cutting to his reaction shot when someone else is talking. Add in some well-chosen music cues, adjust the color levels—you can turn an audience against someone without him saying a single wrong word.

You can also show things totally out of context. We try not to do that. But it happens.

Casey Hawthorne (*producer*): We grinded out the episode. Sent it off to LA as the sun came up. I went to sleep and woke up in time to see it hit the air in prime time that night.

Ezra Phillips (*pop culture critic*): If the pilot was a nuclear bomb, Episode Two hit like a punch to the gut. They made it seem like the father had done in his daughter! I found it very bleak. Depressing, to be honest. But to Casey's credit, I couldn't turn it off.

If it was really true—if this bozo had done this unspeakable crime and then agreed to a reality show—I had to see it all blow up in his face. I was totally hooked. And obviously, everyone else agreed. Trending on Twitter, memes about Dave flying around, a think piece in the *Times* the next day. America was officially obsessed.

Dave Parcell (*father*): Episode Two was tough to watch. I really felt like Casey had betrayed me. The way they cherry-picked all my facial expressions or random little things to make it seem like I was a sociopath . . . it was dirty. She came over to the house the morning after it aired, acting totally normal, and I confronted her about it.

Casey Hawthorne (*producer*): He accused me of stabbing him in the back. I challenged him—was there anything in the episode that wasn't true? We got into a fight about the mud.

Dave Parcell (*father*): Yeah, my truck had mud caked in the tires. And there was some dried mud on the garage floor. The way she filmed it, the freaking music they had playing over that footage . . . the whole thing made it seem like my tires were covered in blood.

Casey Hawthorne (*producer*): It hadn't rained any time recently. There was no mud around. Unless, of course, Dave was driving off-road. Hey, the camera can only capture what's really there. If that leads to uncomfortable questions, so be it. But Dave was arguing about this and that, complaining about how he was portrayed. I listened without pushing back too hard. I knew he was just blowing off steam. Then, after he calmed down a bit, he changed the subject—he asked me about the ratings.

I told him the truth: By any measure, the show was a smash. And everyone was talking about the second episode. We had hit the zeitgeist, so to speak. The freaking *New York Times* was writing about us! He did his best affable shrug and said, "Well, I guess that's better for Sara . . . if it helps for me to be portrayed like this, then I'll let you do your job."

And that was that.

Dave Parcell (*father*): I saw what Casey was doing, and I made my peace with it. I even told her, "Let me know if I can help. We're on the same team, we want the show to be successful, we want to find Sara. If you think it's good TV for me to act a certain way or say something, whatever, I'll do it, just tell me." There was no need to go behind my back, that was my point.

Casey Hawthorne (*producer*): You're probably wondering if I thought he did it at that point, killed his daughter. Like how could I make an episode implying that so strongly, then stroll right back into his house and have a civil conversation about ratings?

Look, I was suspicious of Dave, I really was. I trusted Felix's suspicions, too. But I thought about it, and at the end of the day, I couldn't wrap my head around it: Who could kill their own child and then invite a TV crew into their home? No one, I still believed.

Alexis Lee (*associate producer*): If Casey didn't believe Dave was guilty, then we never should have done that episode. And if she did think he was guilty at that point, and kept making the show with him . . . well, then she's crazier than I thought.

Dave Parcell (*father*): I was ultimately fine with what Casey did to me in that episode. Jeannette, on the other hand . . .

Jeannette Parcell (*mother*): I had stopped in to see my doctor, and she prescribed Xanax for all the stress. But it wasn't helping. Sara was gone. Jack was traumatized. Casey and her crew were in my hair night and day. And now they were making it seem like my husband was a murderer. It was too much. I wasn't sleeping, I had headaches all day. I needed help taking the edge off. Something stronger than Xanax.

Travis Haynes (*bus driver*): Yeah, Jeannette showed up at my apartment one day. No cameras, obviously, she had slipped away from them. I started selling to her. It was fucking crazy. One minute this family is railroading me, the next minute she's a customer. But I don't hold grudges. It's bad for business.

Jeannette Parcell (*mother*): Where else was I gonna go? He was the only person I knew who had Oxy. Detective Calderon was the one who told us!

Jack Parcell (*brother*): Everything inside our house was weird. The hopeful energy started to disappear. There was tension between my mom and dad, and Sara wasn't around to explain it away for me. I was confused. After that second episode, they wouldn't let me watch the show anymore. I think they kicked me out of the room halfway through it. I had thought the show was about finding Sara . . . why was it showing my dad like that?

Becca Santangelo (*SareBears*): We freaked out when all of a sudden it seemed like Dave had done it. But of course it was the father! It made us all so angry. He had manipulated us. For Pete's sake, we were sending donations to the reward fund he'd set up, I had taken up a collection in my dorm. But Casey sniffed him out because she's the best.

Evelyn Crawford (*Manny's wife*): Episode Two was damn near the only thing that show got right. Dave, the monster. They had the whole thing figured out, and they didn't even know it.

Beverly Geary (*grandmother*): Now, look, you know I didn't watch that awful show, but that particular episode was the worst. I could not help myself, I called my daughter and lit into her for inviting this abomination into her home, into all of our lives. She hung up on me.

Jeannette Parcell (*mother*): Who knew my mother was a TV critic? A TV critic, kidnapping expert, marriage counselor, media consultant . . . she fancies herself a quick study.

Bruce Allen Foley (*Unfounded*): Everyone talks about Episode Two because it's when the spotlight got turned on Dave. They all missed the real bombshell. This was when we knew for sure that the whole thing was being staged.

The seventh scene, ten minutes in. Jeannette's in the kitchen with Jack. They're being filmed, of course. Jack's talking about what he wants to do with Sara when she comes home. And every time he says the name Sara, you can see Jeannette's hands, and she's crossing her fingers! Whether she's holding her mug of coffee or opening the fridge, her fingers are uncrossed for the whole conversation but crossed each time Jack says "Sara."

She was telling us as clearly as she could: "I'm lying . . . this isn't real."

We've had reports that some of these crisis actors want out. But they can't just leave. Like what, walk away and tell the truth on *Oprah*? Come on, they know for a fact they'll be killed. And not in a way where anyone would suspect foul play. Look at what Russia does, they put some nerve toxin on your shirt, and then you drop dead. You think our spooks can't do the same thing? Please.

The people caught up doing these jobs, they're like prisoners, they can't get out. That's why we've never heard a full accounting from an insider. But I knew that was exactly what people needed to hear. A confession.

It got me thinking . . .

Felix Calderon (*detective*): Casey's second episode comes out, and I know everyone thinks I look like an idiot again, right? First she beat me to Frank Grassley. And now she's the first to sniff out Dave. Well, not so fast. No, no, no. This time she was doing my bidding.

I assume she told you about when I pulled her into the elevator? I only did that so I could put a bug in her ear about Dave. And yeah, I ended up kissing her. But that was just to mess with her equilibrium a bit. She's a savvy operator. I couldn't risk having her see through my play.

And man, did she take the bait. Better than I could have ever expected, I really owed her. After the episode she ran off to make—all the shadows, the music, the cryptic threats—Bell would have let me walk Dave straight to the electric chair. I got a call from her office first thing in the morning, and she told me to haul his ass in.

I never told Casey I programmed that episode for her. She wouldn't like hearing that.

Casey Hawthorne (*producer*): Wow. Okay. That actually makes sense now.

I bet he was so proud of himself. I can totally picture him gloating as he told you that.

But you know what? Good for him. He got his ass into the game and won a round. I'm happy for him.

Alexis Lee (*associate producer*): I love hearing this. Calderon giving Casey a taste of her own manipulative medicine. But even so . . . big picture, fuck those two and their weird psychosexual head games.

Casey Hawthorne (*producer*): It does make you wonder, though . . . at least it makes *me* wonder, now that I'm hearing this . . . Felix let me take that ride alone with Dave, right when he believed Dave was most dangerous and desperate. He thought he was teeing up my next episode, I get it. But did he really let me get in that truck with a man he was starting to suspect of murder?

Yeah, he did. Noted.

Felix Calderon (*detective*): I . . . I don't see it that way. I was using all my tools to break the case. Casey was never in danger. At least not then. Later, when she actually was, she knows what I did for her.

My focus was on the case. My focus was on nailing Dave. The plan worked.

Christine Bell (*district attorney*): I thought Dave was involved all along, well before Detective Calderon wised up to it. Any fool could have seen that. Once the proper boxes were checked, I instructed him to proceed.

Felix Calderon (*detective*): I picked up Dave at his house, drove him in for questioning. No public perp walk or anything, we weren't confident enough for that. He wasn't happy, but he cooperated. Jeannette was hysterical.

Jeannette Parcell (*mother*): To assume Dave murdered our daughter because of how he was portrayed on the show? Without any evidence? The detective should have been ashamed of himself. If he wasn't already, I let him hear it.

Felix Calderon (*detective*): We brought him down to the station and let him stew for an hour alone in the room. Then I made my run at him.

Dave Parcell (*father*): It was a joke. On the day Sara went missing, I had been at work all morning, then with Jeannette all afternoon. There was no way I could have done anything to her.

Yeah, Calderon had seen me with a burner cell phone. I keep those in my truck for emergencies, in case the battery dies on my regular phone. And yeah, there was mud on my tires. I cracked the case wide open for him: I drove through a puddle. I asked if he was doing any real investigating or just watching TV all day. He didn't appreciate that.

Felix Calderon (*detective*): He had an answer for everything, but the answers were too quick. I had been doing the job a long time . . . suspects with all the right answers made me suspicious.

Take Frank Grassley, for example. When we had questioned him the week before, he was flustered, he didn't have every detail at the tip of his tongue. He had to think. Everything he said ultimately checked out, but he wasn't rehearsed.

Dave was too calm. It felt like the interrogation was just something he needed to check off his to-do list.

Dave Parcell (*father*): We went around in circles. He kept me up late to the point where I was getting tired, trying to trip me up. I reminded him that my daughter was missing, and I would never forgive or forget being treated like a suspect. I could tell Calderon didn't trust me. But he didn't have another card to play. He let me go as the sun was coming up.

Felix Calderon (*detective*): I was discouraged. We hadn't nailed him, and now he knew I had him in my sights. To be honest, I couldn't figure out what was going on.

Dave Parcell (*father*): Even though I was exhausted, I left the police station with a spring in my step. In my mind, I had just gotten over the hump. The hard part was over, and I thought it was smooth sailing from here.

Everything was under control . . .

The cops had taken their shot and missed.

Casey's checks were coming in, just like she promised.

And most importantly, Sara was doing great. I had just seen her the day before.

She was safe and sound and up to speed on the new plan.

CHAPTER 9

"This Awful Idea"

Dave Parcell (*father*): The whole thing was a scam. But I hope you'll believe me, we never set out to do something like this. We're not bad people. It was a small idea that just got totally out of control. The original thought . . . I mean, I still think it was reasonable.

It was the middle of winter that year. You know, dark, depressing, after the holidays. Sara came down from her room one night. It was late. I was by myself, watching whatever stupid college football bowl game was playing on the West Coast. She sat down next to me and tossed a brochure onto the table.

"I want to go to this," she said.

It was a summer residency program at Juilliard. For gifted high school students. The best music academy in the world. Sara really wanted to go. And she thought she had a chance of being accepted. God, just her having the confidence to believe in herself like that, it made me so proud of her. She thought she was one of the best young musicians in the country. And she was.

I flipped through the brochure. Her music teacher had given it to her, Mrs. Rosen. I mean, what could I say, it looked great. Practice sessions in Lincoln Center. Classes outside in Central Park. Outings to Carnegie Hall. I had never been to these places, but I'd seen movies. Sara deserved to experience that world.

And then I got to the last page. Where the tuition was listed. Now, remember, this is just a summer program, it's not college yet, there are no scholarships or financial aid. Twelve grand for six weeks. Twelve grand. And God knows how much more we'd need to give her just to be able to eat, get around New York City. Obviously, we didn't have twelve grand.

Sara knew it. I guess she was kinda hoping for a miracle. Like I had a secret piggy bank to break open specifically for this. When I saw the price, I looked at her, and I could see she already knew. This program wasn't for families like ours. Seeing how much she wanted it . . . it broke my heart.

"Maybe I could pick up more shifts at Olaf's," she said. This poor girl was already stretched so thin, between the music, the track team, school, working weekends. I barely saw her! I told her I didn't think that would make the difference. But I promised that me and her mom would think about it. We'd think about if there was some way to make it work. Her face fell, and she went back upstairs knowing I was just saying that. She knew there was no chance.

I had seen that look before. The first time, Sara must have been only seven or eight. Her friend had a birthday party at one of the farms outside of town. There was a little petting zoo area, and all the kids got to take a turn riding a horse. Well, not a real horse, a pony, I should say. And there were two options, the fast pony and the slow pony. You know damn well which one Sara picked. To see her bouncing around on that thing as she did her lap around the pen, the squeals of laughter, the love in her eyes. It was pure happiness. Of course, at the end of the day, the farm director tells the whole group they can sign up for regular riding lessons. On the real horses. And I see Sara's eyes light up, and now some of the parents and kids are huddled around the clipboard, leaving their information, and Sara drags me and Jeannette over, going, "Can I? Can I?" Well, we saw how much it cost, and you can probably guess what happened.

That was the first time I saw that look. It wasn't the first time our little girl cried, just the first time she cried because she was disappointed in us.

Now here she was at sixteen, same look, same disappointment. And it was breaking my damn heart.

I stayed up that night, getting angrier and angrier. Here was the perfect child. Had done everything right. Had this beautiful gift. All she wanted was a chance to pursue it. And she knew that meant leaving Frederick, going out into the world, facing challenges, chasing dreams, even if it scared her.

And the only thing stopping her? We couldn't afford it. But here's where I still take issue—we couldn't afford it because it had been ten, twenty years of getting screwed out of every dime we tried to save. Always being the nail, never the hammer. Hell, it started the day Sara was born, when the hospital dropped some bogus bill on us that our insurance didn't cover. Cradle to the grave, it never ends. The taxes I paid to start my roofing business. The license fees I had to pay every year to stay certified. The way lumber prices skyrocketed because of some trade deal halfway around the world. The loan I was forced to take at the bank to try and stay afloat. Those freaking interest rates. Then the way they came after me when I couldn't make the payments. The suggestion they made to redo my mortgage to get some breathing room. And then how they squeezed and squeezed and squeezed until I had no choice: Give up our house or shut down my business. Predatory lending . . . there's a name for it.

Picking up hours at Jeannette's father's store wasn't cutting it. We weren't starving, but we certainly weren't saving. And for the first time, this was finally landing on Sara. Sure, she already knew we didn't have money to spend on a cool new cell phone or jewelry or riding lessons. But this was a real fork in the road: The direction of her life was gonna change because her parents were broke. She didn't deserve that.

I know you won't believe me, but my goodness, you should have heard Sara play music. She played from the tips of her toes to the top of her pigtails. Another parent called her a virtuoso once. I always loved that fancy word—"virtuoso." I'm telling you, it was magical listening to her. She was just . . . I'm sorry, excuse me, give me a minute here. I'm just . . . remembering what she sounded like. I haven't heard her play in so long, but I remember. I still have some videos saved somewhere—maybe I'll be able to watch again one day.

Anyway, sorry, I'm good now.

Back to that night with the brochure. I stayed up thinking, there had to be a way.

Another loan. Ask around to friends and family. But none of it worked, it was either impossible or too ridiculous—you can't ask for handouts for a fancy summer program in New York.

And then, out of the blue, I remembered Daryl from softball. A few years earlier, a guy on my beer-league softball team messed up his leg real bad. Sliding into third, that thing snapped like a twig. Compound fracture, he's screaming, ambulance driving right onto the field, it was a whole scene. Game canceled, of course, even though we were winning. Anyway, poor Daryl couldn't walk for like a year. And couldn't work, he was an electrician. So instead of just passing the hat around one time at a bar, someone on the team set up this thing, a GoFundMe. I had never heard of it, but it was a website where everyone could contribute a little to help pay his bills while Daryl was laid up. He told me afterward that it was a lifesaver. And that he couldn't believe how much money had come in!

So there it is. I think, Let's do a GoFundMe for Sara's Juilliard tuition! I wake her up the next morning and tell her my idea. She wasn't too enthusiastic. I mean, yeah, it's embarrassing for your family to be begging for money, no kidding. But she agreed to think it over with me.

We went on the site and scrolled around looking at the other campaigns. She made a great point as we poked around. All of the successful campaigns—the ones raking in the bucks—she said, "Dad, these are all sob stories . . . no one's gonna care about helping me take music classes." She was right. It was all kids with cancer, families whose house burned down, that kind of stuff. Sara didn't want to put her problem up against theirs. She made a joke, though: "Maybe if I fell off a cliff and broke my neck, we'd actually be able to raise some money." She laughed, closed the computer, and walked away. And that was almost the end of it.

But of course I kept thinking. She was right: People wanted to help only after something unlucky happened. Human nature, I guess. Okay, so what if we just *pretended* something unlucky happened and then used the money for the program? Yeah, it would be a lie, but the end result would be deserved: Sara would get to go to Juilliard. This girl born with no lucky breaks would get a chance to change her life. That wasn't a bad thing, right?

I don't mention any of this to Sara, but I start thinking about how we can pull it off. Obviously, we weren't going to throw her off a cliff and break her neck. But I thought, What about a little car accident where Sara hurts her neck? And then she's in one of those giant neck braces. Everyone is sympathetic to the sight of that! So now it's a fund for a young violin virtuoso who busted her neck and needs money for physical therapy or she'll never play music again. Boom! Who doesn't want to help that story?

I knew I'd need Sara to participate if this was going to work. And I knew she wouldn't like it. She's a much better person than me, and plus, the world hadn't ground her down yet. She still believed you could work hard and get somewhere. It would be tough to convince her, but I thought I could do it.

And then, totally unrelated, my brake light went out. Talk about another fork in the road. It's sick how much these things can change our lives and we never know it at the time. Well, this was a big one.

My brake light went out, and I went to see Manny Crawford.

This was the day before I was going to talk to Sara, to convince her. The back taillight on my truck fritzed out, and I stopped at the Shell station on the way home from work. The last thing I needed was a stupid ticket for this bullshit. Would have needed a separate GoFundMe just to pay that.

I get to the gas station and pull into the garage area. Manny says he can deal with it right away, just sit tight for a few minutes. See, Manny wasn't a friend or anything like that. But I had been taking my trucks to him for ten years. Great mechanic. Honest as the day is long.

Well, honest about cars, I guess.

Anyway, you shoot the shit with a guy that many times, and you're gonna have some kind of relationship. Not friends, but friendly. I trusted him. Like I said, super-loyal, honest guy. So I'm standing around, he's fixing the brake light, and for some reason I ask him the stupidest question: "What's more expensive to fix, a front bumper or a rear bumper?"

He looks at me like I've got two heads. "Planning on getting into a fender bender?" he asks.

Well, I didn't say it right away, but yeah, I was! See, I was planning to get into this fake little one-car accident, you know, with a tree or something, and I needed to have some minor damage to the car to make it seem like Sara could actually be injured. And I'm so hard up that I am trying to figure out the cheapest way to do this. So that's how I got to asking my mechanic for advice on how to pull off an intentional car accident.

Manny notices me acting all weird and asks what the hell I'm talking about. And again, there's no excuse for this, in hindsight, it ruined my life, but standing in that garage, I decide to tell Manny about my plan. I knew I could trust him, and I hadn't talked it through with anyone, and maybe I was looking for someone to stop me or help me make it better, but I needed to hear someone else's reaction to this ridiculous idea.

It was dumb, it was a mistake, but I did it.

Of course, by the time I'm done explaining everything, Manny is dying laughing. "Your daughter in a neck brace," he keeps saying, howling, "that's your big idea?"

And now I'm feeling like an idiot, and we're both kind of chuckling, and he goes back to fixing the truck. Honestly, the way he laughed at me, that was probably enough of a wake-up call. I was halfway to abandoning the whole stupid plan. And then he just says it, out of nowhere . . .

"I know how you can make some *real* money."

He sees my face, knows how desperate I am. Puts down his tools, walks over to me, looks around. And then he lays it all out. It was almost as if he'd been thinking about this for years. He says if I want people to really pony up some serious cash, Sara needs to disappear. Nothing like a pretty, white teenage girl to make the world go crazy. He said he watches all these crime shows, Nancy Grace or whatever, and whenever one of these girls goes missing, a huge reward pot builds up for whoever finds her. "Hundreds of thousands of dollars," he says. Snaps his fingers, "like that."

I am only taking him half seriously, but I'm at least thinking along with him now. "But Sara would actually have to disappear," I said. "That's easy," he said, "she can go camp out in the woods or something . . . remember, there's no actual crime, so there's no evidence, as long as she's not in your house for a few days, no one will know where she is." And he thought it wouldn't take long for a real pot of money to build up. Put Sara's photo on the news one night and that would get the ball rolling.

"Yeah, yeah, that's great," I said, "but what good is the reward money to *me*? I can't be the one to find her and collect the reward, it would look ridiculous."

And that's when he smiled. Lit up like a lightning bug. "You're right," he said. "What you need is a Good Samaritan to find her. A Good Samaritan you can trust. *That* person will collect the reward money, no questions asked. And then maybe split it with you," he said with a wink.

We stood there staring at each other, not talking for a while. It just made too much goddamn sense.

I went home and bounced this idea around for a few days. Didn't talk to Manny again for a while. It was crazy, but the more I thought about it, the more I knew we had to do it. Forget the summer program, this could set Sara up for *life*. Jack, too. And yes, it was a lie, just like the fake neck injury, but all the same justifications applied. No one would get hurt. Sara deserved it. And besides, all the other ways to get ahead in this country had been closed off. I was proof of that.

But Sara . . . Sara needed just one lucky break, and then she'd be flying. This would be it. Hell, once she was a rich, famous professional musician, she could spend her life giving back to charitable causes, you know, kids with cancer or whatever. Pay it forward. But first she had to get to New York that summer. This was the ticket.

After I worked through it a few times, I sat Sara down to explain everything. I had figured out where she could hide for a few days. There was this Boy Scout camp up in the mountains, Timber Ridge, they called it. Jack had gone there a few times over the summers. And like five years earlier, I had put a new roof on their mess hall. Worked for a month in April, just me and my crew. No one else ever came around, it was shut down until the summer season. I knew we could set her up in one of the cabins there, a suitcase full of food, some books, and she could hang tight. At least she'd have a bed and a roof and all that. Manny would secretly drive her out there after she slipped out of school that morning. It was totally isolated and totally safe.

In the meantime, we'd get everyone running in the wrong direction by leaving her backpack on the school bus. The cops would pounce on that for a while, and of course it would lead nowhere. And then I couldn't help myself . . . I had to take a shot at Frank Grassley. I told Sara to spend a few weeks texting her friends, making it seem like he was harassing her. It was all bullshit, but I knew the cops would get wind of that and give him hell for a bit, and that seemed like the least he deserved. He had ruined my family's life, now he'd have his time in the barrel.

So yeah, everyone would be chasing their tails for a few days, I would bait the hook with a tearful statement to the news crews and offer a reward of my own, and then presumably a real reward fund would get set up.

After a few days of the money building up, Sara could hike down to a road where Manny would pick her up. She'd have to tell a story to the police about being thrown in the trunk of a car and locked away somewhere, but that she was blindfolded the whole time, and she didn't have more details to share. Manny would talk about seeing someone straggling around in the trees and bravely going to investigate. We were going to portray it as sort of an incompetent abduction where the guy got cold feet and let her go.

Was it the most believable story ever? No. But once Sara was back home, once Manny was recognized as a hero, it wouldn't matter if some of these questions never got answered. We, as a family, would simply say we were grateful for Sara's safe return and just wanted to move on with our lives. I'd block her off from any authorities that wanted to press her further.

I laid this all out for Sara. She was horrified, obviously. First off, just on a basic level, she didn't love the idea of hiding out in the middle of nowhere by herself! But much more than that, she was disgusted at the idea of lying and, as she put it, stealing other people's money. I tried to explain that everyone would only be giving twenty bucks here, fifty bucks there, no one would be suffering from this. And that she deserved this opportunity. In a broad sense, the whole community wanted this for her anyway, so it wasn't stealing. It was *fair*, if you really thought about it.

She wasn't convinced. I wasn't going to make her do it, but I tried to push her. I was honest: This might be the only chance she had of going to Juilliard. I told her we didn't have the money, not even close. Our family was owed a break, it was okay to make this happen.

Sara didn't believe that. She wasn't bitter, like me. The world was her oyster, still—she would find a different way to succeed even if she missed out on the summer program.

She said no. And then worst of all, she said, "I'm sorry." She knew it was going to crush me. And then she walked upstairs.

I had another night where I sat up alone the whole time. Thinking. Stewing. Feeling sorry for myself, embarrassed that I'd even pitched it to her. I was out of ideas. And only one thing was clear: I was failing my kids. That right there, that's shame. Pure shame. I never felt so low.

And then, like a miracle, Sara came downstairs in the morning, looked at me, and said, "Let's do it."

I was shocked. Then relieved. Then energized. You have to realize, after she was on board, the weeks we spent planning this, Sara and me, those were some of the best days of my life. Having a secret with my daughter, just the two of us. Working together, driving around, strategizing, seeing how smart and brave and capable she was. We scouted the camp . . . found a spot for her to get picked up by Manny . . . refreshed some of her camping skills . . . rehearsed her story for the police. And also just hung out, I guess. There's nothing like getting your teenager trapped in a car, it's the only place you can really bond with them. No eye contact, some music on the radio, a little boredom—your kids just crack wide open.

And best of all, I was imagining the future she'd have, how she'd go on to do so much more, live so much better than I ever did. It was a parent's dream. I couldn't stop smiling.

I never talked to her about what made her change her mind. I had a guess, but I couldn't bring it up with her. I was too much of a coward. Even now it's . . . it's hard for me to talk about.

Something happened three or four months before this. Sara saw something that I think she misinterpreted. Well, maybe not misinterpreted but misunderstood.

It was late at night. I couldn't sleep, that was pretty common around then. I was in a really dark place. We had no money, the bills I was sneaking out of the mailbox were past due. Herb had said something to me at the store that stuck in my craw. Jeannette and I weren't getting along. Everything was awful, if I'm being honest. Everything except for my kids.

So I'm up late, moping around, and I decide to clean up some things in the garage. I'm organizing, sorting through boxes, tossing shit, and I come across the case with my hunting rifle. I hadn't used it in years, didn't have the time or the energy anymore. But I open up the case and figure I might as well clean it up, maybe I could sell the thing. So now I've got it out, and I'm making sure everything's in working order, and . . .

Look, I promise I wasn't going to kill myself. I wasn't. But yeah, it suddenly occurred to me that this was a possible answer. If I didn't want to wake up the next morning and deal with all the same problems, well, here you go, boom, this is one option. And again, I wasn't going to kill myself, I don't think the rifle was even loaded. It wasn't, I'm telling you. But I couldn't help myself, I had to see how it would feel, how I'd react.

I flipped it around and put the muzzle in my mouth.

That's when I heard Sara. "Dad," she cried out, but in a whisper. I turned around, and she was standing in the doorway, terrified, crying.

I jumped up and tried to tell her I was just goofing around. I laughed and put the gun down and said, "See, it's nothing, it's not even loaded." She ran up to her room. And we never talked about it.

So you asked what made Sara change her mind after saying no. What made her go along with this shameful scam. I'll never know for sure, but here's what I believe: I think, after I pitched the plan, Sara stayed up all night also. I picture her tossing and turning in bed. She knew how ashamed and embarrassed and desperate I was. God, it is so awful to have your kids see that in you. It's truly the worst feeling in the world. For a long time, I wanted to believe that Sara was convinced we had a good, reasonable idea. But no. That was my pride, my delusions. I know why Sara did it. I know all too well.

She thought if she didn't do this, her father was going to blow his brains out in the garage. And when that happened, it would be her fault.

Sara was a sweetheart. She agreed to this awful idea because she thought it would save my life. She would have agreed to anything for me.

Well, here I am, ten years later. Still standing. And she's the one gone. How's that for fair?

CHAPTER 10

"Never Forgive"

Evelyn Crawford (*Manny's wife*): Dave's plan was the stupidest shit I ever heard. There is no way my husband conceived of it.

Yeah, we watched Nancy Grace and would talk about these cases, and Manny would lecture the TV, criticizing this person or that person for screwing up the crime or the investigation. My husband was smart, I know that much. And he was fascinated by all the ins and outs of the cases. He had an older brother who disappeared when Manny was a little boy. Walked out of their house one day and never came back. Always sounded to me like he took a train to Chicago or whatnot and never looked back. But Manny didn't see it that way. He wished there had been a whole search-and-rescue operation.

So yeah, he had his little obsession, if you want to call it that. But lying about a missing girl? Deceiving everyone? Stealing from his neighbors? That was not my husband. We have two daughters of our own. Dave must have put him up to all that, I know it in my bones.

Jeannette Parcell (*mother*): I was kept out of the loop originally. Certainly while Dave and Sara were planning this. If I had one inkling what they were doing, I would have smacked the living daylights out of both of them.

He had so much pride, that man. Hard to understand for someone who never accomplished anything, but he had so much pride. Twelve thousand dollars. The cost of that summer program. I know we didn't have it in the bank, but I can think of a hundred better ways to get it than faking our daughter's disappearance. Dave needed to make it about himself, though. He needed to be the hero who figured it out instead of asking for handouts. I'll never forgive him.

Jack Parcell (*brother*): When I found out that it all started as a lie, I was very confused. This was only after Sara was dead, obviously. Everyone was so traumatized, they didn't exactly do a good job explaining how it all happened. My mom told me that Sara and Dad had been playing a game at first, and then an accident happened. This was before the divorce, before she had fully come around to blaming my dad and testifying against him.

The detective asked me questions about what I had known. I was truly too confused to help him at all. He was the one who ended up doing the best job of explaining things to me. He told me that Sara was never really kidnapped, that my dad lied about it to steal money, but now Sara was actually dead. I didn't believe it. How could I? But when I asked my mom, she said it was all true.

To be honest, there was no way for me to try and wrap my head around the details. My big sister was gone. She . . . she always used to tie my shoes for me. When I was little. A million times a day, it felt like, I was definitely *that* kid. She was always there for me . . .

That was all I thought about. My big sister was gone.

Jeannette Parcell (*mother*): Dave destroyed our lives. Took a wrecking ball to a perfectly happy family. And the worst part? It was totally unnecessary. I'm sure he gave you the whole sob story about his dignity and always being the nail and never the hammer. About the shame he felt, knowing our kids were missing all these opportunities. It's a crock of shit. Our kids were fine. They were happy. They never missed a meal in their life. So what if we couldn't afford things rich people can afford? The kids didn't even know that, it was always Dave pointing it out! He thought it was a tragedy that Sara didn't take horseback riding lessons. Please. Sara would have found her way in life even if she missed out on Juilliard that summer. That was Dave's dream, not hers. Sure, she wanted to go, but Dave was the one obsessed with it.

Dave's parents were poor, dirt poor. Double-wide trailer with a pipe sticking out from the toilet into the yard. He was always proud of the fact that he managed to get out of that kind of backwoods type of living, you know, that he had done better than his parents. And to his credit, he wanted that for our kids. He always said, "If we do our job right, these kids will be embarrassed by us someday." It turns out he was the only one embarrassed by how we lived.

Jack Parcell (*brother*): It took a while for me to finally understand everything. And then I realized: Sara was dead because of my video. The version that her and my dad planned out . . . she'd still be alive if that was all that happened. I'm not saying it would have worked and they wouldn't have been caught, but she definitely wouldn't have been killed. She would have been back home in a few days. She would have never been famous. The whole thing changed once Casey saw my video and came to find us.

I know there's a lot of blame to go around. But no one can tell me this would have happened if I didn't post the video of my parents crying in the doorway.

Beverly Geary (*grandmother*): I spat in that man's face more than once after everything came out. And Lord knows I'll do it again if we cross paths. I had told Jeannette when they started going together: "This idiot is going to ruin your life."

Jeannette Parcell (*mother*): That's not true at all. My mom always liked him, right up to the day she found out why Sara died. To her credit, though, she did spit in his face.

Beverly Geary (*grandmother*): He's not a real man. A real man doesn't sneak around trying to trick people in order to provide for his family. He goes out and works. I don't care that his business went under. Pick yourself up and do better. My husband—who, by the way, hasn't lied once in his life—he gave Dave plenty of opportunity at the store. Dave was too prideful to take it.

Ezra Phillips (*pop culture critic*): The fragility of white masculinity is a real thing, something I feel more than qualified speaking to, and I see Dave as the tragic embodiment of it.

This is a demographic that has always occupied the highest stratum of society—financially, politically, physically, socially. And while people don't like to admit it, social change is a zero-sum game. The gains of other demographic groups come at a cost to those previously advantaged. I hope we can all agree that it is necessary and commendable for these power shifts to occur, but the velocity of change has been brutal for white men.

I call this moment we're in right now "the great leveling." Yes, the playing field is becoming more level for so many marginalized groups. But there's another reading of the phrase: White guys are getting absolutely steamrolled. All of the built-in advantages of white masculinity are being rendered moot or, worse, toxic, and it's no surprise how these men are reacting. They are the group with the least practice at managing setback, the least institutional resilience to hardship. Sometimes there is a real human toll to modern progress, and the resultant death throes of white male supremacy have proved ugly to watch.

I keep hearing the word "grit" used as a catchall term for perseverance . . . adaptability . . . the strength to overcome obstacles. White men don't have any grit because they never needed it before. I don't mean to suggest that none of them ever faced a challenge. Or that working a job in manual labor or enduring a personal tragedy doesn't require toughness. I'm saying that white men are literally the only demographic that has never faced prejudice, and therefore their grit muscles are atrophied.

So what does that lead to? Dave Parcell had a few bad breaks, no doubt. He lost his business. His opportunities narrowed. His identity as a provider and leader had been taken away. And how did he react? He tried to cheat his way into something he didn't deserve. Instead of finding a way forward that didn't disadvantage others, he thought he was entitled to get ahead. He believed he deserved it because that was all he had ever known. And when that status was threatened, he was capable of anything.

That's the fragility of white masculinity. And after all those rationalizations and justifications, we're left with a complicated question: Do these people, this newly challenged generation of white men, do they deserve any sympathy?

I can't get there.

Jeannette Parcell (*mother*): I know why Dave did it. I don't need all that fancy language. He felt like a loser and couldn't take it. Everyone saw that, once the truth came out. And they had every right to judge our family. How could you not?

Tommy O'Brien (*employee, Geary Home & Garden*): Not cool, man. That's what I thought when I found out. I was busting my ass looking for her, you know what I mean? I was spending money on gas, driving around, hiking through the woods, missing work, and it was all fake? It hurt, I'm not gonna lie. I lost a lot of respect for Dave.

Mike Snyder (*local news*): Frederick is an honest town. Dave took advantage of that. Before the scandal, no one ever assumed the worst in their neighbor. It's different now. He stole our innocence, in a way. You can't put a price on that. No jail sentence can fix that. I think he really woke this town up to the evils in the world. That'll be his legacy.

Miriam Rosen (*teacher*): When they found Sara dead, I was in shock for days. It took a while for the whole story to come out. And when it did . . . it was terribly hard for me. Juilliard, Juilliard, Juilliard. People really latched on to that part of it. The program has created a scholarship in Sara's name. No one knew that I was the one who pushed her to apply. I didn't even tell my husband. I just wept.

Veronica Yang (*principal*): Our students were put on a traumatic roller coaster. First Sara was missing. Then she was dead. And then we found out it was all supposed to be fake and Sara was in on it? Part of healing for a community is having a place to direct our sympathy. These events made that impossible to find. Our kids felt lied to and taken advantage of. Many of them were angry at Sara.

Olivia Weston (*friend*): It really hurt. We never kept anything from each other. And then she literally used us as pawns in her little game. Even the last thing she ever said to me—"I need to run back to get my backpack"—was a lie. It ruined all the other memories from our friendship. I started to question what else she had lied about.

Nellie Spencer (*friend*): I forgive Sara. Olivia never understood—her family was rich compared to mine and Sara's. I get what she was trying to do. It was a cool idea, in a way, it just got out of control. I just wished she would have told us. I would have helped.

Olivia Weston (*friend*): I wish I could have shaken her and told her she didn't need to do it! She was pretty and popular and talented and happy . . . it made no sense.

Nellie Spencer (*friend*): It didn't occur to me right away, but eventually, I remembered and put it together. Sara had said something to me about her dad, maybe a year before. I don't feel comfortable sharing all the details, but I know she was scared for him. She had seen something that freaked her out. My grandpa committed suicide when I was eleven. If I had to go camp out in the woods for a week to stop him from doing that, I would have, too.

Olaf Leclerq (*ice cream shop owner*): I was the one who set up the local reward fund. Put my own money into it. Every local business chipped in, almost every family, too. People around here don't have a lot to give, but they all scraped up something. And how could you not? Who wouldn't want to help find Sara? We had it up to sixty thousand dollars. And then we were all humiliated.

Molly Lowe (*professor of sociology*): Whether he knew it or not, Dave Parcell was tapping into a cultural sweet spot. The journalist Gwen Ifill actually coined the term in 2004—"missing white woman syndrome." It refers to the sensationalized news coverage and disproportionate attention given to the disappearance of white women.

Front-page newspaper stories. Twenty-four-seven TV coverage. Social media campaigns. Celebrity advocates. This treatment is almost solely reserved for missing white women, even though their numbers pale in comparison to women of color. The breathless coverage creates a feedback loop: more attention, more demand, more engagement, more profit. It incentivizes news organizations to sensationalize these exceedingly rare events.

There is thinly veiled racism at play here, of course. White women are more likely to be portrayed as victims rather than complicit in the circumstances that led to their disappearance. They are more likely to be described with positive attributes—say, beauty queen—rather than negative ones—single mother, college dropout, et cetera. Even as they suffer from the same crime, the stakes for white women are implied to be higher, the fall from civilized society into a criminal underworld more jarring, more tragic. This trope is embedded into America's foundation myth—go watch John Wayne ride around in *The Searchers* if you don't believe me.

Sara Parcell fit this archetype perfectly. A happy, pretty, white teenager, relatively well off, from a quiet, mostly white community. Dave had to know how the world would react to the idea of her going missing. "Activate the search party!" He chummed the waters perfectly that first night on his doorstep—a beatific photo of his daughter, an appeal for help—and then he sat back and let the machine do the rest. Before long, everyone in the country knew Sara's name.

Becca Santangelo (*SareBears*): We fell in love with Sara when we thought she was kidnapped. It was easy to think something like that could have happened to me or my little sisters. For those weeks she was missing, I spent pretty much every minute thinking about her. One night, out of solidarity, I went into my closet, scrunched down in the corner, and stayed there for the whole night, cramped, dark, uncomfortable. I thought that might be what Sara was going through. I thought that if she could sense someone else was going through the same thing with her, she'd feel a little stronger. That's how much I related to her.

Then, when we found out she was lying to us, that she was part of it . . . I didn't believe it. It took me a while to finally accept. It was like she died twice—first she died for real, and then, when the truth came out, the version of Sara that we all knew, the girl we loved who was honest and perfect, she died after that.

The second one hurt worse.

Bruce Allen Foley (*Unfounded*): Well, well, well. Didn't I tell you this stuff was all fake? I'm not your average Internet crackpot—Yale undergrad, poetry major, if you can believe that. Then a fellowship year abroad in Hungary. Then Dartmouth Law. I know my stuff. Sometimes there's a detail here or there that we don't have figured out, but we knew this girl wasn't missing. Hardly any of them ever are. It just turned out that besides doing the Deep State's bidding, the dad was also trying to make a buck or two. That sums up America for you—don't believe what you see on TV, and keep a firm grip on your wallet.

Now, even after the dad "confessed" to everything—please note my air quotes there—I'm still not sold that's how it went down. No way. He might still be in character even in prison. Hell, they probably don't even keep him there, I'm sure he just makes an appearance once in a while, and then they sneak him out the back door. Yup, I think it was a lot more complicated than how they made it sound. This was no random small-town grift. I think it goes up a lot of levels.

Brandon Grassley (*neighbor*): Dave and Sara's scam ruined our lives. Notice I say Dave *and* Sara. A lot of people just talk about it as Dave's idea and give her a pass, but no, Sara was in on it from the beginning. I can't ever forgive her for that.

When I was told the truth, I was enraged, obviously. What they had done . . . it was personal to me. And looking back now, it's just sad. None of this awfulness needed to happen. My dad would be fine. Sara would be alive. The trick they played on all of us, that she was really missing, truly in danger . . . it felt so real, especially to me. She was my neighbor, we grew up together. I was desperate to find her, to help in any way I could. I joined the SareBears group, I was messaging with them every day. We all had different skills, we thought if we teamed up, we'd be able to figure out where she was. But it was more complicated than we ever imagined. That's why it ended in tragedy.

Olivia Weston (*friend*): I feel bad about what we did to Mr. Grassley, about the role I played in that. And sometimes I think about how we always treated Brandon . . . we should have been nicer.

Travis Haynes (*bus driver*): Fuck Dave Parcell and his sketchy-ass plan. What did I ever do to deserve getting dragged into it and attacked like that? Nothing but serve this country honorably and drive his daughter safely to school, back and forth, every day, picking up that endless stream of trash. He tried to make me out to be a child molester! Well, karma's a coldhearted bitch . . . look where he is now.

Felix Calderon (*detective*): Dave told us everything after we found Sara's body. No more lies or obfuscating, it all poured out of him. My first reaction? Just sadness. It was so pointless, so unnecessary. The really lucky people in this world, they can go their whole lives without being touched by violence. This family had that life, then they pretended they didn't, and ultimately, it was thrust upon them. They tried to dabble in make-believe violence. Then they learned it could be real. I was truly just sad for them. And it was a bleak reminder: Our capacity to imagine what people are capable of is always surpassed by reality.

Casey Hawthorne (*producer*): It turned out Dave was a hustler. And he was hustling me. Beyond the obvious tragedy, simply on a personal level, I was rocked to my core to be manipulated so badly. I was the sucker, and it changed me. As a person, and how I do my job.

Humility, that's the word. It was a reminder that I don't always know everything.

Felix Calderon (*detective*): Later, after the sadness, the humiliation and the rage set in. Dave had played me from jump street. Made me out to be a fool when all I ever did was try to help his family.

Of course, he wasn't doing it literally right under my nose, like he was to Casey. She's the one who should have known sooner.

Casey Hawthorne (*producer*): Oh, that's rich coming from . . . let me check . . . an actual detective!

I wasn't investigating Dave, Felix was. I was filming him. Whatever Dave wanted us to see, that's what he showed us.

Felix Calderon (*detective*): Dave said it himself: Sara would have been home in a few days if Casey never showed up.

Casey Hawthorne (*producer*): There were good guys and bad guys in this whole mess. Of all the good guys who could've stopped it, who *should* have stopped it, Felix is at the top of the list. It was pathetic that he didn't. Thank God he's barely a cop anymore. The streets are safer, I'm sure.

Felix Calderon (*detective*): She's the poster child for this whole dead girl content boom. Her entire career now is finding these tragedies and turning them into entertainment. Dollars for trauma. She's the reason people like Dave think they can get rich by playing cops and robbers. Hell, I wouldn't be surprised if she found out the truth from Dave and kept her mouth shut. It made for good TV, right?

I do wonder about that sometimes.

Casey Hawthorne (*producer*): Fuck him for suggesting that. Me? In on it? Seriously, he can kiss my ass.

Dave Parcell (*father*): It was me, it was only me. No one else is to blame.

Manny only planted the seed. Sara went along with it for my benefit. Jeannette found out too late to stop it. Casey was totally in the dark. It was my plan, I was in charge, and I take full responsibility for what happened.

But the plan was supposed to be one specific thing—I never expected it to turn into what it did. I never expected Jack's video. I never expected Casey and her show, then the spotlight and all the attention. When that happened, I thought I could manage the new version. After my interrogation, I honestly thought we were home free.

That's what I hoped, at least, but the reality was much different: Things were spiraling out of control everywhere I looked. Those next couple weeks were a nightmare.

And I hope it goes without saying: I never meant for any of them to die.

CHAPTER 11

"Fires Everywhere"

Dave Parcell (*father*): I had a lot of problems to deal with. Every time I turned around, there was a new crisis.

The scariest one was Jeannette. She was falling apart. Look, I understood—she was worried about Sara, and then you add the pressure of the TV show, it was a lot to take. She was staying up all night, constantly looking out the windows. Sleeping all day. Picking at her nails, tiny dots of blood on all her clothes. Disappearing for hours at a time. She wouldn't let the camera crew go with her. I'd ask what she was doing. She'd always say, "I need some breathing room." I was worried.

The craziest part was that for so long, Jeannette had stressed out about money, and now we were rolling in it. I think she was just prone to finding something to work herself up about, in good times and bad.

Jack Parcell (*brother*): My mom was turning into a different person. She was jumpy, she snapped at me. She used to cook us dinner every night. Now she gave me frozen pizza over and over. And I don't think she ate once while Sara was gone.

Dave Parcell (*father*): I was getting suspicious about where she was going. It's not that I didn't trust her, I just wanted to make sure she didn't accidentally screw things up.

So one day after she left, I followed her in my truck. Told Casey and her crew they couldn't come. It wasn't easy trailing her, but I stayed back and out of sight, half the time worrying if I was being followed myself. She drove across town to this run-down apartment complex. Parked in the lot, went up to one of the units. At this point, I was a little scared. I didn't know what she was doing there.

I walk up after her. Get to the door. My heart's pounding. I knock. I can hear the people inside stop moving. I wait. Nothing. So I finally take a step back and slam my shoulder through the door.

I end up sprawled out on the floor inside the apartment. And I'm looking up at my wife and Travis Haynes—the freaking bus driver! Thankfully, they're not fucking or anything like that, I know what you're thinking. But it was still ridiculous.

Travis Haynes (*bus driver*): This family, man. It was like they were obsessed with me.

Dave Parcell (*father*): Travis grabs a liquor bottle, starts swinging it around, screaming at me. Jeannette jumps in front of me, tries to calm him down. I have no idea what's going on, so she's also trying to reassure me. She pushes me out of the apartment, Travis yelling at us, and we make it out to the walkway, go downstairs, I throw her in my truck and peel out. I pulled over a few minutes later and just looked at her. She starts crying and then explains why she was there.

Oxy. My wife was hooked on OxyContin. And I was the person who pushed her there.

I realized then: I had to tell her.

Jeannette Parcell (*mother*): Sixteen days. Sixteen days he let me believe our daughter was missing.

He was never even planning on telling me. But I got so bad, he tracked me down and found out I was popping pills like breath mints. Well, excuse me! I'm reading stories about my daughter being in some sex dungeon or dead in a ditch, and yes, I was freaking out about it.

And then Dave told me she was fine. He said, "She's fine, it's all fake, we did it together, me and her . . . I promise you, Sara is fine."

I didn't understand. He kept explaining, over and over, and finally I just started sobbing. Staring into his eyes, I knew he was telling the truth—Sara was alive . . . she had never been taken. Instantly, the awful sickness that had been gripping my body fell away. I hugged Dave, I squeezed him, I threw myself into him. It was about thirty seconds of pure relief, joy, gratitude, before the anger came. I started hitting him, screaming. He let me tire myself out, absorbing all the blows. When I was done, I sat back, chest heaving, weeping, snot and tears and happiness all mixed together. We sat there in his truck, catching our breath, and then he apologized for keeping it from me for so long.

Dave Parcell (*father*): It was a relief to tell Jeannette. The whole time I was figuring out the plan, I knew this would be the hardest part— making Jeannette go through everything as if it were real. But I had to keep her out of it, she never would have let it happen. I knew once I told her, she wouldn't be happy with me, but at least I could relax around her. And I think I saved her, too . . . she was going down a dark road.

Jeannette Parcell (*mother*): I demanded to go see her, but Dave wouldn't let me. He thought it was too risky—it might freak Sara out, and it would be too difficult for us both to disappear for half a day. Okay, then forget visiting, I wanted to bring her home! I threatened to tell the cops, but he kept explaining that I should be relieved—excited, even. He said we were in great shape. Sara was fine. Money was coming in. No one else knew.

He told me I had to get on board. If we blew it up now, Sara would be in trouble. He'd go to jail. But not if we followed the plan. He had a valid point, but I never should have listened.

Look, you have to understand—he convinced me there was no danger, that Sara wasn't at risk. That she was in the safest place in the world, no one else even knew where she was. "Two more weeks," he said. Then he painted a picture of our life after this was over: all of the stress and tension gone, Sara at Juilliard, Jack getting braces from the good orthodontist instead of the strip-mall guy, a real vacation for the two of us! I wanted to believe that was possible. I know I should have gone that very moment and scooped Sara up and dealt with the consequences. But I believed Dave.

Dave Parcell (*father*): Jeannette was handled. But I still had a more complicated problem: Sara was getting restless.

I had never planned on visiting her at the Boy Scout camp. But after we made the deal with Casey, I had to go up there. I had to tell Sara not to leave and meet Manny three days after she went off the grid, like we had planned. And I had to bring her some more supplies. And even if it sounded crazy, I had to tell her they were filming a reality show about our family while she was gone. Man, did she get a kick out of that. Sorry, not a "kick," I just mean she couldn't believe it. Like it blew her mind that me, Jeannette, and Jack were going to be on TV. And that Jack had caused the whole thing by posting one of his videos. The last time she'd seen him, he was filming himself eating cereal off his nose!

Then she stopped me, a serious look on her face, and asked how her brother was doing. She had always known that, for the plan to work, Jack would have to believe she was really missing for a few days. She hated that part of it, and now it was dragging on even longer, weighing on her. I told her, trying to set her mind at ease, that he was hanging in. I couldn't tell her anything that would make her want to rush home.

Sara's setup at Timber Ridge wasn't too bad. The cabins were all closed for the winter, but it was easy enough to pry open a door. There were bed frames inside. She had a sleeping bag, an inflatable camping mat. No plumbing, but there was an outhouse. She needed a lot of water, but it's not like she had to hike it in herself. A week before this all went down, back when no one in the world cared what we did, we drove up together, stocked the cabin with plenty of water. Books, magazines, crossword puzzles. A few MREs I got at a military surplus store. We practiced opening them up and getting them heated. Sara liked the spinach fettuccine the best. I had a bite—not too bad. Look, it wasn't the Ritz out there, but it was fine for a few days.

When I went that first time, I told her she had to sit tight for another week. But a week had come and gone. Casey was talking about doing ten episodes, maybe more. Each episode was fifty thousand dollars in our pocket. I needed to tell Sara she would have to be a little more patient, and I wanted to bring her a phone so we could communicate more easily.

The second time I got there, it was clear she was going stir-crazy. She had read all of this thousand-page Russian novel, *Anna Karenina*. Her food was running out. She couldn't look at any more spinach fettuccine. I restocked her, brought a few other luxury items. A better pillow, a hot pot for boiling water, stuff like that. Remember, we knew we had to get rid of all this stuff eventually, I was hauling bags of garbage down that mountain every time I left. She asked if I could bring her violin. It had been weeks since she'd practiced, and she was worried about getting rusty. I told her I couldn't risk bringing it and someone noticing it was gone from the house. She almost started to cry.

And there was something else going on. Of course I didn't know the full extent of it until later, but Sara, during her endless time alone, had been realizing how big this lie had grown. She processed that the reality show wasn't just a goofy whim; millions of people now thought she was missing. The magnitude of her dishonesty was eating at her. Whatever she had told herself about doing this to save me . . . I think it became harder for her to keep believing that.

Yeah, point-blank, Sara was over it. She didn't want to do it anymore. She . . . she asked if she could come home. And I had to say no.

I told her to hold out a little while longer. Things were working out so well. And to be honest, I needed to figure out exactly how to wrap things up. I had never planned for Casey and her cameras to be around when Sara was found. It was more complicated now.

Sara just looked at me. She said, "Dad, don't we already have enough for Juilliard?"

She was right, of course. But it was so easy to keep going. I told her to trust me. I made her stay there.

Jack Parcell (*brother*): Sara and my dad had a special relationship. I think he loved her more than me because she was so talented. I wasn't really that good at anything. He wanted me to be good at baseball. Made me play Little League. But then I would always get put in right field, and I could tell that embarrassed him.

And on the other end, I think Sara loved him more than my mom because he was the smarter of the two. Sara was really smart, and my mom drove her crazy sometimes. I don't think Sara ever wanted to do this stupid idea. It wasn't easy to say no to our dad, but she could do it. Not me, but Sara would. I don't know what made her too afraid this time.

Dave Parcell (*father*): I had Jeannette and Sara under control, but I still had to keep playing the part for Casey. She had made me out to be a monster. The show was a success, so I leaned into it. We were on the cover of *People* magazine. But I knew I would have to get the public back on my side eventually. When Sara returned home, there would be scrutiny, questions. I wanted viewers to be happy for us, not suspicious.

For Episode Four, I decided to make a big show of mailing in Sara's Juilliard application. You know, like as a gesture of faith that she was going to come home and get back to her life. Me, Jeannette, and Jack went to the post office together and sent it off. With Casey's crew, obviously. Said a little prayer, dropped it in the mail slot. I thought it was a cool moment.

Becca Santangelo (*SareBears*): We all thought that was a stunt. He was so thirsty to deflect suspicion, it was obvious he was doing that for the cameras. You can tell on these shows when people are just doing things for the audience.

Dave Parcell (*father*): It was nice that Jeannette was able to paddle in the same direction with me now. She got her sanity back once she knew Sara was fine. No more pills, crazy behavior. I explained to her that before Sara came home, people needed to like me again. She was a big help in framing me in a different light. We had a talk in front of the cameras where we thanked each other for being such a strong partner.

Jeannette Parcell (*mother*): I think it was only a few days when I was— what do you want to call it—acting. Dave said I had to. And now, because of those few days, no one will ever talk to me again. I lost all my friends.

Casey Hawthorne (*producer*): Dave and I had settled into a nice groove. He started thinking as a producer, almost, staging moments that made for great TV. If an exchange or moment didn't feel right, he offered to do it again. To shoot a second take, essentially. I know people at home like to think reality TV is all organic, but that's not how the sausage gets made.

Ezra Phillips (*pop culture critic*): Let's be honest . . . we never should have believed anything in Casey's show. Truth and entertainment are antithetical to each other. Once the profit motive comes into play, everyone has to become a carnival barker. Even the news networks need to play this game! The marketplace is ruthless. Survival of the fittest. Whoever tells the best story wins, truth be damned.

Alexis Lee (*associate producer*): I found all of Casey's artifice nauseating. She was treating the parents like creative partners. I thought we were there to document a tragedy. I thought the voyeurism was supposed to be a Trojan horse for something more meaningful. Maybe we could reveal some humanity to our viewers, inspire them to be kinder people. But Casey fell back onto all of her *Arm Candy* tricks. It felt like Dave and Jeannette were acting. Which, it turned out, they were.

Casey Hawthorne (*producer*): Alexis is a great example of a very specific type in Hollywood: someone who always has a critical thing to say but never a solution. It makes them feel smart to point out problems, but they never have the balls to be a leader, to take responsibility, to actually *solve* problems. Her attitude in Frederick was awful the whole time. And please spare me the holier-than-thou routine: Her actions essentially set in motion the events that got Sara killed.

Alexis Lee (*associate producer*): Wow. That claim would be laughable if the whole thing wasn't so sad.

Dave Parcell (*father*): As hard as I was working to get Casey to frame me in a better light, I didn't do any planning for the last part of my rehabilitation tour. The fake-missing-kids wacko did it all for me.

Bruce Allen Foley (*Unfounded*): We went to demonstrate in front of the Parcells' house. Big signs, I had a bullhorn, dozens of our Unfounded members had made it out to Frederick. The news crews ate it up. We were just trying to spread the truth: Sara Parcell wasn't missing . . . this was all a lie.

Mike Snyder (*local news*): I know it only encourages them when we put that footage on our broadcast, but it's still news. We tried to give it context: grieving family harassed by conspiracy theorists. Sadly, even with the negative framing, it just makes them more popular.

Dmitri Russo (*patrolman*): We can't do anything if they're assembling on public property. We can't do anything about the signs. They're despicable, but they have their rights.

Dave Parcell (*father*): I couldn't believe those people dared to come up to our house. Now, look, don't get me wrong, I realize I can't really be upset about what they were saying about Sara. There was a kernel of truth to their claims. But what they do to other families, the ones who are legitimately looking for their kids? It's barbaric. I couldn't let that go unchallenged.

I went out there with my softball bat. Casey and Zane were right behind me, filming.

We got into a shouting match. I grabbed his sign—"Sara Parcell Isn't Real"—and smashed it to pieces. He tried to grab it back from me, we fell onto my property, rolled around for a bit, and then the cops broke it up. Local guys, they were all on my side, they threw him in a cruiser. So I became known as the dad who fought the crazy people off my lawn. Not bad for my image.

Dmitri Russo (*patrolman*): Once Foley instigated a physical altercation on their property, we finally had cause to arrest him. We brought him down to the station. Started to book him for trespassing, but then the call came in from way above my pay grade. We had to let him go. I didn't understand it.

Bruce Allen Foley (*Unfounded*): I had friends in high places. District Attorney Christine Bell. We had a meeting the day before. She had a tough election coming up and was looking to bolster her grassroots donor list. Not only that, she had some bigger political ambitions. I assured her that my group had some very generous and loyal political donors. She got me out of that fix, and in turn, she can thank me for winning her race.

Christine Bell (*district attorney*): I am proud to have a wide-ranging donor list. Accepting political contributions is not an endorsement of any individual donor's beliefs. I don't recall ever having a formal meeting with Bruce Allen Foley, and I do not and have never had a relationship with the group Unfounded.

Felix Calderon (*detective*): It drove me nuts when Bell let Foley walk. But at that point, I still thought of him as a sideshow. I didn't have time to get in the mud with those two.

Dave Parcell (*father*): Jeannette. Sara. Casey. The Foley asshole. I had fires everywhere. I was running on fumes, sneaking around at night, but somehow I got it all under control. And then came the big problem: Manny called me. The guy who started it all suddenly wanted his money.

I slipped away and met him at the garage that night. I was already upset that he'd called me. We had agreed to have zero contact after that first planning session, and he had already tried to pin me down with the flat tires trick. When Manny eventually found Sara, I needed it to seem like he was just a guy I barely knew from around town, not some close friend. But now if anyone checked the phone records, we'd have to explain this call. I was pissed.

He was pissed, too. Remember, the original plan was supposed to play out over three or four days. But things changed. Manny saw what was going on with the show, obviously, the magazine covers and all that. Meanwhile, he's sweating it out, stuck answering uncomfortable questions from the cops because someone spotted the car he had taken from the shop. Manny thought we were getting rich, and he wanted a piece of that money. To skip town or I don't know what. And now he was saying he deserved credit for the whole idea, that he had led me straight to a jackpot and wanted a "finder's fee" on all our TV money, ten percent.

I told him I was happy to pay him what we'd agreed to . . . half the reward fund. And even that was generous . . . I hadn't figured out how to bring Sara back, but I didn't even need Manny involved anymore.

Manny didn't want to hear it. He wanted a taste of the money right then. He said he was at risk, too, being involved in this whole conspiracy, this fraud. I was like "Whoa, slow down there!" That was the first time he was using this language. He had presented the idea as a victimless little scam. But now he was like "Damn right, we are in the middle of a serious criminal conspiracy, and if you want me to keep my mouth shut, I'm going to need some money." He was blackmailing me, essentially.

I got angry. I told him there better not be a question about whether he was keeping his mouth shut. My life, my family, it hinged on him keeping his mouth shut. This wasn't negotiable. He told me that getting paid right away wasn't negotiable. Things got tense. He stepped into my space. He tried to make it out like he was in control, that he had all the leverage. In a way, he did. But I told him I was still calling the shots. He poked me right in the chest and demanded a bag of cash the next day. I pushed him off. He came back at me. I threw a punch. He grabbed a wrench. I tackled him so he couldn't smash me in the face. We crashed into something. And when we landed on the ground, he wasn't moving. Like, seriously not moving. Blood was pooling underneath his head. An awful groan came out of his body. I looked up and saw that he had smashed the back of his head against the edge of a steel tool chest. I had driven him straight into it.

I tried to wake him up. I tried to bring him back. Shaking him, shouting his name, doing the basic CPR I knew. But he was . . . gone. My God, the blood was just spilling out of his head. I didn't know what to do. If I'd thought he was still alive, I would have called for help, I swear. But I could tell there was no point. I ran out to my truck and drove away. Left him lying on the floor in the repair bay.

We were just arguing. It didn't need to turn physical. And even then . . . it was an accident. It wasn't murder. That's what they always called it afterward. They say I murdered Manny. No. It was an accident. A stupid accident, I swear. And everything else that happened from there on out . . . with Sara, with all of it, I promise, it was all . . . it was all just an accident.

Felix Calderon (*detective*): I arrived the next morning, after another mechanic found him and called it in. It was an ugly scene . . . and a shock to see in Frederick.

I thought there was a good chance we could solve it. There was a lot of evidence. Footprints, potential DNA, maybe surveillance footage. It was obvious that whoever killed Manny Crawford had not planned to do so and had not covered their tracks.

I started to work the scene. Then I got a phone call. My boss. I listened, my anger building and building, then hung up and walked away from Manny Crawford's body.

Thanks to Casey, I didn't have a job anymore.

CHAPTER 12

"Hashtag CaseCal!"

Casey Hawthorne (*producer*): *TMZ* had it first. I didn't have any warning. My phone just exploded.

Look, I shouldn't have been surprised. In the previous few weeks, other outlets had started generating content around our show, like little feeder fish riding a shark. It was the typical stuff: podcasts, recap blogs, Twitter polls. So I knew our show made news, and I was grateful for it. We were the center of a content ecosystem! I just never expected the news to be about me.

Ezra Phillips (*pop culture critic*): *TMZ* put out a breaking-news alert, you know, siren emojis, the whole nine. I remember the headline: "Producer and Detective Caught in Romantic Conspiracy." And then they spelled it all out, essentially that Casey and Detective Calderon were sleeping together. Canoodling, cavorting, secret tryst, "He's working the Case-y" . . . they had a lot of ways to describe it. Details from their date nights, speculation about their sexting from an unnamed source "close to the situation." I wanted to dismiss it as trashy gossip about two consenting adults, but something stopped me. And many others, I'm sure. It was more than gossip. One of them was investigating the disappearance of a teenage girl, and the other was making a reality show about it . . . there was something undeniably wrong about these two pairing off.

I think for a lot of people, this was the moment when the Sara Parcell case turned from mystery to circus. The public was already fascinated, but now they suddenly had opinions about the personal lives and behavior of the people surrounding it. It took on a meta quality and turned Casey into both chronicler and subject of her show.

Casey Hawthorne (*producer*): At first I didn't know how they found out. We had been discreet. I thought the only people who knew were Felix and my crew. Well, there you go. The answer became obvious after Alexis quit. She threw a grenade and then ran to the airport.

Alexis Lee (*associate producer*): Casey had a tiger by the tail, and she lost control of it. She was putting out a product that pretended to be this truthful look at a real investigation. But she was manipulating events, framing innocent people, doing anything to juice the ratings. And she still walked around with this haughty air of journalistic superiority.

Well, I know this: You can't be an objective observer when you're fucking the lead detective. Can we agree on that? I thought everyone—our audience, the Parcells, the people in Frederick—deserved to know the truth.

I had always made a little bit of extra cash feeding items to the tabloids. All of us did. Whenever I was working a show, a bunch of reporters would check in, and sometimes I'd give them a story. You know, so-and-so threw a tantrum on set, or this other chick had her boobs done. This is a common practice in our industry, and it's usually a win for all parties: Websites got content, our shows got publicity, and I got paid. My guy from *TMZ* happened to call when I was in Frederick. He asked if I had anything juicy. It was the same day Casey had made me return a salad with the wrong dressing. I was over the whole fucking thing. So I gave him the scoop, sat back, and waited for the show to blow up.

Casey Hawthorne (*producer*): And she wonders why she's never had another job in this town. I hope the two hundred bucks was worth it.

Zane Kelly (*camera operator*): We all knew something was going on. It didn't bother me or strike me as newsworthy. Good for Casey, I thought. Calderon was hot, he had those male-stripper-in-a-cop-uniform vibes. I wish I had been the one caught in a scandal with him.

Marcus Maxwell (*executive*): Oh, God. Casey's infamous misstep. It certainly didn't make me happy. I had been nervous about the concept to begin with. All my faith was in Casey. She was out there with no oversight, no safety net. I didn't think I had to tell her "Don't screw the help."

My assistant sent me the *TMZ* link. That kind of email landing in your inbox . . . you instantly know the rest of your day is ruined, can already hear the parade of lawyers, HR folks, marketing people in a panic. Everyone goes into siege mentality. But before all that started in earnest, I called Casey. Screamed at her. Got that off my chest.

Does the screaming ever make you feel better? I say yes, it is an important part of my crisis-management process. And then, because Casey is smarter than me, I asked what we needed to do next.

Casey Hawthorne (*producer*): It's sad but it's true: Any publicity is good publicity. I hadn't lied. I hadn't broken the law. Felix was never even featured in our show. If people wanted to gossip about me, that was their prerogative. But I wasn't going to dignify it with a response.

I told Marcus to mind his own business and keep letting me do my job.

Zane Kelly (*camera operator*): The paparazzi started showing up. They were taking photos of us while we filmed, it was a bizarre house of mirrors. For me, stuck in that bubble, I didn't realize *Searching for Sara* had become such a sensation. I guess it was the number one show at the time.

I'm not gonna lie, it sucks being filmed like that, not having privacy, worried you can't scratch your nose without looking like an idiot. I know that might sound hypocritical, but at least the people we filmed had signed up for it.

Anthony Pena (*editor*): Casey was playing with fire, and she got burned. I'm sure that was half the appeal to begin with, and I'm not the guy who's gonna look down my nose at a proper dangerous liaison. But I did ask her what we were going to do about it. She said, "We are going to keep doing what we came here to do: find Sara . . . document the search . . . share the Parcells' ordeal with the world." She leaned harder into our work. I think before the news broke, she felt her professional reputation was at stake. Now it was personal. If our show didn't help Sara come home safely, Casey was going to get blamed. Her choices, her decisions, were going to be part of the failure. Everything was on the line for her.

Molly Lowe (*professor of sociology*): The conflict of interest is obvious. That's not what fascinated me about it, however. I'll leave that to the legal experts. To me, the Casey-Calderon scandal was the apotheosis of the interplay between sex and violence in our entertainment landscape. It was Casey and Calderon saying the quiet part out loud, an inadvertent admission of the central tenet of the true-crime explosion: Violence turns us on.

One of these people was there to investigate a crime. The other to document it. They were as close as you could get to the crime without being literal participants. By falling into bed together, they demonstrated the intoxicating effects of being proximate to danger. The universal truth they were proving—violence as a stimulant, physiologically and emotionally—is something that our country has never properly reckoned with. Quite the contrary: We've normalized it to the point where it is the most popular form of entertainment. Casey and Calderon took this one step further—the violence they were proximate to . . . it was real. Then to use that real violence as an aphrodisiac? It's chilling.

Becca Santangelo (*SareBears*): We all loved it when the news dropped about Casey and Detective Calderon. A few people in the group were already shipping them, hashtag CaseCal! I always hoped they would get back together, they were a cute couple. And I know from following Casey's Instagram all these years . . . it's not like she's found anyone better.

Bruce Allen Foley (*Unfounded*): Isn't that a big thing in Hollywood— on-set romances? These godless showbiz heathens can't help themselves. And can you blame them? These are fundamentally broken people, leading lives of profound loneliness that they paper over with the stories they make up and the superficial relationships they jump in and out of.

I'm not saying I know for sure whether this particular relationship was real or staged, but I'll say this: If you're trying to distract people from a fake investigation about a fake crime, a good old-fashioned sex scandal will do the trick. You'd be surprised at how dumb average Americans are. Wave a shiny object in front of them, and they'll follow you blindly while the real world passes them right by. Do you have any idea what Bill Clinton did to Fort Knox when the Lewinsky chick had everyone's attention?

Mike Snyder (*local news*): Totally unprofessional on Casey's part. But that's the type of behavior the Parcells signed up for when they sided with the Hollywood interlopers over the local pros.

Nellie Spencer (*friend*): I heard "sex scandal" and "*Searching for Sara*" and I almost fainted. But it wasn't about me and Coach Walker, thank God. Turns out that was like the only secret in Frederick that never came out.

I didn't think the Casey news was that big of a deal. Props to her for getting it in. People hook up, it's no one else's business.

Olivia Weston (*friend*): I was disappointed in Casey. I looked up to her. She was supposed to be helping to find my best friend.

Brandon Grassley (*neighbor*): It made me lose faith that we'd ever find Sara. If this was what the cops and TV show were doing . . . there had to be a better way.

Travis Haynes (*bus driver*): Casey's a baddie. Can't stop, won't stop.

Felix Calderon (*detective*): What is there to say? It was awful having everyone in the world invade my private life. No warning whatsoever, it all crashed down on me at the Shell station while I was looking at Manny Crawford's body. My boss called and told me to come see him ASAP. I could see everyone else at the garage looking at their phones, then at me. When I hung up, I saw the story. Absolute pit in my stomach . . . I knew I was screwed.

Freaking traveling salesperson . . . I should have known better from the start.

I got back to the station, and the fallout was pretty quick: Suspended without pay pending further investigation. Leave your badge and gun, go home and wait to hear from us. Walk of shame through the station, out to the parking lot, drove home, sat down, and suddenly, I had nothing to do. Sara still missing, Manny Crawford dead but still warm, and I'm on the couch, told explicitly to stay away from these cases. It was humiliating.

I blamed Casey, of course. I hadn't told anyone, so it had to come from her side. Maybe she didn't leak the story herself, but she definitely ran her mouth. For all I knew, this was part of some game she was playing—with me, with the show, I didn't know. I opened a bottle of whiskey and got pretty lit, thinking about what I was going to do the next time I saw her.

Christine Bell (*district attorney*): Detective Calderon humiliated law enforcement with his lewd and dishonorable behavior. We had no choice but to relieve him of his duty. The vigilante escapades that came after he was no longer employed by our county . . . I didn't approve.

Dmitri Russo (*patrolman*): I couldn't believe it. He had always been so by the book. And he was like a robot, emotionally. Worked all the holidays when everyone wanted to be with their families. Never came out drinking with us. I can't even really picture him on a date. To carry on with Casey after he found out who she was . . . I guess he was really into her.

Dave Parcell (*father*): Oh, man, that was some interesting news to get, wasn't it? My first instinct was to panic. These are two people I'm bending over backward to deceive, and now I find out they're romantically involved? It didn't seem good. If they wanted to compare notes, put their heads together, I was sure they'd be able to poke some holes in the story I had cooking. But on the other hand, I had seen them together— they hated each other! So once it seemed like this was a love connection gone wrong, that they were enemies now, I started to see that this spat was actually helpful to me. They were already so territorial about access and information, nothing was being shared between them. Now that I knew about their little secret, I figured I could exploit it.

Jeannette Parcell (*mother*): Looking back, I see it as another lie we were fed by the people who were supposedly helping us. That detective berated us and judged us for letting Casey into our lives . . . and at the same time, he was chasing her tail?

Dave started the lies, and one after another, everyone else piled on with their own lies, always looking out for themselves. And then, at the end of all the lies, Sara was dead.

Dave Parcell (*father*): The timing of the story could not have been better. It was the morning they found Manny's body. I had left him that night in a rush and had no idea what the cops would find. I was waiting for them to come arrest me. If a cop car had pulled up to our house that day, I was ready to tell Jeannette to get Sara. The jig would have been up. But now, out of nowhere, the two people sniffing around me were distracted and wasting energy on their own personal stuff. And the only competent detective in town was thrown off the case. It was a miracle.

I'm sorry, I don't want to make it seem like I was happy. I was torn up about what happened to Manny, I really was. What happened to him, accidentally, because of me. I knew he had a family and all that. Daughters. I had always said from the get-go, no one should actually get hurt in this little scheme. Aside from Frank Grassley being run around a bit, but I meant no one should get physically hurt. Now Manny was dead. My family was getting paid and Manny was dead, it wasn't right. I had to let go of the fantasy I'd been telling myself, that this would all work out. But I couldn't dwell on it, either. It's not like I could go back and fix it. We had to press on.

Evelyn Crawford (*Manny's wife*): My husband was killed in cold blood and left on a dirty garage floor. Dave can go on talking out his neck about how Manny was threatening to blackmail him. I'm not trying to hear it. I learned a long time ago: You know how you can tell Dave Parcell is lying? His lips are moving.

Felix Calderon (*detective*): Me and the whiskey bottle in my living room. Manny Crawford, dead—take a shot. Sara Parcell, still missing—take a shot. Casey Hawthorne, Hollywood queen of manipulation and destruction—take a shot. After a few hours stewing alone, I took my pity party to the hotel bar. I knew Casey would have to pass through at some point.

Casey Hawthorne (*producer*): When I got back to the hotel after we were done shooting for the day, Felix was at the bar, loaded for bear. He screamed at me across the lobby, "What the hell did you do?"

Felix Calderon (*detective*): I didn't scream. I don't ever raise my voice.

Casey Hawthorne (*producer*): He wobbled over and put a finger in my face. Literally was poking my chin. I was so embarrassed for him. Everyone was watching, people were taking their phones out to film.

Felix Calderon (*detective*): I asked her why she was trying to ruin my life.

Casey Hawthorne (*producer*): I told him that the leak hadn't come from me.

Felix Calderon (*detective*): I told her she was a liar and a whore. I meant it in the context of her show, her career, but I think she took it the wrong way.

Casey Hawthorne (*producer*): He said some things that were unforgivable. I fired right back at him. I told him he was a joke and a failure. That he ran away from a real city because he couldn't handle the pressure, and the same thing was happening all over again. I told him he just wanted someone to blame for not being able to find Sara. I told him to look in the mirror.

Felix Calderon (*detective*): I asked her how she could look at *herself* in the mirror. Coming to our town to profit off the misery of others. She was the failure who couldn't cut it as a real artist, so she quit and started cashing checks making mindless drivel for zombies. I called her a death merchant.

Casey Hawthorne (*producer*): I said Sara probably *was* dead, because of his incompetence.

Felix Calderon (*detective*): I told her I bet she was happy about that, it would make for a nice end to her show.

Casey Hawthorne (*producer*): I told him to get out of my way and never speak to me again.

Felix Calderon (*detective*): I told her it'd be my dream to never lay eyes on her again.

Casey Hawthorne (*producer*): And I thought that would be it. I hoped that would be it. That we never had to cross paths again.

But thank God we did. Otherwise I probably wouldn't be alive.

CHAPTER 13

"Time to Fight for Your Life"

Casey Hawthorne (*producer*): What I remember most about that particular time is the general malaise that had settled around the town. It was raining every day. Everyone caught the same cold. My crew was starting to resent being stuck in Frederick. We were reeling from Alexis's betrayal, and now we were shorthanded. I had been humiliated on the Internet and screamed at by Felix. My energy was waning. The Parcells weren't being as cooperative with the show. I was getting the sense that we didn't have much more story to tell.

And most of all, there was that one specific dark cloud hanging over everything: It was starting to feel like there was no hope of finding Sara.

Olivia Weston (*friend*): I had been going every day to where we had the vigil in the town square. I would leave something different for Sara each time, a note or a small gift. I burned a mix CD with all of our favorite songs. But after a few weeks went by, I couldn't do it anymore. Life kinda went back to normal. We had our first track meet without Sara running the relay with me. We hung her singlet, you know, her running jersey, on the fence. But then some people said that made it seem like she was definitely dead. There was a whole argument about it, so we stopped bringing it to our meets. It was like she was already starting to fade away.

Miriam Rosen (*teacher*): We were entering that moment when maybe it made more sense to grieve rather than hope. No one wanted to say it out loud, but you felt it in the air. The tight-knit community that had mustered into action . . . we were exhausted and ready to face reality.

Tommy O'Brien (*employee, Geary Home & Garden*): We had stopped the searches. I was actually relieved. After the first few days, you started to realize, "I'm not looking for Sara anymore, I'm looking for a corpse." I really didn't want to find her body.

Mike Snyder (*local news*): I think it was day nineteen. That's when we finally led our broadcast with a different story. A new zoning law that allowed people to build an additional unit on their property. I remember the debate we had in the newsroom: Is this more important to people's lives than the same disappointing update on Sara Parcell? The answer was yes.

We still checked in on the story here and there, but after the initial frenzy, there wasn't anything new to say. Sara had disappeared into thin air. Once Travis Haynes and Frank Grassley were cleared as suspects, and once they couldn't make anything stick on Dave, there were no new leads. It was confounding, but there was nothing to report.

Casey Hawthorne (*producer*): I needed a plan for our sixth episode. I decided to focus on Sara's peers at school, how they were coping with everything. It was boring. Marcus called me and asked where the series was going. I didn't have an answer. We had a massive audience who wanted resolution. But this was the risk we took, producing the show in real time—we made an implicit promise for closure before we knew if it was possible. I was starting to feel like we'd lost the bet.

Anthony Pena (*editor*): I was ready to bounce from Frederick. Coachella was coming up. I wanted to be back in Cali by then.

Casey Hawthorne (*producer*): I was already on thin ice with Marcus after the Felix story broke. He stuck his neck out for me and let me keep going. I promised him I would figure something out for a series finale. He wanted to hype the shit out of it with promos, but I told him to hold off. Not until I figured out how to end things.

That's when I was summoned by Dave and Jeannette.

Dave Parcell (*father*): I was starting to breathe easier about not being connected to Manny. No one had come to ask me about it, let alone haul me off to death row. I saw that Casey and her show were running out of steam. I figured it was time to wrap things up.

Jeannette Parcell (*mother*): Dave wanted to bring Sara home. He thought it was time. I was thrilled, but I was also nervous. Of course I was desperate to see her, but I knew this was the moment when we had to do everything right or it would all blow up. Dave had a plan. It wasn't very good, but I thought it was good enough.

Dave Parcell (*father*): We had always planned for Sara to make her way out of the woods to a specific spot on the road where Manny would pick her up. When Manny died, I thought we were screwed. But then I realized: Manny was only important because he was the silent partner we needed in order to split the reward money. Remember, we originally set this up to take advantage of the local reward fund that would pop up. Our family didn't need to collect that anymore, we had the money from Casey's show. That payout could go to an honest-to-God Good Samaritan! I would even chip in the chump change I had promised from my bank account.

But the point is, we didn't need Manny or anyone else in on the plan. I went to visit Sara one final time and filled her in on the new marching orders. She was supposed to wait one more day, then pack up the camp, and leave. When she made it down to a road, Sara could be found by anyone, really, and she would follow the same script when the authorities questioned her: a vague description about her ordeal, extreme fatigue, relief to be home. Once we had her back, Jeannette and I could protect her from repeated questioning. Her reluctance would be understandable and hopefully respected. Yes, the mystery of who had taken her would never be solved, but we would all focus on the miracle of her coming home.

Jeannette Parcell (*mother*): I hated the idea of having to be fake about everything in front of the cameras. Can you imagine us pretending to celebrate when Sara came home? I thought it would be impossible to pull off. So I pointed it out to Dave and said, "Why not end the show now, so we don't have to deal with them when all this goes down?"

Dave Parcell (*father*): Jeannette was right. Bringing Sara back after Casey was gone made more sense. Less attention, less scrutiny, less pretending, less chance we get caught. We had plenty of money already. There was no need to get greedy.

We knew Casey wouldn't like it, but we called her over to the house to tell her we were done.

Casey Hawthorne (*producer*): Out of nowhere, they canceled the show. Pulled the plug like they were suddenly these network big shots, and without any good explanation. I was suspicious. They said the idea had run its course, they were looking forward to regaining their privacy, and they didn't feel like it was helping to find Sara.

I was disappointed. I didn't know what was motivating them, but I couldn't tell them they were wrong. The vision we'd had of millions of people on alert to find Sara hadn't borne any fruit. We got thousands of tips to the social media accounts we set up—Sara is hiking through Australia, a lock of her hair is in this rental car, everything you can imagine—but none of them amounted to anything.

Dave and Jeannette had the contractual right to stop at any time, but I still gave a half-hearted plea to keep going. Pulling the plug right then felt so . . . unfulfilling. I explained there were millions of fans invested in their family. If we couldn't get closure on the search for Sara, we could at least end with an intentional statement of hope and gratitude.

Dave Parcell (*father*): Casey made her case, gave us the whole song and dance again. But we didn't need her anymore.

Casey Hawthorne (*producer*): They said no. And just like that, I was screwed. I had promised something special to a lot of people—the Parcells, the viewers, my boss—but now I had nothing up my sleeve to wrap up the show.

I went back to my hotel defeated and humiliated. On my way into the lobby, Marcus called. I picked up and reluctantly started to share the news. He started screaming at me, but we lost service and got cut off when I stepped in the elevator.

I was distracted. I should have been more careful. But I didn't notice who was following me or what was happening to me until it was too late.

Felix Calderon (*detective*): I don't remember how I got home after my fight with Casey in the hotel lobby. I certainly didn't drive myself, thank God. But that meant I'd left my car behind in the parking lot. I woke up the next morning, nursed a pretty bad hangover, didn't have to report to work, obviously, so in the late afternoon, I took a long, depressing walk back to the hotel.

I noticed something in the parking lot. Bruce Allen Foley's car, an old, scratched-up beige minivan. A dozen bumper stickers proclaiming the world is flat or whatever. The kind of car you give a wide berth on the highway.

Over the previous few weeks, I'd gotten in the habit of keeping an eye out for him. Our department had caught on pretty quickly: No matter where he showed up, it always ended in trouble. There was nothing crazy about the van being parked at the hotel, but when I saw it, I went out of my way to walk past and do a once-over. The car was empty, but there was a pile of cigarette butts under the driver's window. As if he'd been sitting there for a while. One of the discarded butts was still smoking.

Not my problem anymore, right? That's my first thought. I'm about to get in my car and drive home, but I can't help myself, I head for the lobby instead. I wanted to make sure he wasn't causing a scene there. I walk in and don't see him. Go up to the woman at the front desk. Ask if she's seen him around. By then everyone in town knew this guy, most people hated him, obviously. She tells me that he passed through the lobby a few minutes earlier.

I think for a second. I had a funny feeling, but there was nothing going on as far as I could see. And besides, I was suspended. No badge, no gun. I couldn't even articulate what I was worried about. So I go back outside to my car.

As I walk through the lot, I stop and turn back to the building. Again, I couldn't help myself. Eighth floor, corner room. Casey's room. I peer up at it and see the shades. Pulled tight, the heavy curtains, too. I stood there staring. Casey and her ridiculous natural-light wake-up routine—when I stayed over in her room that first night, she had given a whole speech about the benefits of waking up from natural light. No alarm clock, shades wide open, just the sun rising . . . "caressing your eyelids." Yeah, real practical, I thought. But she made me do it that morning. To activate our serotonin or whatever.

Now I was standing in the parking lot, looking up at the curtains in her hotel room, and it didn't make sense. Casey would never have them closed like that. I didn't want to, but I called her, fully expecting her to pick up and yell at me—you know, "Stop stalking me, asshole." But there was no answer. Text her, no response. I almost got in my car, maybe I did, but I couldn't drive off. Before I knew it, I'm back in the hotel, walking quickly through the lobby.

Elevator, heart pumping, starting to sweat, jabbing the button over and over as if that makes it go faster. I get out on the eighth floor, start down the hallway, now I'm jogging. Reach Casey's door. Listen for a second, don't hear anything. Knock. Call her name. At this point, my sincere hope is that Casey answers in her sweatpants and curses me out all over again. That would be so much better than what I'm worried about. But she doesn't answer.

I take out my phone, try Casey again. Nothing. I'm thinking I need to call down to the station, have them send a unit over. But that's fifteen minutes. I'm already at the door. Maybe this can't wait fifteen minutes. I want to break the door down, but I can see it's too heavy. Solid steel, reinforced. I decide to try. I have to. If Casey is in there, in trouble—if anyone was in there, in trouble—I have to do it. I take a few steps back and brace myself to smash into it. And just as I'm ready to charge forward, I realize . . .

I'm wearing my jacket. Casey had slipped her key card into my pocket.

I reach in and there it is. I've got the key and I'm at her door. I don't hesitate—I slide it in and push the door open.

Casey Hawthorne (*producer*): When I got off the elevator and tried calling Marcus back, I realized the other person riding with me got off, too. I could sense him following me down the hallway.

Unfortunately, every woman alive has dealt with this. I knew what to do, how to kick him in the balls, punch him in the throat, all that good stuff. I was hoping it wouldn't come to that, that maybe I was being paranoid. I desperately wanted to get Marcus back on the line, I figured that would be enough. But just as Marcus picked up, the guy in the hallway caught up to me. I was about to turn and fight, about to scream, when I felt him press the gun into my back.

Very calmly and quietly, he leaned in to my ear and whispered: "Hang up the phone, keep quiet, and walk into your room." Feeling his breath on my neck like that . . . it was awful. I didn't know what to do. I had only bad options. I felt the gun jab firmly into my rib cage. So I followed his demands.

I unlocked my door, we stepped inside, and my heart sank when it closed behind us. I was terrified at what might come next. Then I turned around and I saw who it was.

That lunatic, Bruce Allen Foley.

Bruce Allen Foley (*Unfounded*): Everything had been building up to this moment. I was calling it the Revelation. I had known our movement needed something like this, a confession from inside the leadership who crafted these lies. Someone to confirm that these child abduction cases were all an excuse to trick citizens into giving up our privacy. We were always looking to find whistleblowers willing to admit they were paid crisis actors, but no one ever came forward. I decided it couldn't wait any longer. The Sara Parcell case was the last straw for me. If someone wouldn't confess voluntarily, I'd put them in a position where they had no choice.

Casey was the perfect vessel. Beautiful, blond, charismatic, telegenic, and it was obvious to me that she wasn't just a bit player, she was in a leadership position. How else could she be trusted to play such a prominent role? Of course I knew there were many levels above her, but those people didn't show their faces as readily. I couldn't very well kidnap the director of the CIA and make him confess on a livestream.

That was my plan. Subdue Casey, set up the camera, and stream her confession out to the world. I had been teasing the event for days—"The Revelation is coming" on Facebook, "The Revelation is coming" on Signal—and people were going crazy, speculating what exactly I had in store. I kept putting hints out there that it would be the coup de grâce of our movement.

So I packed up some equipment, waited for Casey in the parking lot, and followed her up to her room.

Casey Hawthorne (*producer*): He kept the gun pointed at me. I asked what he wanted. He said he'd explain everything after he put zip ties around my wrists. I was shaking, I didn't want him to, but I let him do it. Then he had me sit at the desk, and he secured me to the chair. He put some duct tape over my mouth so I couldn't scream. He pulled the curtains closed and disconnected the phone.

I realized I had made an awful mistake and started to cry; I suddenly remembered something from years earlier, some self-defense expert talking about home invasions, and he was adamant about one point: When the tape comes out, it's time to fight for your life. To scratch and claw and do whatever it takes to get free or kill them. Because it will probably be your last decent chance. But the tape had come out, and I had let the moment pass. I was bound and gagged and at his mercy.

Bruce Allen Foley (*Unfounded*): I never intended to hurt Casey. I'm a pacifist!

Casey Hawthorne (*producer*): Once I was secure, Foley opened his bag and started taking out all this camera equipment. He set up a tripod, a ring light, got the camera on, connected it to his laptop. Asked me for the Wi-Fi, but my mouth was taped shut. He found the hotel binder and flipped through it until he got the Internet info. Commented on the room service menu. It was surreal, something so mundane in the middle of a hostage situation. And then, once he had his precious Wi-Fi signal, he finally explained what he wanted from me.

Look, by this point I had known vaguely about these people for years. And had known about Foley specifically for the past few weeks, obviously. The head nutjob, the semi-famous one, the poster boy of Unfounded. He had been harassing the Parcells, had gotten in a fight with Dave, had shown up with his cronies wherever we were shooting and generally made a nuisance of themselves. But I thought of them as weirdos and idiots, not terrorists, not violent criminals. Clearly, I underestimated him. I should have known the first time I ever heard his name—who uses their middle name besides serial killers?

I sat there totally tied up as he broke it down for me: He wanted me to confess to helping facilitate a global conspiracy of fake child abductions. He wanted me to say that none of these events were real, they were orchestrated as a tool to take away civil liberties, and that by making a big deal of these fake crimes and putting them on TV, I was intentionally tricking the American public. And then he wanted me to explain the whole operation from top to bottom. I almost laughed through the duct tape. But I didn't. I was too scared.

Bruce Allen Foley (*Unfounded*): I didn't expect Casey to willingly confess everything. I knew she had been trained to resist and obfuscate. That's what the gun was for.

Casey Hawthorne (*producer*): He told me if I didn't do it, he'd kill me. I didn't fully believe him. But I also realized this person's brain was so addled, he might be capable of anything. His entire life was tied to this theory—I wasn't exactly keen to debate him when he had me so vulnerable.

I thought about just agreeing to say what he wanted. I tried to imagine the fallout: I'd survive, presumably—that was good! The Unfounded groupies would think they'd been vindicated—okay, so what? Everyone else would realize I was lying to save myself. All in all, an outcome I'd gladly take. So I started to think about how I could tell a story that would satisfy his grand delusions. You know . . . the president has a Secret Service agent put chalk on a mailbox, and I wear a disguise to go pick up instructions for the next fake child abduction. I knew I needed to really put my back into it. I got ready to spin the wildest and most important yarn of my life.

That's when we heard a knock on the door.

Bruce Allen Foley (*Unfounded*): I looked at Casey and whispered that she better not make a sound. I brought the gun to her head.

Casey Hawthorne (*producer*): I did not enjoy that, having a gun pressed to my temple. I heard someone in the hallway call my name. I realized it was Felix.

Bruce Allen Foley (*Unfounded*): The freaking detective. I guess he was really in love with her or something. Hanging around and stalking her. He knocked again, and I could feel him waiting there.

Casey Hawthorne (*producer*): It was a giant relief knowing he was out there. On the other hand, I started to realize that the most likely way I was going to get killed was if he broke down the door and Foley panicked. I couldn't stop shaking. All I could do was sit there, waiting, hoping he'd find a way to save me.

Bruce Allen Foley (*Unfounded*): A minute or two passed. I started to relax. Just when I thought he was gone, I heard the key card. And then, click, the door was suddenly unlocked, swinging open, and he walked right in. Are you kidding me? He had a key?

Felix Calderon (*detective*): I walked in and saw Casey gagged, facing a camera, tied to a chair, Bruce Allen Foley holding a gun to her head. I stopped in my tracks. The door closed behind me. Now it was the three of us.

Bruce Allen Foley (*Unfounded*): I welcomed him to our little streaming party. We could always make room for a costar! But I warned him, he had to listen to me—"Don't do anything crazy, just secure your wrists and attach them to the bed frame."

Felix Calderon (*detective*): I told him I wasn't going to do that. I looked at Casey. She was talking to me through her eyes. She was scared.

Bruce Allen Foley (*Unfounded*): I said he better do it or I was going to kill Casey.

Casey Hawthorne (*producer*): The barrel of the gun was literally pressed to my head. I sat as still as possible.

Felix Calderon (*detective*): I started moving toward them. Casey told me to keep coming. I saw that she needed me, that she trusted me.

Bruce Allen Foley (*Unfounded*): I yelled and pointed the gun at him. He kept moving in.

Felix Calderon (*detective*): I was close enough to touch Foley. Instead of tackling him, I reached out and put my hand on his shoulder. I put my other hand out, palm open. I asked for the gun.

Casey Hawthorne (*producer*): All I could do was watch. I didn't dare take a breath.

Bruce Allen Foley (*Unfounded*): I gave him the gun. It wasn't even real, just a cheap plastic toy. Like I said, I'm a pacifist!

Casey Hawthorne (*producer*): I started crying. It all washed over me.

Felix Calderon (*detective*): I moved Foley to the bed. Flipped him over, put the zip ties around his wrists. Then laid him down on the floor. He was as meek as a lamb, it turned out.

I went to Casey, took the tape off her mouth. Asked if she was okay. She said yes. I cut her free. She leaped up and squeezed me and wouldn't let me go.

Casey Hawthorne (*producer*): I didn't expect to be that emotional. I had been scared, but I thought I had a plan to survive. I believed that if I told the story Foley wanted to hear, he wouldn't hurt me. But Felix didn't know that Foley was bluffing, that the gun was fake. He walked into that room defenseless, not knowing what he'd find. He did it to save me. You can call me a stupid fairy-tale princess, but I loved him for it.

Bruce Allen Foley (*Unfounded*): Get a room, you two, am I right? No, I'm just kidding. It was actually kind of sweet seeing them like that.

Felix Calderon (*detective*): I had to peel Casey off me so I could call down to the station and alert them. They made it over, took control of the scene, took our statements, hauled Foley off.

Bruce Allen Foley (*Unfounded*): I apologized to Casey when they led me away. Not for trying to make her confess, I stand by that. But for scaring her, threatening her. That wasn't nice. Ugh, we were so close to getting the Revelation! That's my only regret.

Another time, I guess.

Felix Calderon (*detective*): Eventually, it was just me and Casey alone in her room. She was still shaken up. Literally shaking. She wouldn't stop staring at me. She asked if I could stay for a bit.

Casey Hawthorne (*producer*): I wanted him to *stay* stay. It was all very confusing. The day before, I had hated him. But there's something about a guy trying to save your life that changes things for a gal.

Felix Calderon (*detective*): I thought about it. She definitely batted those baby blues at me. But I remembered what she had said to me in the lobby the night before. I remembered that because of her, I didn't have a job, my career was ruined, Sara was still missing, and she was making a TV show about the whole thing. I remembered how much she disgusted me.

I told her no.

Casey Hawthorne (*producer*): It hurt. Watching him leave, I realized for the first time I had genuine feelings for him. But I also knew I had hurt him. I had blown through his life and fucked everything up, and he'd still stuck his neck out to save me. I owed him, and I knew there was only one way to fix things between us. It was nothing I could say. No sweet, soul-baring speech about love and chemistry and a lifetime of kisses in the olive groves of Spain.

There was only the one thing: I had to find Sara.

CHAPTER 14

"Eureka Moment"

Casey Hawthorne (*producer*): Sara Parcell was a real person. Despite what Bruce Allen Foley believed, she wasn't a crisis actor. She wasn't a figment of anyone's imagination. She was a sixteen-year-old girl with friends and family who went to school one morning and didn't come home. No one seemed to know where she was, but she was, in fact, *somewhere*. I had to figure out where that was.

I had promised Marcus I would wrap up the series with a worthy finale. I had assured Dave and Jeannette I would do their family justice. And I owed Felix a chance at redeeming himself. Even more than that, I was desperate for him to see me differently. All of it hinged on me finding Sara.

I went back to what I knew beyond any shadow of doubt: Sara, walking back to her school bus and then never being seen again. No explanation, no evidence, no suspects that made any sense. I started to see that this was the defining characteristic about the case: None of it made sense. I was missing something. We all were.

The more I thought about it, the closer I got to admitting it—the answer had to start with Dave. His behavior, his demeanor from the moment we met, it had all been too unexplainable. I couldn't figure out exactly what he'd done—was he a monster? a con man?—but I knew that was where I had to focus. I decided to dig as deep as I could into who he was, what he was hiding.

I sat down at my laptop. Same desk where I had just been held hostage, scuff marks on the chair from where I had been pulling against my zip ties. I began to compile every known fact I could find about Dave Parcell. After five minutes, I was at a dead end. For whatever reason, this man barely had a digital footprint. No social media, no Google hits, no criminal record, no public life, it seemed. I was frustrated.

Then something occurred to me. I had seen Dave countless times on Instagram, Facebook, everywhere else. I realized it was never his account. It was Jack's. Jack was a typical tech-obsessed eleven-year-old boy. His social media was an almost daily log of his family's life. I pulled up all his accounts in different tabs and dove in.

I scrolled and I scrolled, going back years. The daily routines of the Parcells came into focus, along with all of their specific quirks. Jeannette's signature wardrobe in the mornings, her oversize sweatshirts and fuzzy pink slippers. Dave's chores on the weekends, his constant battle with one specific roof gutter. Sara's activities where Jack got dragged along, her recitals and track meets.

I took notes. My legal pad started to look like one of those crazy bulletin boards with red string connecting all the criminals. An idea began to take shape in my mind, a guess, really, one that I couldn't ignore. I kept digging through the digital bread crumbs. Certain posts jumped out and started to seem more and more significant.

An Instagram photo of Dave, Jack, and Sara camping in the woods.

A tweet where Jack complained about missing Orioles opening day because his dad was doing his "secret project" with Sara.

Facebook photos that show Jeannette falling apart at the beginning of this whole ordeal and then, two weeks later, with her hair done up and a full face of makeup.

My wheels were turning. I kept clicking and clicking. I suddenly had the urge to go back and watch the viral video that started everything: Dave and Jeannette in their foyer, embracing, crying, promising to be strong for each other. It was still so moving. But I realized there had to be more than the snippet that went viral.

I went to Jack's YouTube channel. Scrolled back to find the full-length version of that moment. It's only a few seconds longer, and the difference is almost imperceptible, but I caught the key frame. It is right there on Dave's face as he hugs and comforts his wife—he doesn't know he's being filmed, of course, and he knows Jeannette can't see him. He lets his guard down and drops the act. I swear you can see it . . .

This is not the face of a man who is worried about his daughter.

With his speech and his embrace, he had been performing for Jeannette. Jack captured it on video, and the whole world interpreted it exactly the way you'd expect. Worried parents, tragic situation, inspiring resilience. But there's a frame at the end of that video where Dave lets it slip. He's lying.

I had chills. I instantly knew that Dave was running a scam. And now so many other things started to make sense.

His reaction when I showed up at their front door. Our meeting at the diner.

His embrace of the show.

The unexplained decision to cancel.

All of these moments flooded back to me, and I finally saw it clearly: Dave had been in control from the start, not concerned for his daughter, only worried about manipulating me and everyone else. It was a shock to admit . . . I was somehow both crushed and elated.

I still didn't know what this meant for Sara. Where she was. If she was alive or dead. I felt so close, but I couldn't figure out the last piece of the puzzle.

I knew I needed to call Felix.

Felix Calderon (*detective*): Casey called. It was the middle of the night. I had already left her at the hotel. I didn't pick up, I knew she was safe. Bruce Allen Foley was locked up, and they had posted security outside her room. I just didn't have the energy for whatever she wanted. But then she kept calling and calling. I finally answered. She told me she was close to finding Sara. But she needed my help.

Are you kidding me? I didn't believe her, of course. And I didn't want to role-play being hero investigators with her. I told her I was suspended and she didn't know what she was talking about and to leave me out of it. She kept saying I had to hear her out, to see everything she found, to help her find the missing piece. I told her no. I was about to hang up.

And that's when she told me that if I didn't step up, this was going to be another Houston. That the blood was going to be on my hands again. I hung up on her and punched a hole through my wall.

Casey Hawthorne (*producer*): I had to say it. I wasn't planning on ever bringing it up, on weaponizing it, but now was the time. I knew it would sting, but if Sara was alive, Felix was the only one who could save her. And that was the one thing I could say to get him off his ass.

Felix Calderon (*detective*): Houston, okay, I'll give it to you as straight as I can.

Six years earlier, I was working Special Victims in the Ninth Precinct there. I caught a missing person case, two little kids, a four-year-old and a two-year-old taken from their grandmother's backyard in broad daylight. Everything told me it was the ex-boyfriend of the mother—the kids' father—who was out of the picture. This guy had an alibi, he held up during questioning, but I fucking knew it was him.

In these cases, every minute that goes by is terrifying. I begged for a search warrant, called in a favor to a judge, got the paper I needed. We went out to the guy's house and turned it upside down while he sat there sweating. Looked everywhere. Didn't find a thing. But even as we walked away empty-handed, I made him for it.

Two months later, someone else in his neighborhood got caught with some coke during a traffic stop. Third strike, Texas sentencing guidelines, no bueno. So this guy starts selling out everyone he's ever known to wriggle out of a life sentence. He's giving up dope houses, chop shops, old ladies running unlicensed day-care centers, anything he can think of. And during the course of this grand civic gesture, he fingers the ex-boyfriend for snatching those kids a while back.

My guys know I'm hung up on this case, so they call me down to the interrogation. Our loudmouth repeats it for me now, that the ex-boyfriend hid the kids away in an attic or something like that. He heard it from a friend of a friend who worked with the guy. My hopes weren't high to begin with, and all he's got is a thirdhand rumor, so I'm ready to walk out. I searched the house already, there was no attic. Jailhouse snitches will try to sell anything, I figure this guy is throwing darts and hoping he gets lucky.

"No, no, I'm serious," he keeps saying. He asks if I know what the ex-boyfriend does for work. Challenging me on my own case. Of course I do. He was a laborer on a contracting crew. We checked out the properties he worked on, no sign of the two kids. "Closets," our guy says, "he was all about them closets . . . my friend heard him bragging about all the secret compartments he could build into your closet . . . heard him talking about what you could hide in these things—secret shelves, safes and whatnot, and then my friend says he got all squirrelly, like he was proud of something else but wouldn't say it . . . everyone knows that dude is a sicko who snatched up his kids . . . go check his closets."

I'm halfway out the door already. Fuck a warrant this time. Race to the house. No one home. Kick in the door, I don't care. Go upstairs. Back bedroom. Find the closet. We looked there already, but now I notice. The whole thing looks too . . . new. Too . . . intentional. I've got my flashlight out, I'm feeling around every inch of this thing, and I finally find the latch. The back of the closet was a false wall. I pull it open to find a hidden compartment behind it. And laying on the floor, bundled up in garbage bags, two tiny corpses.

Caleb and Ashley.

I was six inches from those kids when I searched the house the first time. I touched that wall. Two days after they'd been taken. They were alive then. I probably could have heard them breathing. Six inches, and I left them there, in the middle of their unspeakable nightmare, to die. Moved right past.

It hit me hard. Panic attacks, sleepless nights, compulsive behavior like checking for false walls everywhere, sitting in my car next to playgrounds and keeping watch. My marriage fell apart. It was destroying me.

I transferred out of Special Victims. It helped, but not much. Just being in that city was too much for me. I moved to Frederick after seeing the job posted online. Was hoping it was a place where little kids didn't get stuffed in closets. And the plan worked for a while. I got better. But Sara Parcell brought it all back.

I don't know why I told Casey about Houston. It was during those first few days before I knew she was a liar. I was being real with her. And then she filed it away and waited for the right time to throw it back in my face.

Casey Hawthorne (*producer*): It worked. He hung up on me, but twenty minutes later, he was at the door of my hotel room. This time he knocked.

I thought he was going to jump down my throat for using the Houston thing against him. But he didn't. He didn't even mention it. He was all business.

"Show me what you've got," he said.

Felix Calderon (*detective*): We went over to her laptop. She had bookmarked all these posts from Jack's social media. She took me through it. I started to see what she saw, to believe her. It was all there. The family was lying to us. Dave wasn't a killer, like I had thought at one point—he was running a scam.

But Casey hadn't figured out where Sara was. I asked her to walk me through everything again. Jack had inadvertently documented his family's entire life, had basically built an effective surveillance operation. Now we were looking for a needle in a digital haystack, and I wasn't going to stop until we found it.

Casey Hawthorne (*producer*): Felix was the one who nailed it, the eureka moment. It was a great catch by him. A Facebook photo from June of the previous summer. And a similar post from the summer before, and the one before that. It was the whole family dropping off Jack at a Boy Scout camp called Timber Ridge, an annual tradition, apparently. They were posing in front of a flimsy cabin, Jack in his uniform, Sara giving him bunny ears.

I asked what Felix was thinking. He turned to me, dead serious. He said he thought Sara was alive. Hiding somewhere off the grid without anyone else around. But somewhere safe. If that was all true, he thought it might be at this Boy Scout camp.

We looked it up, found the location on a map, an hour away. Saw that it was closed down in the offseason. Empty, presumably. Familiar to Sara and Dave. Middle of nowhere, isolated but safe. We couldn't be sure, but we both smelled it. We gathered our stuff and headed out the door. Hopped in his car at sunrise and set off for the camp.

Felix Calderon (*detective*): No cameras. No more funny business. I could see a change in Casey, she was finally taking things seriously. I hit the gas and didn't let up. I didn't know what to expect once we arrived, but I knew that every minute mattered. I knew that all too well.

Casey Hawthorne (*producer*): We barely spoke. I think we both knew there was too much to get into. The *TMZ* leak. The unforgivable things we'd said to each other when we fought in the hotel lobby. The Foley ordeal. Houston. The Parcells tricking us. If we cracked open that door, we would lose the fragile peace and momentum we had.

We hoped that what we were about to find would put all of that other stuff behind us for good.

Felix Calderon (*detective*): I wasn't thinking about any of that. Casey's the one to turn everything into a therapy session. I just wanted to find Sara.

We made it up to this winding dirt road in the foothills of the Appalachians. Reached the entrance, there was a rusty chain hung across the road. I parked, and we walked into the camp area.

Not a soul in sight. Just a big mess hall–type building. A firepit, picnic tables, tetherball courts, those sort of things. And then a horseshoe of small wood cabins surrounding the perimeter, with an ocean of thick spruce trees behind them. The cabins all had shutters tied down over their windows.

Except for one.

Casey Hawthorne (*producer*): Felix and I looked at each other, holding back proud smiles.

We knew it. We had found her. I could already feel him thinking about me differently.

Felix Calderon (*detective*): Casey and I approached the cabin. The door wasn't locked like the others. Footprints in the mud outside, lots of them, men's boot prints, too. I reached for my gun . . . but I didn't have one. Fuck it. No stopping now. We edged up the three stairs. I called out: "Hello, Sara, it's the Frederick Police, we're coming in." No answer. I pushed the door open. I felt Casey breathing down my neck. We stepped inside.

And that's when we saw her.

Casey Hawthorne (*producer*): Sara. Dead on the floor. Eyes wide open. I would say peaceful, if not for the dark strangle marks around her neck.

Felix Calderon (*detective*): I couldn't help turning to look back at Casey. It really was my first thought.

Casey Hawthorne (*producer*): He didn't have to say anything. I felt his rage and judgment. Knew exactly what he was thinking: This girl was dead because of me.

And I knew he was right.

CHAPTER 15

"It Was All Over"

Casey Hawthorne (*producer*): I was in absolute shock. I screamed. I rushed over and knelt down next to her body. Felix pulled me back. I yelled at him to help her. I didn't understand why he wouldn't help her.

"She's dead, Casey," he said. "She's dead. We need to preserve the crime scene."

I couldn't believe there was nothing to do. I couldn't believe he was so cold-blooded about it. I guess he would call it professional. It didn't make sense to me . . . we thought we were going to that camp to find Sara hiding out, participating in a scam. But instead we found her body.

Felix Calderon (*detective*): I pulled Casey away from her and knelt down and felt for a pulse. She was gone. Cold already. There was nothing we could do. Sara Parcell was no longer missing, she was murdered.

The cabin was a crime scene now. It held our best chance of figuring out who'd done this. I looked around and tried to take it all in: a bunk with a sleeping bag on it, a collapsible camping chair, a suitcase filled with clothes, some books, magazines, a radio, lots of food, a stove, jugs of water, toiletries, tidy bags of trash. Exactly what you'd expect if a teenage girl had been living there for three weeks.

I headed for the door to go outside and call it in to the state troopers. I held the door for Casey, but she had sat down on one of the empty bunks. She was holding her head in her hands, weeping softly.

Casey Hawthorne (*producer*): I needed a moment. It hit me with the full weight for the first time. This was Sara Parcell, the real person, not the hook of a TV show. Sixteen years old and now dead. Brutally murdered, from the look of it. We had never met, of course, but I felt so . . . connected with her. Like I really knew her, like we had our own little bond. I wanted to sit there with her, but Felix dragged me outside. In hindsight, I wish we had filmed Sara in the cabin. I could have at least taken out my phone or something. It was part of the story and deserved to be documented. But in that moment, I was too shaken up. I didn't have the heart to fight for it.

Zane Kelly (*camera operator*): Casey had put us on standby to shoot that day. Told us to be ready for something big. But that morning came and went, and the call never came. I'm not sure why.

We did make it up there the next day, when it was a locked-down crime scene. Couldn't get too close to the cabin, but I shot some B-roll and wide shots of the camp. I hear that people still make pilgrimages to pay their respects.

Becca Santangelo (*SareBears*): Of course I've been to Timber Ridge. We all have. Cabin Four, I have a photo in the doorway. Laying on the floor, too. I could totally feel Sara's presence when I was there.

Felix Calderon (*detective*): I went back into the cabin and took one last look around for myself. Snapped some photos with my phone. Remember, I was still suspended, I didn't know if I'd have access again.

I stood there with Sara for a moment. Closed my eyes. I waited for that familiar feeling to hit me, the one from Houston. Guilt, disgust, shame, horror. I let it wash over me. Somehow it wasn't as bad this time, wasn't as overwhelming. Maybe because it was so familiar—I had lost it, and now it was back. There was a sick relief in experiencing it again.

Casey Hawthorne (*producer*): I tried to say something to him outside the cabin, but he cut me off. I could see the torture descending on him, I wanted to help, to share in our suffering. But Felix clearly wanted nothing to do with me. I walked away and left him there standing guard.

Felix Calderon (*detective*): I waited on the stairs of the cabin doorway until the cavalry rolled in. Within a couple hours, there were dozens of people there.

My captain showed up. DA Bell, too. I briefed them on how we got there and what we found. They agreed to put me back on the case. It was contingent on me not having any more contact with Casey. They had already removed her from the property. She had been instrumental in locating Sara, but I understood their concern. The decision was more than fine with me.

Look, I give Casey credit for sniffing out the scam. But I had no doubt that this whole tragedy happened because of her TV show. She wanted to come off as a hero, but all Casey did was bring a bucket of water to the fire she had been feeding with gasoline. As far as I was concerned, she was a moral accomplice to the murder.

Casey Hawthorne (*producer*): Moral accomplice? That's . . . that's hard to hear. I'm sorry he still thinks that. All I ever wanted was to save Sara. But I know it's a lost cause with him . . . my desire to change his mind about what I did faded a long time ago.

Felix Calderon (*detective*): While the techs handled the scene, I knew there was something I had to do straightaway. The worst part of the job. I had to drive back to tell the Parcells.

Dave Parcell (*father*): There was a knock on the door. I opened it, and I knew it was all over. I didn't even notice the squad car and the cops waiting at the curb. It was just from Calderon's face. He had disgust in his eyes.

I still wasn't prepared for what he actually told us; I only thought we had been caught. That he'd figured out the scam. I guessed that Sara might even be with him. If they'd finally found her, I'd hope they'd drive her home! So, yeah, maybe the scam was over, but my life, my family, our dreams—I didn't think all of that was about to shatter, too.

Jeannette Parcell (*mother*): He stood in the living room. Told us to sit down. Jack was watching something. He told us we might want to ask Jack to give us some privacy. That was the moment I started to feel sick.

Jack Parcell (*brother*): I didn't sense anything at first. It was normal during those days to have cops, all kinds of people, coming through the house. I took my iPad and went upstairs.

Felix Calderon (*detective*): I told them as clearly as possible that we had found their daughter and that she was dead. And then I watched them react. I knew these next few moments might reveal everything.

Jeannette Parcell (*mother*): When he said they'd found a body, I was relieved. Thank God, I thought. If they found someone dead, then it couldn't be Sara. It had to be someone else's body. Someone else's Sara. Sad, of course, but I knew our daughter was safe.

Dave Parcell (*father*): I didn't believe it, either. It wasn't possible. I was the only one who knew where she was.

Jeannette Parcell (*mother*): I told him there had to be a mistake. Sara wasn't dead.

Dave Parcell (*father*): Then he mentioned the Boy Scout camp. And my world just totally ended.

Felix Calderon (*detective*): It hit Dave first. Jeannette saw that and freaked out. She started screaming. She attacked him. Wailing, swinging, scratching. He didn't move a muscle to stop her, absorbed all the blows, the life drained from his face, almost detached from reality. She sobbed and sobbed and punched herself out and collapsed on the floor.

I held my look on Dave and asked him point-blank, "You knew she was up there, didn't you?" He didn't answer. Jeannette sobbed louder.

Jeannette Parcell (*mother*): I said I needed to see her. He told me I could be escorted to the morgue after her autopsy. For a supervised identification.

Felix Calderon (*detective*): Her wailing started all over again. I wasn't trying to antagonize them. I was sympathetic that they had lost their daughter. But they were suspects now.

Jeannette Parcell (*mother*): The thought of our baby girl on some frigid metal table, being poked and prodded . . . it was too much. I just wanted to hold her. I wanted to hold her peacefully one more time.

Felix Calderon (*detective*): Dave was calmer. I couldn't tell if he had given up on the act or not.

Dave Parcell (*father*): I asked Calderon who did this to her. He said I should know. But I really didn't. For the life of me, I didn't know how it could have happened.

Felix Calderon (*detective*): I didn't believe him. He had no credibility. I informed him that he was under arrest. Mirandized him.

Dave Parcell (*father*): It was over. I wasn't going to fight anymore. I told him it was all me, the scam part of it, Jeannette didn't know anything.

Felix Calderon (*detective*): That obviously wasn't true.

Dave Parcell (*father*): But that I didn't kill her.

Felix Calderon (*detective*): Didn't believe that, either.

Dave Parcell (*father*): I asked if I could see Jack before leaving the house. If I could go upstairs with Jeannette and tell him. Calderon said no. It broke my heart all over again.

Felix Calderon (*detective*): He didn't deserve any considerations. I put him in cuffs and led him outside.

Jack Parcell (*brother*): I heard all the yelling downstairs. My mom finally came up and told me. Not the whole truth yet, just that they found Sara and she was dead. My sister was dead. My big sister was gone. It was . . . I mean, what is there to say? She was my favorite person in the world.

Felix Calderon (*detective*): Casey and her crew were out front by now. She was back to her old self, with Sara's body barely cold. When I came out with Dave—handcuffs, squad car, the whole thing—they had the cameras rolling and got the perp walk they always wanted.

Casey Hawthorne (*producer*): I wasn't going to miss that. I thought it would be the final scene of the series. But, goddammit, it happened again—Dave's face! The man had the uncanny ability to say everything with his face. And what I saw as he was dragged out of his house—the sadness, the shock, the devastation—this time it was all real. For weeks it had been fake, but now I could see it was genuine. True grief at losing his daughter.

I didn't believe he was the one who had killed her.

Felix Calderon (*detective*): I was back in the box again with Dave. It didn't take much prodding, he confessed to everything except Sara's murder, and walked us through each step: the stupid GoFundMe plan, the day she disappeared, the media stunt on his doorstep, the reward fund, Casey's unexpected arrival, even Manny Crawford's death, which he claimed was accidental.

Dave Parcell (*father*): Sara was dead. My family was ruined. I had caused all of it. There was no way to hide it and nothing left to fight for.

Felix Calderon (*detective*): He insisted that he had no idea how she'd died and seemed genuinely confused, shocked, and devastated. Said he had seen her a few days prior and nothing was amiss.

He was obviously our top suspect again, but I slowly started to believe him. I didn't want to, but I did. I had seen him as a liar, and this was different.

If my instinct was right, it meant we still had to find the real killer. I finished taking Dave's confession, then went to call DA Bell.

Christine Bell (*district attorney*): We finally had a body, and it was obvious who had killed her. But Detective Calderon, Frederick's newly redeemed renegade hero, insisted the case wasn't solved. I couldn't announce anything. Look, he ended up being right, that's fair, but let's not give him too much credit—it's not like he was the person who solved it.

Felix Calderon (*detective*): Bell wasn't happy. She wanted a victory-lap press conference. I didn't care. I went home, caught a couple hours of sleep, and then got right back to work. We had gone from an unsolved missing person case to an unsolved murder.

Miriam Rosen (*teacher*): It was the middle of a school day. I don't know how word reached the school, but once someone found out, it spread through the whole building in minutes. I know I stopped teaching. I think we all did. There was a lot of crying. Our grief was still pure at that point, before we learned all the other details. Before we learned that Sara was partially responsible for what happened to her.

Olivia Weston (*friend*): I was in the biology lab. Someone came back from the bathroom and had heard in the hallway. He told us that Sara's body was found in the woods. I threw up in a garbage can.

Nellie Spencer (*friend*): The rumors were out of control. That she was raped and tortured. Carved up in a satanic ritual. I heard people in the locker room say she was eaten by wolves. It was like the deeper you went into the school, the crazier the story got.

Brandon Grassley (*neighbor*): I'm not sure how people at the school found out. I just remember the principal coming over the loudspeaker, making a short announcement, and canceling the rest of the day. But then everyone sort of hung around. They set up a kind of informal group session in the auditorium, with some of the teachers leading the conversation. I went and listened for a while.

Olaf Leclerq (*ice cream shop owner*): A shadow fell over the whole town. All those yellow ribbons, they had become tattered and dirty in the weeks outside, they suddenly seemed so depressing. I closed the shop and walked home. Before I did, I took the black-raspberry ice cream out of the display case. Never sold that flavor again.

Evelyn Crawford (*Manny's wife*): I still had people coming over to see me at the house, it had only been a week or two since Manny was killed. My daughters, other family, friends. A whole group of us heard the news together. It was sad, but I had no room for it. We talked about it for two minutes, then we moved on. What did Sara Parcell have to do with my husband? Not a thing, I believed. I'd be lying if I told you, in the moment, I thought there was any connection.

Tommy O'Brien (*employee, Geary Home & Garden*): I was crushed for Dave, of course. But mainly, I started to get angry. For weeks we had all held out a little hope, but now it was clear that Sara had been murdered. I wanted to find the asshole who did it and tear him to bits.

A lot of us did. We congregated at Lenny's Tavern, waiting on any word if they had a suspect. We were ready to roll out as vigilantes and deliver justice ourselves. And then we heard they arrested Dave. That he was the main suspect. What the hell? I didn't believe it was him.

Beverly Geary (*grandmother*): Someone came into Herb's store and told him. He drove home, and I remember noticing that he sat in the driveway for a while. Then he finally came inside and told me. I wailed and I wailed. My only granddaughter. My sweet little pigtailed angel with the buckteeth and extra serving of sass. God help this awful world.

They told Herb that Dave was the one who'd done it. I decided then and there to kill him. I just knew the next time I saw him, I would claw his eyes out.

Mike Snyder (*local news*): Of course it was our top story again. But I had some good sources, and the details I was hearing didn't make sense. Found at the Boy Scout camp . . . strangled . . . but she had been living there? The father was arrested, but the investigation was ongoing? We didn't report all the rumors, but I had enough sense to know that another shoe would drop.

Becca Santangelo (*SareBears*): Everyone in the Facebook group started freaking out, and I don't think I left my computer for like forty-eight hours. We were all posting tributes, making photo montages, consoling each other. I know I had never met Sara, but I really loved her. The day her body was found was one of the worst of my life.

Bruce Allen Foley (*Unfounded*): I was being detained in the Frederick jail, of course, after the whole Revelation snafu. No friendly bailout from my DA pal this time. I guess the hostage-taking charge had made me persona non grata in the political world. Too bad for Christine Bell, she went nowhere without my support.

Anyway, the word spread through the jail, and I shrugged. Okay, yeah, sure, they found a body. Sometimes they find a body, sometimes they don't. It didn't prove anything.

Ezra Phillips (*pop culture critic*): It was a national story. Breaking-news alerts on my phone, all that stuff. And I immediately noticed something unsettling: Suddenly everyone was super-pumped for the series finale of *Searching for Sara*. Planning watch parties, making predictions, almost gleeful at this morbid update. It was like the greatest tease of all time—we finally have a body, come see for yourself how it all went down!

I had to catch myself, because I was excited, too. But then I remembered this wasn't like some season finale of *The Sopranos* where you tune in to see who gets whacked. Those were fictional characters. This dead body was a real person. The promos, the headlines, the breathless anticipation . . . I know I work in a sleazy business, but it left a bad taste in my mouth.

Still, I'm sure Casey was ecstatic.

Casey Hawthorne (*producer*): I was an absolute mess. We raced from Timber Ridge to the Parcells' house, filmed Dave's arrest, then I finally got back to the hotel. Anthony wanted to start editing right away, but I needed a moment. I went to my room, curled up in bed, and lay there for a while.

I kept thinking about the accusatory look Felix had given me after he saw Sara's body. Was she dead because of me? Had I come into town and turbocharged what was supposed to be some minor-league scam? Had Sara been kept in that cabin by Dave so we would keep filming our show and lining their pockets? I feared that all the answers were yes.

I was ashamed and heartbroken. All the pride I felt from figuring out what was really going on? Gone. Sara's body had seemed so fresh, like she had only been killed the previous day. I had taken too long to uncover the scam. I know I'm being hard on myself, but I did feel a pang of responsibility. How could I have been so dumb for so long? If I had just gotten my act together a few days earlier . . .

This soul-searching went on for the entire night. I had set out to find Sara only to find her dead. I knew I couldn't fix what was already broken. She was gone forever, and I would always be partially to blame. But I started to realize I could still honor her. And maybe in doing so, I could redeem myself as well.

I owed it to Sara, to my audience, and to myself to do one last thing: find out who killed her.

And I thought I knew exactly where to look.

CHAPTER 16

"I Got My Confession"

Casey Hawthorne (*producer*): Earlier that morning at the Boy Scout camp, after we had found Sara's body, I stumbled on something major. I didn't know exactly what it meant when I saw it, but I thought it might be the key to finding Sara's killer.

While Felix stood guard in front of the cabin, I wandered around the Boy Scout camp. All the other cabins were locked up and shuttered. The large mess hall, too. But there was a little annex attached to that building, and I noticed one of the windows had the shutter propped up.

I walked over and peered inside. It was a bare-bones office — couple of desks, file cabinets, ancient copy machine. I could picture an old man in Crocs and suspenders making announcements over the PA system during the summer. Nothing too exciting. But as I was about to move away from the dirty window, I noticed something.

An old computer, sitting on a desk . . . and the monitor light blinking green, green, green.

I looked over my shoulder. Calderon couldn't see me from where he was waiting. I went to the door, turned the knob, and walked right in.

It was dark and dusty inside, stale air and cobwebs. I went over to the desk. An empty water bottle sat next to the computer. An old dial-up modem sat behind it, lights flashing. I touched the mouse, and the screen came to life. And suddenly, I saw how Sara had been spending her days.

She had been reading about herself on the Internet.

Of course she was! What teenager gets famous and doesn't check their mentions? Sara had a dozen tabs open, some of them practical, like the weather forecast and a Google search for how to give yourself the Heimlich maneuver. But most of the tabs were websites talking about her and the case and the show.

For the first time, I realized how surreal this experience must have been for Sara . . . her father comes up and tells her she's the focal point of the most popular TV show in the country. Surprise, sweetheart! Front-page news. Magazine covers. And then, obviously, all the Internet saturation that comes next. Sara was famous but invisible. So she started monitoring her story from her forest hideaway. I couldn't help but smile as I pictured her taking this all in. Yeah, she had scammed everyone—including me, first and foremost—but I still hoped that she had been happy with how she was being portrayed.

I didn't know how much time I had in the office alone. State troopers were on their way. I knew I had to tell Felix and whoever else showed up what I had found. This was important evidence, after all. But I clicked around for another minute. That's when I saw that Sara wasn't just following her story . . . she was interacting with people, too.

From the looks of it, Sara was neck-deep in the *Searching for Sara* Reddit thread. I knew this was a popular place for fans of the show to interact, share theories, make jokes and predictions. It had thousands of daily users. One of them was InThePines22, a username that Sara had apparently cooked up. This was insane! Sara was being an anonymous fangirl on the Reddit board for the show about her disappearance.

I was about to scroll through the page when I heard sirens in the distance. I knew I'd catch shit if anyone saw me in the office. I wiped the mouse off with my shirt, used a pencil eraser to turn the monitor back off, and booked it out of there. I walked back and told Felix that there was an office on the other side of the camp, and it looked like someone had been using a computer. He barely acknowledged me. He conferred with some of the other police who had shown up. They kicked me off the premises. As I was being escorted out, I saw Felix rush back to where we'd left his car at the entrance. I knew where he was going. I hitched a ride back to Frederick with some nice EMTs, got my crew together, and raced to the house just in time to film Dave's arrest.

It was a crazy day. But even amid all that chaos, I was preoccupied by one thing: getting back to my hotel, opening my laptop, and figuring out who InThePines22 had been talking to.

Molly Lowe (*professor of sociology*): It was unique but shouldn't have been surprising that Sara became obsessed with her own story. She was as susceptible as anyone else to the siren song of true crime. The story was personal to her, and she couldn't resist weighing in.

Over the years, there are countless examples of audience members influencing real events—it has almost become a signature trope of the genre. Creators have come to expect that their content will be crowd-sourced at times, diverting and meandering down different paths as information filters up from the bottom. These projects become collaborations, with creators getting the ball rolling and then the audience taking up the mantle of pushing the story forward.

But this was the first time that audience and victim overlapped. That's why this is the apex of the "true crime as entertainment" era. Or some might say the rock bottom.

Casey Hawthorne (*producer*): When I finally had a moment that night, I pulled up the Reddit page. The archives went back weeks, to the premiere of *Searching for Sara*. It was a typical fan page. Sara wasn't commenting at first, who knows if she was even reading. But around

Episode Two, when people started getting suspicious of Dave, the thread took a turn. It exploded with wild predictions, conspiracy theories, claims that people had seen Sara in their town on the other side of the world. There was intense scrutiny on all of the Parcells. And suddenly, Sara, under her anonymous ID, started to chime in. She would defend her family members . . . shoot holes in offensive theories . . . generally engage in the debates of the day.

As I kept reading, I started to realize how much time Sara had spent there. Hundreds of comments, maybe thousands. Hardly a surprise, considering her boredom. And it became clear that she was getting familiar with some of the other regular posters. Exchanging jokes, veering into topics beyond the show. She was forming relationships. When anyone asked about personal details, Sara would either lie or dip out of the conversation.

Looking at the more recent posts, it was clear she was interacting most with one other specific poster. Mars_Volta_Man. They were always upvoting each other's comments and going on long riffs whenever one of them posted. The exchanges were sweet. Flirty.

Mars_Volta_Man was an ardent defender of the Sara presented on the show. They teamed up when other posters attacked. They reveled in good news that might bring Sara home. I read every word they exchanged, and they struck me as a cute little Internet couple. I understood how they could have gravitated to each other: Sara, stuck alone in this camp, desperate for connection and validation . . . and this lonely viewer, whoever it was, obsessed with the show and delighted to find a kindred spirit.

And then I saw their last exchange.

I'm not sure I would have caught it had it not been the final one. I went back to it only after I didn't find any new posts from either of them in the last few days. It was so subtle but then suddenly so obvious.

It was L-O-L. But not a normal L-O-L. It was L-O-L with a twist, written with the numerical digits one, zero, one. 101. So that the numbers looked like a lowercase L-O-L. Mars_Volta_Man had made a joke, and that's how InThePines22 had responded. 101.

I got chills. 101 was a signature quirk of Sara's.

I had seen it countless times on Jack's social media pages, on Sara's own accounts, in texts to Olivia and Nellie. It was mildly clever. Or cute or whatever. Nothing that memorable. But now I saw that Sara had let this typing tic slip out under her anonymous name. It was like a fingerprint; it could only belong to her. And I saw that she had used it in the last exchange she had with Mars_Volta_Man.

It hit me all at once, what this meant: If I had been able to recognize this quirk, someone else could have as well. Mars_Volta_Man had figured out he was messaging with Sara. And that meant he already knew her.

As soon as that hit me, I realized the username gave him away. The Mars Volta was a semi-obscure rock band. I had heard of them, even if I couldn't think of anyone I knew who listened to them. But I had seen those words once before since I arrived in Frederick. I had seen a sticker inside a locker. In the middle of a hundred other peeling stickers, I had seen the band's logo, half obscured, and my subconscious had somehow filed it away. And I suddenly remembered whose locker it was.

Brandon Grassley.

It all made sense. Of course he was on Reddit obsessing over the show. Of course he was defending Sara's honor—thirty seconds after meeting him, you would have known he was in love with the pretty girl next door. Of course he and InThePines22 bonded over their shared proximity to the case, even as they didn't reveal their identities or know who they were talking to. Of course he recognized Sara's signature laugh, 101. And then of course he knew broadly what that meant—if Sara was whiling away her days chatting on the Internet, she was surely alive and well, and the whole disappearance was a scam, with his own family targeted and ruined as intentional collateral damage. And of course that would have enraged him, motivated him to confirm his instinct, find wherever Sara was hiding, and confront her. Sadly, as I already knew, that confrontation had ended in violence.

I didn't know how he had found her, but I knew it in my bones: Brandon Grassley had killed Sara Parcell.

I knew what I had to do. I had to confront Brandon, with the cameras rolling. But not before I told Felix.

I called and called. No answer. Finally left a voicemail.

Felix Calderon (*detective*): I listened to it. She was practically breathless, claiming she knew who killed Sara. I was done with Casey. Even if I had been allowed to speak with her, I was done. I blocked her number.

Casey Hawthorne (*producer*): I was the person who found Sara. Not him, not any other cop. He could have been a little more open-minded. Now I had found the killer. Again, not him, me! I wanted Felix to be part of the closure, to share the glory, so to speak. After all the problems I had caused him, and everything he had done for me, I owed it to him.

Felix Calderon (*detective*): Sara was dead because of Casey and her show. Dave had confirmed as much. She had lost the right to be involved in this case. She had lost the right to be a hero.

Casey Hawthorne (*producer*): He texted back: "I'm blocking your number . . . don't contact me again."

I know he blamed me for Sara's death. And what could I say? He was right, in a way. I stared at his message and began to accept that I couldn't fix what was broken between us. I had lost his respect so deeply, and he was so stubborn about having the moral high ground, it was hopeless. It hurt, the way he thought about me. It hurt to have him cut me off. Call me crazy, say it's sappy, I don't care—I knew we could have had a special life if we'd given it a try. I could have playfully argued in bed with that man forever. But we would never get there with me begging him to change his mind about me. That type of change, it can't be asked for . . . it needs to come sincerely from the other person.

Felix . . . he never came around. It's okay. The world keeps spinning. I honored his request. That was the last interaction we ever had.

Felix Calderon (*detective*): Correct. I haven't spoken to Casey since the day we drove up to Timber Ridge.

Casey Hawthorne (*producer*): If Felix didn't want in on solving the murder, that was his problem. I made a plan to confront Brandon Grassley first thing in the morning. I got my crew up early, and we headed over to the high school. I explained to the principal that now that Sara was dead, I wanted to bookend the series with interviews from all of the students I spoke to for the first episode. Nellie, Olivia, her other friends . . . and Brandon, of course. The principal set me up in the same classroom and arranged to have the students come by. Didn't force them but asked them. As I anticipated, Brandon didn't want to draw any suspicions by refusing.

Veronica Yang (*principal*): I always thought of the students' participation in the series as an alternative form of therapy. I was happy to facilitate Casey's interactions with them. However, I was not made aware that the final interview would essentially be an illegal interrogation.

Brandon Grassley (*neighbor*): They told me I had to do another interview for the show. I didn't want to, but I also didn't want to fight about it. So I went to the room. I obviously didn't realize what I was walking into.

Casey Hawthorne (*producer*): We started with the same generic questions I had asked the others: the mood at school; Sara's legacy; their reaction to the news; how their lives had changed during this saga. That last question was touchy for Brandon. I saw him tense up. He gave a clipped response. I pressed him. Then he came out and said it: Sara's disappearance had ruined his life. I got him to elaborate. He talked about the stalking accusations against his father, which had turned out to be false. The online vigilantes who had targeted his house. The SWATing, the doxing, the secrets that had been exposed, his father's humiliation. I truly felt for him as he got emotional talking about it. He was unburdening himself, it was therapeutic for him. I saw that he had every right to be angry.

But I also pictured Sara dead on the floor of that cabin, eyes locked in fear, purple rings around her throat. The horror of that image inspired me to push forward.

I asked Brandon if he had become obsessed with *Searching for Sara*. He said no. I asked if he followed any of the coverage online. He said sure, a little.

I asked if he ever looked at the Reddit message board devoted to the show. He said maybe, he didn't remember.

I asked if he ever posted there. He hesitated. Said no. I held my gaze on him.

I asked if he was a fan of the Mars Volta. He said yeah, kind of.

I asked if he ever used Mars_Volta_Man as a user ID. He said no, eyes narrowing. I asked if he was familiar with a Reddit user named InThePines22. He said he didn't think so but that he didn't remember every person's ID who posted on Reddit.

I asked if he thought he knew the real identity of InThePines22. He didn't answer. I asked if he knew anyone who typed LOL as 101. He looked at the floor.

I asked if there was anything about Sara he wanted to tell us. I asked, "Did you kill her?"

He looked back up at me, eyes burning.

I told him it was all over. I had figured it out. And the cops would, too. DNA samples, evidence at the cabin and on Sara's body, forensic analysis of his phone and laptop, motive. It was all clear now. I asked him again: "Did you kill her?"

Brandon kept staring at me, raging, eyes welling up, realizing the gravity of the situation. He didn't say another word. He didn't have to, though. We had the camera rolling, and his face said it all.

I had the confession to end my series.

That's when Felix and the cops came in. Perfect timing, as far as I was concerned. They arrested him, read him his rights, walked him handcuffed through the school hallway with all the other students standing in shock. It was surreal. And Felix never even acknowledged me. I had solved his case, and he wouldn't even look me in the eye.

Felix Calderon (*detective*): We received a call thirty minutes earlier at the station. Casey was already at the school, I guess, filming with the students. It was a tip with credible evidence that Brandon Grassley had murdered Sara Parcell. It was enough to obtain a warrant. I immediately went to the school to effectuate the arrest.

Jeannette Parcell (*mother*): Casey called me that morning. She told me she knew who killed Sara. She explained everything. It was excruciating to hear. Then she told me that Calderon wouldn't listen to her anymore. That someone else had to tip him off. She went to the school to film her last interview, and I immediately called the police station.

Beverly Geary (*grandmother*): I told you. I never liked those Grassleys.

Felix Calderon (*detective*): Casey nailed it. I give her credit for figuring out it was Brandon Grassley. But we would have figured it out also, probably within hours. She did it first and turned it into content. That was her priority. And none of what she did brought Sara back to life.

Casey Hawthorne (*producer*): I had a finale to cut together. We raced back to the hotel and got started.

Marcus Maxwell (*executive*): Casey called me and asked if I was wearing a diaper—the implication being, I guess, that when I heard what she had for the finale, I would shit my pants. She brought me up to speed, asked for an extra hour, told me to go crazy with the promos, and I listened to her. The stage was set. I was excited but managed to control my bodily functions.

Anthony Pena (*editor*): We had thirty-two hours to turn in a final cut. There was a lot of material to cover. The discovery at Timber Ridge . . . Dave's arrest . . . reaction from the town . . . Brandon's interview. It was haymaker after haymaker, an editor's dream. But it had to be handled sensitively. The backdrop was that a teenage girl had been murdered. I give Casey all the credit here. The episode could have come across as a victory lap for everything she had figured out. But we laid it out more as a requiem. It was classy.

Felix Calderon (*detective*): We brought Brandon down to the station and sat him in the same chair his father had been in three weeks earlier. Took blood, saliva, hair samples. Fingerprints. Sent it to the lab, where samples taken off Sara's body were already waiting. I left Brandon to consult with his father and the lawyer he brought down. It was clear by that point that we had him dead to rights.

When I walked back into the interrogation room, Brandon was ready to confess in exchange for a plea deal. That wasn't up to me. I told him I could put in a word with the prosecutor, but I needed to hear his story first.

Brandon Grassley (*neighbor*): I have no problem talking about it now. It was an awful period in my life, and I did something unforgivable. I accept that. But when I look back at it today, it almost seems inevitable, you know? Like it was just a perfect storm that led me to kill her.

I guess I should start before Sara disappeared. We grew up across the street from each other. I can't remember a time when she wasn't part of my life. Same classes, same school bus, same birthday parties. I always liked her. And yeah, eventually, that became a crush. How could I not have one? She was smart and funny and beautiful and nice.

It was the nice part, most of all. Other girls at school were cruel sometimes. If I wore the wrong kind of shoes or had the wrong haircut, I'd always hear about it. Even from Sara's friends. But never Sara. It wasn't like she'd go out of her way to invite me to a party, but she'd smile at me in the hallway. If I asked her a question on the bus, she wouldn't roll her eyes. I played a song at the Spring Jam talent show once, and she told me good job the next day.

When she went missing, I was terrified. I would have done anything to help find her. Then Casey and her show started up. I thought it was so cool that I was, like, a character. I know everyone else who got interviewed was really friends with her, and I was just there because we lived on the same block, but it was really exciting. People were jealous of me for the first time.

As soon as the show premiered, and my father was mentioned at the end of that episode, it kind of took over my life. I was seeing everyone reacting on Twitter. People posting memes on Instagram with my dad as a serial killer. Eventually, I checked out the Reddit page. I started posting, trying to defend my dad. People would talk shit about Sara there, and I defended her, too. Another user started liking all my comments. We started replying to each other. I didn't know who it was. It felt like it could be a girl my age. No one had ever flirted with me before. I mean, maybe it wasn't even flirting, but I felt connected to this person. We sent hundreds of messages back and forth. It sounds ridiculous to say now, but I swear I thought it at the time: Whoever it was, they reminded me of Sara. If I'm being honest, I would have said I was falling in love.

Then she laughed. LOL. 101.

It was the craziest mix of emotions I ever felt. For an instant, it was the happiest I've ever been: My secret Internet girlfriend is Sara

Parcell! And I made her laugh! My dream had come true. Sara was alive and she liked me!

But within a few seconds, I started to realize what it all meant. If InThePines22 really was Sara, and I was pretty sure it was, then this was actually my nightmare. I didn't have all the details, but I saw the broad truth pretty clearly. If Sara was capable of posting on Reddit all day, she wasn't kidnapped. It was all fake. And it meant she was in on it. She lied about my dad being a sexual predator. Led to him being outed, losing his job, becoming a recluse. She was the driving force that ruined my father's life.

And then to top it all off . . . the one person I wanted to tell about this . . . my new confidant, the person who I thought genuinely liked me, who would understand all the ins and outs, who I fantasized about meeting someday? That was taken from me, too. She had somehow managed to ruin the first relationship I was ever excited about. I was enraged.

It didn't take me long to track down the IP address from where Sara was posting. You can buy a software patch online, go into Reddit, take some of the accessible metadata, and reverse-engineer it. It all led back to a modem registered to a postal address—the Timber Ridge Boy Scout camp. I looked it up. An hour away. I took my dad's car and drove up that Saturday.

I made it to the gate, left the car, and walked into the camp. It was obvious which cabin she was in. In fact, she was sitting outside, reading in her camping chair, when she saw me. She jumped up, surprised. And then I guess she recognized me.

She said, "What the hell are you doing here?"

I asked what she was doing there.

She said it was none of my business.

I told her what had happened to my father. I told her how I was being treated at school. How people were grabbing my backpack in the hallway, dumping it on the floor, checking for her body parts. I asked if she knew about that. Was that my business?

She went to the cabin door, said, "I think you should leave." Ducked inside and tried to close the door, but I stopped her. She tried to push me out of the way, but I forced my way in.

"What do you want?" she said.

I looked around the cabin. She had been living there. Had access to a computer somewhere, obviously. Had been lying the whole time, lounging around, eating snacks. While the rest of us searched for her. Donated money. Had our lives turned upside down. She had her feet kicked up at Timber Ridge, reading in the sun. I had hoped there was an explanation that I hadn't thought of. But no. It was the worst version of what I had imagined.

I asked her to explain it. I was still hoping she would say something that would allow me not to hate her. But the more she tried to justify it, to downplay it, the angrier I got. It was pure selfishness. Greed. Disregard for others.

I told her it was over. I was calling the cops.

She yelled for me to stop. She told me that I was going to ruin her life, that she and her parents would go to jail. I told her she had already ruined mine. I took out my phone. She tried to grab it. We started fighting over it. We fell to the floor. She was on top of me. Screaming in my face, "Don't do this to me! Why did you come here?" I couldn't believe she was making me out to be the bad guy. I had been the one defending her! Over and over again, defending her! She was the one who came after me and my family!

I flipped us back over. I was on top. I snatched my phone back. She was hitting me. Screaming at me. I tried to hold her arms down. She wouldn't stop. Kept attacking me. I don't remember the next part. I saw the photos later. It looks like I strangled her. But I honestly blacked it out. My lawyer called it trauma-induced dissociation. The next thing I remember, I was lying next to her, gasping for breath myself. Sara wasn't moving. She was dead.

I ran out of the cabin and didn't look back. Got in the car, started driving. Vomited all over the steering wheel. Drove home, cleaned the car, and tried to pretend that nothing happened. Went about my life like normal. Until I sat down for the last interview with Casey. She had figured it out, and I knew I was caught.

I'm sorry it happened. I was sorry right away. I didn't drive there wanting to kill Sara. I don't even remember doing it. Even after everything she did, she didn't deserve to die. But I also understand how I did it. I can still feel the rage I felt that day.

Molly Lowe (*professor of sociology*): Some people chalk up every violent act against women to a boy who never got kissed in middle school. They think it's really that simple. I hate that framework because it implies that it's somehow every teenage girl's responsibility to dole out just enough romantic attention to not get murdered. It's lazy, misogynistic, and reductive. But I live in the real world. And goddamn if that doesn't feel like the truth most of the time.

Felix Calderon (*detective*): I listened to Brandon's whole story, left the interrogation room, and went downstairs—I thought Dave deserved to hear it from me. He was a liar and a criminal, but he was also a father who'd lost his daughter.

He took it about as badly as you'd expect. Those sobs, after the shock, after he put it all together . . . they still haunt me.

Dave Parcell (*father*): I've read a lot about the case, big surprise, there's not much else to do locked away in here. And there's always someone wanting to write a new article or revisit things. I noticed that anyone trying to sound smart always uses the phrase "tragic irony." I'm not a genius, I can't give some fancy definition of what that means. But then I remember Calderon coming down to tell me it was Brandon Grassley. That he and Sara had been chatting online or whatever. And that Brandon was pissed off about what we had done to his father, the cheap shots I had taken at Frank that, in hindsight, had been totally unnecessary. I remember the feeling that seemed to hollow out my entire body as I looked back on every decision that paved the way for this boy to wrap his hands around my little girl's neck. That feeling . . . it wasn't no "tragic irony." It was white-hot rage. Anger that can never be fixed.

Not at the boy. At myself.

Casey Hawthorne (*producer*): The finale aired the next night. We finished editing just in time. I knew it was perfect.

Ezra Phillips (*pop culture critic*): Remember how many people were glued to their TVs for the O.J. chase? Now imagine if something like that—a national moment of true-crime obsession—was scheduled and promoted and you could communicate in real time with all your friends and follow along on social media. This was the Super Bowl of reality TV.

Becca Santangelo (*SareBears*): The first part of the episode was all about Timber Ridge—how Casey figured out Sara was hiding there, then finding Sara when she went up with Detective Calderon.

Mike Snyder (*local news*): The second part revealed the scam they were running. Dave, Jeannette, Sara . . . they were all in on it. They exploited every part of this community—local media, the school, small businesses, law enforcement. Regular citizens who donated their hard-earned money. Search-and-rescue teams traipsing through frigid creeks. Innocent people whom they framed. Everyone in town was impacted. And it was all fake. Shame on that family.

Olivia Weston (*friend*): Then Casey showed how she figured out who the killer was. I cried when I saw it. Sara's laugh, 101—it was such a small thing, but I missed it.

Nellie Spencer (*friend*): I wasn't surprised it was Brandon. He was a fucking weirdo.

Travis Haynes (*bus driver*): So the killer *was* on the bus. Ain't that something?

Miriam Rosen (*teacher*): The end of the episode destroyed me. It was a memorial, of sorts, to Sara the person. Yes, she was complicit in this crime, but I think we all recognized she was doing her father's bidding. She was a victim worthy of our compassion.

Marcus Maxwell (*executive*): It was a masterpiece of emotional story-telling, if I do say so myself. And I do.

Olivia Weston (*friend*): The end montage took you through Sara's whole life. It reminded everyone how special she was. Brilliant, sweet, talented, fast, funny, generous, goofy, terrible dancer. It really just showed how happy she was.

Miriam Rosen (*teacher*): And that last image. Oh my God. The Parcells' home. Framed against the blue sky of a perfect spring day. And then it zoomed in closer and closer. You could see there was a bundle of mail dropped on their doorstep. Closer still, and you saw what was on top.

A welcome packet from Juilliard.

Marcus Maxwell (*executive*): Cut to black. Chef's kiss.

Felix Calderon (*detective*): I watched. I remember the ending. Everyone always talked about the letter from Juilliard. Sure, very touching—if it wasn't a prop that Casey cooked up. But either way, that's not what I remember most. I remember the screen going dark and then a single credit popping up, filling the whole screen . . .

Produced by Casey Hawthorne.

It sat there for a long time. Produced by Casey fucking Hawthorne. Damn right it was.

If you ask me, you couldn't summarize the whole tragedy any better than that.

Casey Hawthorne (*producer*): My work was done. That was a wrap on *Searching for Sara* and a wrap on Frederick. It was a bittersweet time, but I'm proud of what I accomplished.

Brandon Grassley (*neighbor*): Sorry for laughing, but I can't help it. It's just funny how Casey portrayed everything in her show. How she tied it up so neatly.

Because that's not what actually happened.

CHAPTER 17

"The Deleted Scenes"

Brandon Grassley (*neighbor*): It's a nice story, isn't it? The way Casey laid it all out? There's closure, a satisfying logic to the whole thing. It made for good TV, and the millions of people who followed the case got what they came for: The weird boy across the street took the fall. I get why Casey portrayed it this way.

But she left out one giant piece of information . . .

I might be the only person aware of this, but did you know that Casey went up to the camp to see Sara before she was killed?

Casey Hawthorne (*producer*): What? What did he say? No, I was never at Timber Ridge before going there with Felix and finding Sara's body. I never met Sara.

Brandon Grassley (*neighbor*): Of course, she'll never admit it. You see what that would mean, right? That Casey would be just as responsible for Sara's death. If Casey hadn't kept the secret, if she hadn't tried to orchestrate events for the sake of her show, I never would have found Sara there. She'd still be alive.

Casey didn't share that part in her little show, did she? But I'm telling you, she was there. She and Sara talked. They made a plan.

Casey Hawthorne (*producer*): He must be confused. Maybe he means when I wandered into the office and found the computer? I revealed that in the finale. But that was the same day we found Sara. So I really don't know what he's talking about.

Brandon Grassley (*neighbor*): Casey was there. And she's been hiding it ever since.

Casey Hawthorne (*producer*): Brandon is a confessed murderer and a known liar. You can't believe a word that comes out of his mouth.

Brandon Grassley (*neighbor*): I can prove it.

Casey Hawthorne (*producer*): I was never there at any other point in time.

Brandon Grassley (*neighbor*): I was as surprised as anyone when I figured it out. It was a few years into my sentence, and it was totally random. I was doing a lot of reading. Books, magazines, anything, really. I picked up an old copy of *Entertainment Weekly.* Yeah, we're allowed to read magazines in prison. This was when Casey was just starting to be hot shit, when she was blowing up. You know, turning into the true-crime queen. So of course this fancy magazine was doing a profile on her. Supposedly it was about exploring the ethics of her professional success, but give me a break, it was basically a puff piece.

I'd read profiles like this before. The journalist follows the subject around, gives some behind-the-scenes insights to their life, gets some quotes, makes some pseudo-intellectual observations. I'm not a fan, generally, but when I saw it was my old pal Casey, I gave it a read. They're talking about her life in LA, her daily routine, how she manages to juggle so many shows, how she chooses her projects, blah, blah, blah, and now they're getting into the details: what car she drives, what time she wakes up, the color of the tiles in her Spanish-style home, her exercise routine. It's all driving me nuts, but

I'm still reading. And then I see it. It was a throwaway sentence, but it triggered my memory instantly—and I knew Casey had seen Sara.

I remember it word for word: "Hawthorne seems to subsist entirely on a never-ending supply of strawberry-rose-geranium snack bars, a specialty item only available at the trendy Moon Juice Café in Santa Monica; they seem to materialize out of the ether on the hour, eventually leaving a trail of neon pink wrappers in her wake like flower petals."

She really loved those bars, huh? Enough for this journalist to mention it. And I believed it. Because I had seen one of those bars before. Which is odd, because I guess you can only get them at one specific place in Los Angeles. But that neon pink wrapper, it was unforgettable.

I had seen one in Sara's cabin.

Think about what that means.

I already told you what happened when I followed Sara into her cabin. I was there for less than five minutes, but I looked around before we got into our fight. Remember, I was trying to piece together what was going on. Sara had a cubby stocked with her food supplies. There wasn't much, it looked like she was running low. But I know I saw that pink wrapper on the shelf. I'm positive. It stood out. I didn't know what it was at the time and never thought of it again. Until the article.

It was a strawberry-rose-geranium snack bar from Moon Juice Café in Santa Monica.

So maybe you can answer this: What the hell was a specialty snack bar from California doing in Sara's cabin on the day I went up there?

I'll save you the time. Sara didn't bring it herself. Casey had been there already. And she conveniently left that out of her show.

Casey Hawthorne (*producer*): I . . . I, uh . . . I mean, that's absurd. What is he even saying? It sounds like he read about a snack I like, and he's making up a colorful story. Or maybe he saw me eating one back in Frederick, I don't know.

Brandon Grassley (*neighbor*): I'm saying that bar was in Sara's cabin. Casey can deny it all she wants, but I saw it.

The only part I never figured out: What was Casey doing there? What happened in that cabin? What did she and Sara agree to? What was the plan? Why would Casey keep the Parcells' secret?

I can't answer that. Only Casey can. And if she won't admit it, there's no way we'll ever know.

Anthony Pena (*editor*): He says he saw one of Casey's Moon Juice bars in the cabin? That doesn't make sense. He's mixing things up. I mean, yeah, she carried those bars everywhere, but I was with Casey when we edited the finale—she was too calm and collected, there's no way she had seen Sara alive a few days before. For her to keep that a secret . . . it would be psychotic.

Marcus Maxwell (*executive*): That's quite an accusation. It would expose Casey and this network to significant legal liability. I'm not going to comment, other than to say I don't believe it.

Alexis Lee (*associate producer*): Oh my God, of course she did! That fits with everything else I saw. Casey tries to present herself as this noble, innocent documentarian, but in reality, she was always the author and engine of this whole tragedy. Good luck getting her to admit it, though. Unfortunately, I think Brandon's right—we'll never get the full explanation of what happened.

Bruce Allen Foley (*Unfounded*): Whoa, whoa, whoa. Seriously? This is too good! Casey saw Sara alive at the camp, and Brandon Grassley can prove it? Well, ain't that rich!

I told you that everyone was lying, didn't I? Maybe I got a detail wrong here or there, but this proves my point: It's all one big conspiracy between the government, the media, and the patsies they trick into being involved. I can tell you *exactly* what Casey was doing up there.

I've been studying these scams for decades. Just hold on a minute, let me connect all the dots here . . .

Okay, I'm ready. You want to know what really went down in Frederick? The deleted scenes, if you will? Make sure that recorder is charged up, I'm gonna lay it all out for you.

Sara and Dave are running their scam. Calderon is trying to crack the case, except there's no case to crack. And Casey is making her show about a missing girl, but the girl's not actually missing. Something's got to give!

As the weeks drag on, everyone is getting suspicious. Casey and Calderon are questioning themselves. Maybe they're logging onto my website and thinking, You know what, ol' Foley might be onto something here. Their gut is telling them to dig deeper. Don't just accept the facts that are fed to you, do your own research. So they do. And then boom! One of them figures it out. Not the detective, who's supposedly trained to do this. The producer! She figures out where Sara is hiding.

But she doesn't tell Calderon—there's the first lie she told you. No, she wants this explosive scoop for herself. She's not positive, though, she needs to confirm it first, so she goes up to Timber Ridge alone. And what does Casey find? Sara, on the verge of ending this charade, ready to leave the camp that very day, per her father's instructions, relieved to be done with her ordeal, and now . . . caught!

Can you imagine the exchange between Sara and Casey? Sara, terrified that her life is ruined . . . but desperately curious to meet the woman who made her famous. Casey, bursting with pride that her instincts were correct . . . and filled with contempt as she confirmed that this family had been playing her for so long. There's a twisted sisterhood between them, two smart young women engaged in separate schemes to get ahead in the world, each obsessed with the other, finally crossing paths. This fateful collision will destroy both of them, but they don't know that. Their minds would be racing: What now? Is this friend or foe? How can I tilt this moment to my advantage? It's delicious!

But it's not a fair fight. Casey, the old pro, has all the leverage. Sara knows it. If her family's scam is revealed, her father will go to jail. Her own good name will be ruined, and the life she seeks will be ripped away. She pleads with Casey: "I was just helping my dad . . . I beg you, don't blow this up."

Maybe a part of Casey is moved to spare the girl. But a bigger part sees an opportunity. A solution to her problem. No ending for her show? Not anymore!

Casey's got ice in her veins. She stares back at Sara—this frazzled, tearful, desperate, homesick child—and Casey knows she owns her now.

And what does Casey do with this power? She strong-arms the poor girl: "I'll keep your secret . . . I'll protect your family . . . but on one condition—*you're not going anywhere.*"

Yup, there it is. Casey is the one who made Sara stay at the camp. Who left her there to be murdered.

She insists Sara remain in hiding against her will, a sacrificial lamb to Casey's insatiable ambition. This will give Casey enough time to return to Frederick, secure permission from the Parcells to keep shooting, and then, once Casey has her ducks in a row, Sara can execute the fake happy homecoming . . . with Casey there to tie a bow on her series.

What choice does Sara have? She's negotiating with a master manipulator from a position of weakness. So she agrees to the deal. A Faustian bargain that each intends to keep forever: The scam will be kept secret, and both will benefit from it. They shake on it, or whatever girls do.

And allow me to interrupt here to deal with Brandon Grassley's claim, the magical snack bar from LA. I believe him. But how did it get there? I think Casey's got one on her when she arrives at the camp. Maybe she's hungry, it was a long drive, and she eats it herself and leaves the wrapper. Or even better, she finds Sara, low on food, sick of eating the same boring things for weeks. As a gesture of friendship, or manipulation, she offers Sara a treat, which is gladly accepted. We don't know who ate it, but we know that Casey brought it into that cabin.

Now back to their deal . . . what happens next? I can't be sure of the details, but I think Casey drives back to Frederick, heart pounding, mind racing. Mission accomplished! Her instincts were right! She's on the verge of a fairy-tale ending for her show. Just a few more things to take care of.

First stop is Dave and Jeannette, where she reels them back in. Maybe a financial offer they can't refuse. Or pure intimidation, hinting that she's onto their scheme. Either way, she gets them back on board.

Dave Parcell (*father*): Yeah, Casey came back to us a few days after we canceled the show. We were done negotiating, didn't want to let her in the house. But she had a different look in her eye. Cold-blooded. Told us we had two choices: Let her get back up and running to film a finale . . . or live with the consequences.

Jeannette Parcell (*mother*): She told us we had five minutes to decide, then left the room. Dave and I looked at each other. We both felt the same thing.

Dave Parcell (*father*): Did I think she was onto us? Maybe. I sure as hell didn't want to find out the hard way. We signed back up.

Turns out it didn't matter. I never found out what Casey suspected. Once Sara was found the next day, Casey and her show were the least of my concerns.

Bruce Allen Foley (*Unfounded*): She got the Parcells back in her pocket, but why didn't she follow through on her plan? How did she end up back at the camp with Calderon the next day?

Something changes for Casey. A dark night of the soul, if you will. Here's how I imagine it . . .

She's alone that night. Everything is teed up for her professional coronation. The finale of her show is going to be gangbusters, and she willed it into existence through sheer brains and charisma. But why does she feel so empty?

I know Casey. I was in her presence several times. And I've followed her every move since—from a legally mandated distance, obviously. I think the answer is simple: She's finally crossed her own line. Gone from passive facilitator to outright liar. Earnest film school artiste to tabloid hack. She's an active participant in the scam, for God's sake! It's all catching up with her. She's become a monster she never could have imagined for herself.

Maybe she goes out for a walk to clear her head. Ends up at the bar where she first met Calderon. But she sits alone this time. And I mean *utterly alone*. No family, no partner, no one to share her secret with. And who's to blame for this crushing moment of isolation and shame? Just her, of course. All of her choices have led her to this lonely barstool. She's over this life, ready to change, but she's trapped. Tears well in her eyes.

But then, a miracle.

As she swirls the dregs of her third martini, the idea takes shape. And in a flash, she sees that it's brilliant. That it solves all her problems. Sets her on a new path. Hurts no one. Puts her on the side of truth. And as a little bonus to get her blood pumping, it even requires a soupçon of the old Casey flair.

Best of all, it wins back the handsome detective. She had ruined Calderon's career, but now she can save it. Save *him*, really. For Casey, he'll always be the knight in shining armor who rescued her from certain death at the hands of a deranged kidnapper. I mean, *I* knew there was no real danger, but that's what it felt like for them. I saw the way they embraced once Casey was untied . . . let me tell you, it was uncomfortable being the third wheel in that hotel room. But Calderon still walked out on her that night, and boy, did that have to sting. This is Casey's chance to win him back.

How? By doing something crazy: Casey decides to reenact her race to Timber Ridge, only this time with Calderon by her side, after she lets him "figure it out."

It's perfect. Calderon will be a hero. The Parcells will face justice. Sara won't have to continue living the lie. Casey will get a great ending for her series, and she will finally be out of the deception business. She'll be redeemed.

It's complicated to pull off, though. Casey has to loop in Calderon and pretend like she hasn't figured out everything and gone up to the camp already. A little acting, no big deal for these types. She hides her first visit from him, just like I'm sure she hid it from you and everyone else. No one knows she went up there!

So Casey deftly steers Calderon to his own eureka moment about where Sara is hiding. Her solo discovery is now a collaboration. Calderon is invested again, and they're off, spurs jangling as they ride to the rescue. They're headed for a showdown at Timber Ridge. Casey is pretending the whole time that she hasn't done this days earlier. "Oh, wow, it's so far," "Is this the right turn?," that type of stuff. Calderon has no reason to suspect anything. The adrenaline is flowing, love is in the air, the end is nigh!

But wait. Let's not lose sight of something essential. Here is the moment when Calderon must have made her choose. The ultimatum that put Casey's new value system to the test: "Me or the cameras," he would have said, "this has to be about finding Sara, not your show."

And Casey agreed. She laid down her weapon! We know she did. That's why we never saw any footage from Timber Ridge. I don't even think it was hard for her. It's what she wanted now. She chose Calderon and the truth over her career . . . the personal over the professional. Casey's new life was right at her fingertips. Until, you know . . . the two lovebirds reach the camp. Enter cautiously. See the cabin. Approach. Call out. Nothing.

They go in. And what do they find? Their worst nightmare. Just a body. Sara is dead.

Calderon is devastated. In his mind, he figured it all out only to arrive too late. But that's nothing compared to Casey's reaction.

She's in shock. She can't believe the body in front of her is the same spirited girl she interacted with days earlier. And then the heavier thoughts start to sink in. The guilt. The shame. The professional and legal consequences. This poor girl, martyred in service to a reality TV show. Casey is responsible for this. She didn't do the deed, but she made it happen all the same, in the waning hours of her craven ambition. She blackmailed Sara into staying. The shame overwhelms her. It will never leave her. Even in those first moments, she knows that she's been given a life sentence.

There's a shred of relief, though, as Casey's mind races. Yes, she realizes with growing confidence, it could be worse. By sheer luck, the judgment will only come from within. No one besides Sara knows that Casey was here earlier. No one will ever know.

And just like that, Casey starts slipping back into her old skin. The new life she dreamed of, the life of integrity and purpose, with Calderon's love and respect—it's gone forever now. Impossible to conjure again. She probably takes only a moment to mourn it, poor soul, and then the old reflexes kick in. She'll pick up the camera again, like the old gunslinger we know can never change. She'll craft a finale that elides the truth. Make a mint on telling the tragedy of this family . . . as only Casey wants it told.

Yes, her regression takes only a second. So easy it'll make you queasy. Casey sees Sara's body and decides to take their first meeting to the grave, just like poor Sara did. She will finish making her show and leave Frederick confident that her secret is buried there.

But now we know that's not true. Casey was betrayed by her tiny moment of kindness or inattention. By the seemingly insignificant decision to offer a hungry girl a snack from the pocket of her leather coat. A snack so out of place and colorful and unique it couldn't help but stick in the memory of the only other person to step foot in that cabin between Casey's visits. A snack so interesting that, years later, it would warrant mention in a magazine profile. A strawberry-flower-macadamia moon, or whatever the hell it was.

Like I said . . . delicious.

Yes. That's it. My best guess on how it all went down.

But who would ever believe me? I'm just a crazy ex-con conspiracy theorist strapped into an ankle monitor.

Casey Hawthorne (*producer*): Wow. It's quite a tale. Foley has a vivid imagination. Maybe he should get into show business. But no . . . none of that is true. Not a word. It's the ramblings of a sociopath.

Bruce Allen Foley (*Unfounded*): Casey will never admit it. Far worse than the self-incrimination, there would be the humiliation of admitting she rejected her old self, took the brave leap for a new life . . . and landed right back where she started. No, she has to keep pretending to be happy, to be fulfilled by how things turned out, to live the lonely lie. Can you imagine how awful that must be? My heart breaks for her.

And Sara . . . Sara can never tell us, of course. But there is a way to confirm that Brandon Grassley is telling the truth about seeing the wrapper there. It would be in the evidence log—the list of items found there, and the crime-scene photos.

Calderon could go back and look. If he finds it there, boom, it's all true.

It would prove that Casey left that girl there to die.

Felix Calderon (*detective*): The case files? Yes, I have access. And yes, all the items found in the cabin were logged as evidence.

Bruce Allen Foley (*Unfounded*): But even if he checks and sees the wrapper, he'll never tell you, same as her. He can't, it would ruin everything for him! I'm telling you, he loved Casey. Still does, I bet.

I bet he looks back at those days in Frederick with her in a sepia-toned mist of longing. I bet it's what he thinks about before he falls asleep. When he hears someone laugh a certain way. When he cooks a certain meal. When the sun hits his face on a cool spring morning and he remembers the warmth of her cheek. I bet he tells himself that the only thing worse than losing a lifetime of those moments is never knowing them at all. I bet it drives him mad and somehow keeps him sane. The poor guy.

And if he found out Casey had seen Sara before they drove up together? Well, first he would be enraged. He'd realize that Casey solved the case before him. That she was faking his heroic discovery and their mad dash to the camp. That her delay in reporting the truth cost Sara her life. This realization would destroy him.

Imagine him on his computer, logging in to check the files. Scanning the inventory and the photos, hoping against hope that Brandon Grassley is wrong, even as the pit in his stomach tells him what he will find. But he can't stop himself from checking, knowing it's torture, desperate not to detect that specific shade of neon pink. And then when he finally sees it, there will almost be a feeling of relief. Part of him, the rational part, was right about this woman all along: She can't be trusted.

But there would be something more powerful than the anger. People aren't rational. If he still loves her, he will see something else in Casey's actions, and it will stop him from betraying her. He will see what Casey tried to do for him, and convince himself of its deep meaning. She could have been the hero alone, but she chose to include him. To restore his dignity. To make amends. To pay him back. *To be his partner.*

He will jump at the chance to interpret this as a gesture of love, one that Casey could never confirm after Sara was found dead. It was the only thing she could do to win him back—and it would have worked, he knows. They came so close to finding their way back to each other, but then it all fell apart, and she could never tell him. And the fact that he was unaware of Casey's gesture until now . . . my God, that bittersweet knowledge will burn a hole right through his soul.

We all see what we want to see, right? Once Calderon sees Casey's decision through this lens, he'll never admit the Moon Bar wrapper is listed in the crime-scene report. He'll lie or make some excuse or delete the files. He'll do it to echo the gesture of love that Casey once tried to pull off for them. It will be too late, no doubt, to restore their bond, but he'll do it nonetheless. Only Casey will know for sure that he's lying. He'll do it for an audience of one.

It will be sweet for them, this little measure of closure, but sad for the rest of us. It means we'll never know the truth.

Casey Hawthorne (*producer*): Wait, what? You asked Felix to go back and check the crime-scene files? My God. That seems like a lot of . . .
   What did he say?
   I'm sorry, not say—what did he find?

Felix Calderon (*detective*): I went back and checked. There was no Moon Juice snack bar wrapper in the cabin. Casey was never there with Sara.

Casey Hawthorne (*producer*): Oh. Wow.
   That's . . . that's really what he . . .
   I mean, of course. Of course he did.
   Like I always said.

"Look at You"

Molly Lowe (*professor of sociology*): The *Searching for Sara* debacle should have been a reckoning. Ten years removed, it is clear that it wasn't. Our culture is just as voracious for true-crime stories, and introspection about the costs of this obsession has never come to pass.

We are left with a dispiriting status quo: a corporate class of entertainment specialists who sort through the violent underbelly of society in the hope of finding a nugget salacious enough to capture the attention of the masses. This is done for profit, in a system where bigger audiences equate to bigger financial returns, so think about what that incentivizes: more sensational stories and storytelling.

There is nothing inherently evil about this model when applied to traditional entertainment. The worst consequence, really, is a glut of bad superhero movies. But when this incentive structure is applied to the true-crime genre, it begs fundamental questions: Is it morally acceptable to profit from these real tragedies? Is this entertainment or exploitation? And if the answer is both, how can anyone involved live with themselves?

I often think about the people involved in the Sara Parcell case. I wonder what they're doing now. How they've come to terms with everything that happened. And most of all, I think about who is most responsible for that girl being dead.

I always start with the parents, of course . . .

Dave Parcell (*father*): All I do is think about what I did. There's not much else to do in here. I am serving a twenty-year manslaughter sentence in Cumberland State Prison for what happened with Manny. I pleaded guilty to several other charges—wire fraud, making false statements, endangering a minor. I didn't want a big trial. And what was the point? Once everything fell apart, I had no defense.

And I kept Jeannette out of it. Made it clear that she didn't know anything. She filed for divorce and got to walk away scot-free, which I think was right.

I spend my days making license plates. Playing cards. Trying to steer clear of trouble. I asked about getting a guitar in here, but it's considered contraband. Those strings . . . I get it. So mostly I just think back. For a while, I tried to tell myself that my only crime was wanting to be a good dad. To provide for my kids, to give my daughter the opportunity she deserved. But when you have to lie and steal and exploit others to do that, that's not being a good dad. I've made my peace with that. I loved Sara, but I didn't do right by her. If you want to say I was a terrible father, I can't argue. She's dead because of me.

Jeannette Parcell (*mother*): I live in Texas, it's been about three years now. Remarried, no more kids, changed my name back. He's an accountant. Not a big talker, I had enough of that. He doesn't ask about Sara or my life in Frederick. Most people don't, actually. I was surprised at how quickly everyone forgot. There's always something new for people to get worked up about. It's just as well with me—it hurts too much to dwell on what happened.

Maybe it helps that there's no word for what I am. You know, something like "orphan" or "widow" . . . we don't have a word to describe a parent who's lost a child. If we did, I'm sure I'd hear it every day. I doubt I could bear that.

I have some peace knowing that when Sara was alive, I tried my best to save her. Once Dave told me the truth, I wanted to see her, to bring her home. But Dave had me brainwashed. Over and over, he told me everything was fine, right until the day she was dead. It was a stupid idea from the moment he cooked it up. I don't wish him a moment of mercy, wherever he's stuck right now.

Jack Parcell (*brother*): My mom and I stayed in our house for a few months after they found Sara. Just us, obviously. There was a funeral, a memorial service at her school. Lots of people over at the house for a while. Then it all kind of tapered off. We moved in with my grandparents, the bank was taking our house anyways. I helped my mom pack up Sara's room. The trophies, the music stuff, that same stupid teddy bear. We brought everything over to my grandparents', for some reason, but it all got stored away in the basement.

There's a nice violin down there collecting dust. I only know that because my dad always asks when I visit him. "You still have Sara's violin, right? It's safe?" Like as long as he can picture where it is, Sara still kind of exists for him. I tell him I'm taking good care of it. He doesn't have anyone else to visit him. I don't have a car, but I go up on the bus when I can. I don't hate him. I know how hard it is to live with this guilt.

I'm taking a year off from community college right now. I have a job at the Verizon store. I'm really just trying to get back on track after what happened last year. I cut myself pretty badly. Almost died. Stayed in the hospital for a few weeks, getting my mind right. I wouldn't call it a suicide attempt, exactly, but I had definitely thought about it before, so I don't know.

Going to classes, being on campus, was hard. All that vibrant life made me think of Sara. I would picture her traveling the world, performing, soaking in applause, going out with her friends after. Laughing. She was supposed to have this big, cool life. But it all got cut short for her, and it doesn't feel right for me to try and have one instead. Not when I knew why hers got cut short. Me and that stupid video.

I tie my own shoes every day. And it gets me emotional each time. It's hard to want to live when you stopped someone else from living. Someone more deserving.

Molly Lowe (*professor of sociology*): After Sara's family, you have to look at the people who helped turn this tragedy into an entertainment product. There is a scientific principle known as the observer effect. It states that people's behavior is impacted merely by the knowledge that they are being observed. Surely this applies to anyone who knows they are being filmed for a reality show. It's easy to see this phenomenon in effect with the Parcells—Sara was supposed to be gone for three days, but once the TV show was set in motion, she was stuck at the cabin for weeks. The Parcells changed their behavior due to being observed. Do the people who went there to film realize that their presence led to Sara's death?

Marcus Maxwell (*executive*): It was a noble idea with unintended consequences. Casey went there to help. I green-lit the show because it was unique. The fatal flaw was that the family lied to us, they lied to everyone. We couldn't have foreseen that. And the result, at the end of the day, was a kill show. It breaks my heart to admit that. But I don't think Sara is dead because of the whims of the TV industry. That's ridiculous.

Zane Kelly (*camera operator*): I still work in reality TV. I'm on a show right now called *Date My Dad*. The point is, I don't take jobs anymore if there's a chance someone might end up dead.

Anthony Pena (*editor*): I'm still ride-or-die with Casey. It's been an incredible run. I mean, she's a genius. The production style she innovated—boots on the ground, instant turnaround—it plays, man. And I know *Searching for Sara* ended badly, but some of the other projects we took on with this brand, we really made a difference. *Cop Killer,* we went on the run with that dude and saved his life. *Man of God,* that whole church owes us for exposing their scumbag pastor. We have more work than we know what to do with, and I'm proud of most of it. I bought a house in Sherman Oaks. My kid goes to private school. All because of the true-crime boom and the lane that Casey carved out.

Alexis Lee (*associate producer*): Casey was right about one thing: I didn't get hired again. I went to grad school and became a therapist. And she got rich making more shows about the worst moments of people's life. One of us is creating trauma, the other is treating it. I'll leave it at that.

Ezra Phillips (*pop culture critic*): People used to say that religion was the opiate of the masses. And for most of human history, that was probably true. But surely the new universal sedative is TV. Or "content," if you will, however you define it and whatever screen you use to consume it. But here's the thing about opiates: As our tolerance builds up, we need to keep upping the dose. For a long time, true crime was the hot new strain, the good shit that made people tune in, sit still, zonk out, and get that warm fuzzy feeling. But eventually, even the thrills of true crime won't do the trick anymore.

I'm afraid about what comes next. For the viewers . . . and also the people tasked with making it.

Molly Lowe (*professor of sociology*): The family and the production led the charge, but Sara wouldn't be dead without a lot of well-meaning people missing what was right in front of their faces . . .

Veronica Yang (*principal*): In hindsight, I never should have let Casey into our school. I thought it would be therapeutic for the kids, that they could process their trauma on a level they were more comfortable with. But after it was all over, I realized Casey just saw our school and our students as plot points in the story she was telling.

Miriam Rosen (*teacher*): I put too much pressure on Sara. I told her about Juilliard and how important it was for her, to get there by any means necessary. I encouraged her to ask her parents. And now I can't hear a violin without thinking about her.

Olivia Weston (*friend*): I live in New York, and I walk by Juilliard all the time. I think about how Sara should be here with me. We should be trying new restaurants together and going to museums and complaining about guys. But then I remember that she was part of the lie from the beginning. I get so angry at her. You don't do that to your best friends.

Nellie Spencer (*friend*): I'm still in Frederick. Just me and my son. No, Coach Walker is not his father. I wish Sara could've met my little guy. I wish she was still around to hang out.

Honestly, after those few weeks when she was missing, everything's just been kind of boring.

Tommy O'Brien (*employee, Geary Home & Garden*): Herb sold the store, but I still work there. Once in a while, someone mentions Dave, and people ask me about it, they know I was there from the beginning. Come to think of it, I was the first person he lied to, when he ran off the job on me. But I tell them the truth. That Dave was a good guy who got in over his head. And I try to take a lesson from the whole thing: Be grateful for what you have, don't go twisting yourself into a pretzel trying to get more.

Mike Snyder (*local news*): Dave played us like a violin. Sorry if that hits too close to home, but he really did. I'm not sure what we, the local media, could have done differently, though. If a family says their daughter is missing, are we really supposed to report that with an "allegedly"? I guess that's the part that still bothers me—this story helped usher us into the age of cynicism, where no one believes what they see on the news. That hurts.

Olaf Leclerq (*ice cream shop owner*): I never got back the reward money I put up. I don't know who got it, it disappeared. And Big Olaf's doesn't exist anymore. We were wiped out by Cold Stone.

Travis Haynes (*bus driver*): I make a decent living going to true-crime conventions, signing autographs, taking photos with fans. I have a few requests on Cameo every week at forty bucks a pop. Some people ask me to threaten to kill them. I try to make a joke of it. Look, people get a kick out of it, I'm not complaining. No, but seriously, America loves me. I was only in a couple episodes, but they see me as an inspiration. The little guy who had everything stacked against him but stood strong and survived. Damn right I did.

Evelyn Crawford (*Manny's wife*): I haven't gone anywhere. Still have to drive by the old Shell station on my way to the grocery store. You would think people would stop talking about all that at some point, but I get phone calls, lookie-loos, every week still. I can tell you one thing I don't appreciate: Everyone always acts like it was the Sara Parcell tragedy. Well, excuse me, my husband was killed, too. That's who Dave is in prison for murdering, that was the real crime, the real victim. Manny Crawford. When the story comes up, folks should say his name, too. And no, I don't believe any of that junk that it was his idea. No how, no way.

Christine Bell (*district attorney*): I don't see the Sara Parcell affair as a failure of the legal system. Quite the opposite. A fraud was perpetrated, and we convicted those who did it. A murder was committed, and we convicted the killer. Justice was done on all counts, and fairly quickly, I might add. If there was a failure somewhere, it was in the fabric of a society that inspires this kind of immoral scheming. This is what I campaigned on when I ran for governor. And I would have won, too.

Really, you want me to explain it? Everyone already knows, I'm sure. I had one little mistake on my résumé, and the lamestream media blew it entirely out of proportion. That's why I'm not governor.

Molly Lowe (*professor of sociology*): Then there are the people with no connection to Sara, but they latched on to the story, made it a part of their lives, and added fuel to the fire . . .

Becca Santangelo (*SareBears*): Fans didn't get Sara killed. Groups like the SareBears didn't cause any of this to happen. We don't change any of the outcomes, we're thousands of miles away and only see everything after it already happens. We watch because we care. It's not like if we stopped watching . . .

Well, it's impossible to know. I can't predict what would happen if people didn't watch things like this, so I'm not going to try.

Bruce Allen Foley (*Unfounded*): Do I take any responsibility for Sara's death? Ha, no. If people had listened to me sooner, actually used their brains and applied some common sense to the situation, the whole farce would have been exposed before it turned grisly. But I'm used to being doubted. It's hard to convince sheep. For the most part, they prefer to just go on eating grass.

Molly Lowe (*professor of sociology*): Then there are those who could have saved her, whose profession requires it, who, in the most technical sense, totally failed Sara. I wonder if they own up to that failure. And if they do, whether it still haunts them.

Felix Calderon (*detective*): I did everything I could to find Sara Parcell, to prevent the fate that ultimately awaited her. Unlike in Houston, I've never tried to run from what happened on my watch. I fucking wear it. I wear it to this day. I shook off that feeling once, I know how hard it is. And I know I don't have the strength to do it again.

So yeah, I think about Sara every day. But I'm haunted more by what I've learned while answering questions for this book.

Molly Lowe (*professor of sociology*): And of course there's the person who actually killed her. He pleaded guilty to the crime, but I always sensed he thought it was somehow justified . . .

Brandon Grassley (*neighbor*): I paid my debt to society. Thankfully, I was allowed to enter my guilty plea as a minor. Did a couple years in juvenile facilities, then the last seven in prison. It was hell. But I had a lot of time to think. I'm sorry Sara died, and I take responsibility for what happened in that cabin. Did she and her family bring that moment upon her? I'm not going to say that. They deserved to be exposed and punished for the lives they ruined and the lies they told. My dad was never the same. He had to leave Frederick. But Sara didn't deserve to die.

My time inside wasn't all bad. I got married a few years ago. Yeah, one of my pen pals proposed to me, then we got hitched in the prison chapel. Lucky me, right? She's a great girl. A SareBear, of course. But she doesn't hold things against me, she gets why I did what I did, sees the bigger picture.

I've been out on parole for a year. We live in Florida. Just had a baby last month.

There wasn't a lot of debate . . . we named her Sara.

Molly Lowe (*professor of sociology*): But when I parcel out responsibility for this sad story, I always end with Casey. It's not just what she did in the moment—rushing to Frederick, manipulating the family, turning their tragedy into a hit TV show—it's what she's done since. She has built an entertainment empire by documenting the bleakest moments in our culture. She is unapologetically the true-crime queen. She's rich. She's famous. She's celebrated, mostly. But at what cost? And I don't just mean the ruined lives put on display and preserved for all time. I mean at what cost to herself?

Can someone hold on to their humanity while devoting their life to selling the tragedies of their fellow man? If you get a chance to ask her, I'm curious what she'd say.

Casey Hawthorne (*producer*): Do I feel responsible for Sara's death? Of course not. Dave was the one who lied about everything. Brandon Grassley was the one who strangled her. Felix and the other cops . . . well, never mind, I'll leave him out of it. The point is, I just stood on the sidelines and told my crew what to shoot. I hate to break it to you, but bad things happen every day, whether or not there are cameras around.

And what was your other question? How do I live with myself doing this job? My humanity? Please. You act like what I do is somehow unique. Look at you, you're doing the exact same thing, earning a living by writing about Sara Parcell's death. Framing it as some kind of retrospective intellectual exercise, give me a break.

Let me guess . . . there will be ads for this book. A marketing budget, a promotional tour. And if all goes to plan, lots of people are going to buy it. What a neat trick! You get to pass judgment *and* turn a profit at the same time!

And your readers, don't even get me started. They're going to pay their hard-earned cash to immerse themselves in this saga. They'll enjoy it, be moved by it, maybe even smugly laugh at it. They'll use Sara's story as a distraction to help fall asleep in their comfy beds, far away from the grim reality it depicts. High thread count, low crime rate, juicy page-turner, "Alexa, lock the front door"—that's the dream, right? And everyone buys into it: you, your publisher, your audience— all of you will be treating this real-life tragedy simply as entertainment to be consumed.

So how do I live with myself? Well, let me ask you something . . .

How are you any different?

ACKNOWLEDGMENTS

My eternal gratitude to two guardian angels, Richard Abate and Jonathan Berry, for their faith, wisdom, and support.

And thank you to all the talented, patient, hardworking people at HarperCollins, most of all to Sara Nelson, for being this book's sharpest critic and greatest champion.

DANIEL SWEREN-BECKER is an author, television writer, and playwright living in Los Angeles. He graduated from Wesleyan University and received an MFA from New York University. His play *Stress Positions* premiered in New York City at the SoHo Playhouse, and he is the author of the novels *The Ones* and *The Equals*.